The Body in the Bath

A Chupplejeep Mystery

MARISSA DE LUNA

Murder, mayhem and Goan village life

For Mum

CHAPTER ONE

'So jealous,' Rosie said, handing a freshly laundered white towel to Indu.

'Why? There's nothing to be jealous of.'

'Nothing? *Che,* I wish I was your age and my boyfriend was taking me dancing. *Danchic, danchic,*' Rosie said, clicking her fingers and shaking her hips. 'Instead I have to go from cleaning toilets at work to cleaning toilets at home, while my good-for-nothing husband rubs his belly like a Buddha demanding hot *pakoras.* I wish I had a handsome man like Garjan to take me out.' She winked at Indu. 'Utterly jealous.'

'Shh,' Indu said, looking from left to right.

'What *sush*? Who's there to hear us?'

'If mama and papa find out, I'll be in solid trouble. And you never know if some aunty or cousin is lurking. These relatives spring up from nowhere, na. If somebody tells them, they'll ground my butt for sure,' Indu said, slipping into the accent from her favourite American TV show. 'Then both of us will be at home making *pakoras.*'

'High five for *pakoras.*' Rosie raised her hand.

Indu laughed. 'Shut up, *men*! Don't you have rooms to clean? You are properly delaying me. If I don't finish fast, I won't be able to meet Garjan.'

'Okay hottie, no more delay tactics. Last room, Madam is out?'

'Reception said there was no key.'

'That doesn't mean anything. That Furtado on reception has *ghee* instead of brains.'

'True.' Indu hesitated. 'Madam is usually out at this time. I'll quickly tidy the bedroom and bathroom then I'm going to do the laundry before I go home. You'll cover for me with the boss?'

'Hari? No problem. But don't forget to tell your grandchildren what I did to help you and Mr Handsome get friendly,' Rosie said. She danced down the stairs of the colonial-style boutique hotel, singing *Tum hi ho*.

Indu knocked twice on the white door in front of her. She didn't expect a response. She polished the brass door handle with a cloth as she waited. She hated cleaning Madam's room when she was around. Madam was always watching with her puffy eyes, and stealing soaps from the cart when she thought Indu wasn't looking. The woman had a filthy tongue and Indu was sure she got her kicks from putting others in their place. These *filmi* people were all the same. Indu slipped her master key in the lock. Her hand trembled slightly as she turned the handle. She looked behind her before shouting 'Madam!' as she opened the door.

No answer.

She took some toiletries and a shower cap from her trolley, placed them on a towel then stepped through the open door. As she headed through to the bathroom, she busied her mind with thoughts of her impending date. Should she wear the green *shalwaar* that brought out the colour in her eyes or should she wear the blue one – the one with the mirrors, which made her skin look fair? She placed the towel on the glass shelf next to the basin and noticed that the curtain had been pulled across the bath. She called out, but there was no response. She peered into the toilet. 'And she thinks she's a lady, *che*, it smells in here. Dirty woman.'

Indu looked up, her eyes widening. She could make out the silhouette of Madam's head behind the plastic curtain. Her heart skipped a beat.

She bit her thumbnail and considered her options. She could feel tiny beads of sweat trickling down her back. It was too late to run. She swallowed and inched her way towards the bath. Carefully she pulled back the curtain, just a fraction.

Indu peered behind the plastic and her mouth fell open. Madam looked beautifully still, her black sunglasses covering her eyes. She expected it, yet the sight of the bloody water made her toes curl. As Indu took in the scene, she let out a blood-curdling scream and then threw up her lunch of *idli sambar*.

Chapter Two

'*Hai, hai*, I'm telling you, no. Someone is blackmailing me and you useless cops are doing nothing about it.' Advani flicked his wrist, rested his chin on his hand and pouted.

'Mr Advani, with all due respect, you only reported this crime yesterday,' Police Officer Pankaj said.

'My life could be at stake. I'm a visitor here in Goa, I should be treated with some respect. You don't know what it's like when you're attacked like this in an unfamiliar place. If I was back in Bombay I would have hired some private security firm, but in Goa I can't just pick up my cell. You know how it is, *yaar*, if you don't know their provenance, they could be the ones to kill you in your sleep. You can't trust anyone in these rural states.'

Pankaj held his tongue. Goa was much safer than Mumbai, one hundred times over. 'If I correctly remember our conversation from yesterday, your life is not at risk, sir. You are being blackmailed for money.'

Advani's assistant, Takshak – a slender man dressed in a light yellow *kurta* just like his boss's white one –

nodded in agreement. Pankaj flashed him a grateful smile before he continued. 'The letter you received demanded that you leave forty *lakh* rupees in the garbage can outside your gallery on Christmas Eve or they would expose your secret. Yesterday was the 15th, which gives us eight days to solve the case. I'm working with my superiors to solve it well before this time. Perhaps, sir, if you can tell us what secret is going to be exposed, we can get a better idea of what type of person is behind this.'

Advani shifted his gaze to Takshak and then back to Pankaj. He shook his head. '*Hai,* I don't know if I can trust you people. This secret could blow apart my career.' He stood up, wrapping his bright pink scarf around his neck. 'Come Takshak, lets go from here. As usual, these cops are not going to help people like us.' Takshak rose to his feet and Pankaj did the same.

'It will take longer if you don't share your secret,' Pankaj said with a sigh. Advani's blackmail case wasn't one that excited him. Homicide was his true passion. But the smaller stations like Little Larara couldn't be fussy about what cases they took. Inspector General Gosht had warned them that in their geographical area, they were responsible for all crime.

Advani made a face. 'You go, Takshak,' he commanded. 'I'll tell this oaf what it is.' The artist sat back down. Takshak adjusted his *kurta* and left.

~

'Why was he back so soon?' Detective Chupplejeep asked as he passed Advani leaving the station.

'I don't know where to start,' Pankaj said, his head in his hands.

'But has he told you the big secret?'

Pankaj nodded.

'And?'

'The long and short of it is that his initial paintings were actually done by another man. An artist he knew when he was younger. He's worried that if this is exposed it will discredit all his work to date, even the work that is his own.'

Chupplejeep took a seat behind his desk. He twisted one end of his moustache, trying not to think about the hot sweet *ladoos* he had seen the *mithai-wallah* selling on his way to the station. 'And the man who did these paintings is…?'

'He's dead, sir.'

'Was the blackmail note posted or hand delivered?'

'Hand delivered, sir.'

'Well, that makes it simpler then. It must be someone who is in Goa at present.'

'Unless the blackmailer got someone to do his dirty work.'

'And risk that person taking off with the four million rupees? Highly unlikely. He would certainly be watching, if he didn't deliver the note himself.' Chupplejeep scratched his chin. 'Perhaps you should start by making a list of all of Advani's acquaintances who are currently in Goa.'

'Sir, I did have one thought.'

'What?'

'D'you think that someone is blackmailing Advani because he is gay?'

Chupplejeep tilted his head as he digested this information. 'Everybody knows Advani is gay.'

'Yes, sir, but perhaps someone who doesn't like homosexuals is doing this.'

'It would be a difficult place to start. Prejudice is everywhere and some people hide it under their smiles. But very rarely have people in Goa publicly demonstrated that they are homophobic. Goa is pretty relaxed when it comes to sexuality.'

Chupplejeep opened his top drawer. He pulled out a packet of lime and masala Lays and opened it. A pungent smell filled the office. 'So that is his big secret?' He put a crisp in his mouth. 'But now the work is his, isn't it? Unless…' The detective made a face.

'What, sir?' Pankaj said. He leaned across his desk ready to listen to his boss intently, hoping to find the answer he was looking for.

'Never mind. Ask Advani how many paintings the other artist created, and how much money had he sold each one for initially. Does he know who currently has ownership of them?'

'Good idea, sir,' Pankaj said, making a note. 'And then?'

'Who was this other artist? Did Advani use his paintings when he was alive? Had this artist given him

7

his consent? Because if he hadn't then this other artist could have told a number of people.'

'And then?' Pankaj said, scribbling furiously on his notepad.

'Then I suggest you…' Chupplejeep stopped mid-sentence. Pankaj looked up. 'Then I suggest *you* think about what else you need to ask him.'

'Sir, I thought homicide was difficult, but with murder there are always more clues – for a start there is often a murder weapon. With blackmail it's like fishing without a net.'

'Extortion's a tricky one, but good experience for you. It's not dissimilar to murder because, like with murder, there is always a motive. Someone has a good reason to blackmail Advani. It may not just be for the money.'

Pankaj pouted. 'I suppose.'

'This is the first case you're working on alone?'

Pankaj nodded.

'Good. But it'll wait until tomorrow. Today, we have something else we need to deal with. Get your things and come with me.'

CHAPTER THREE

Chupplejeep peered into the bathtub at the Golden Orchid Hotel, located in the heart of Dhesera. Room number 13, unlucky for some – definitely unlucky for washed-up actress Subrina Basi.

'The maid threw up in the bath, Detective, so the scene is already contaminated, eh,' Kulkarni said. 'This hotel was really putting Dhesera on the map. Everybody wants to stay where the celebrities are staying, but not where they are dying, eh. What a shame.'

'Subrina Basi was not so much of a celebrity.'

'You're correct, sir,' Pankaj said from the doorway. 'Basi was what *Icon Bites* called a D-list celebrity.'

'A double D-list celebrity, I would say,' Kulkarni said with a wide grin.

Subrina Basi's body lay limp in a bath filled with red water. Mucus, tiny pieces of coriander and *idli* were floating on the surface and a malodorous smell of faeces, urine and death filled the room. Subrina's perfectly-made face didn't match the chaos around her. Her signature red lipstick and dark glasses were firmly in place.

'Why has she still got her sunglasses on?'

'You know how these trendy, modern women are – always with their sunglasses on, even in nightclubs.'

'It looks like suicide,' Pankaj said.

Kulkarni made a face. He carefully lifted up the victim's left arm with his gloved hand. 'Slashed wrists usually point to suicide, 'es.'

'She was troubled,' Pankaj said, still hovering by the entrance to the bathroom.

Kulkarni lowered the victim's hand back into the water.

Pankaj inched a little closer now. 'Her career wasn't much to write about. She was always full of drugs and booze.'

'You knew her personally, did you?' Chupplejeep asked.

'No sir, *Icon Bites*.'

'They report things like that, do they? A few years back they would never dare to publicly defame a Bollywood star in the press.'

'Sir, they still don't. Bollywood stars are still like gods.'

'You're not making any sense.'

'Subrina Basi was not Bollywood, sir. She was Dollywood. As in, the Delhi-based film industry.'

'No wonder she was on drugs, eh,' Kulkarni said. 'Double D-list celebrity in a D-list film industry, eh.'

'Dollywood is emerging,' Pankaj said. 'You shouldn't laugh. One day it'll overtake Bollywood. There is solid money in Delhi. She may have been D-list but she had a certain style and family wealth so she got into quite a few press releases. She made it to all the right parties too.'

Chupplejeep raised his palm. 'Okay, enough Bollywood, Dollywood. Instinct tells me this isn't a suicide.'

Pankaj frowned.

'Kulkarni? Tell us.'

'Look at the colour of the water,' Kulkarni said.

Both Chupplejeep and Pankaj did as they were told. 'Look at the way the wrists have been cut – big vertical cuts at least four inches long from the base of the hand to mid-point on the forearm, severing the ulnar artery.'

Chupplejeep nodded.

'I would expect to see a lot more blood from cuts such as these. The water should be a deep red colour. And the cuts themselves, they appear smooth and deep on both wrists. There are no hesitation marks, just one small nick on the right wrist. It would take a lot of strength and determination to do this to yourself, no matter how high on drugs you were. The first cut would have definitely sobered up our celebrity and the second cut, well, unless the victim was ambidextrous I would have expected the cut to be shallow and jagged. Also, if you cut one wrist and it was bleeding, it would be difficult to cut the other with the same precision, don't you think, eh?'

Chupplejeep smiled. His instincts were still in working order. He had been worried that working in the villages, with so few homicides to solve, he may have lost his ability to pick up the small nuances which alerted his attention to foul play: the way Subrina looked in the bath, like she had been placed; the bath water that wasn't as red as he had seen in other genuine suicides. He had noticed all this and made his deduction within seconds. What Kulkarni was saying made perfect sense.

'Plus, there's some fresh bruising on the legs and some bruising made not too long ago on the arms. I could be wrong but these could be defensive wounds, suggesting a struggle.'

Chupplejeep nodded. 'Time of death?'

'You always ask this. This is not the movies, Detective. I can't just estimate time of death instantly, like that,' Kulkarni said, clicking his fingers.

'I need to know roughly for when we interview people. I need to know who was around when she was murdered.'

Kulkarni rubbed his chin thoughtfully. 'The body being submerged in water like this may have slowed the rate of decomposition. Plus the air conditioning has been on. I estimate that she died in the last twelve hours.'

Chupplejeep looked at his watch. 'It's two in the afternoon now. So we need to know her whereabouts from last night. Any sign of a break-in? The bathroom window is secure with that metal grille. Was the door of the room locked from the inside?'

'No. The maid had no problem gaining access,' Kulkarni said.

'So, Subrina either let her attacker in or they had a master key.'

'Ya,' Kulkarni said.

12

'Or they climbed over the balcony. The balcony door was open.'

'But the air con was on?' Pankaj said.

''es,' Kulkarni replied.

'Hmm.' Chupplejeep looked at Subrina's limp body. It was certainly uneconomical to leave the air conditioning on while doors were left open, but it wasn't unheard of. Especially when it came to the rich.

'There is enough reason for me to do a full autopsy,' said Kulkarni. 'This is not going to be an open and shut case, if that is what you were hoping for. I know Christabel has been keeping you busy these days.'

Pankaj laughed. Chupplejeep narrowed his eyes at the medical examiner.

'Sorry, Detective.'

'Sorry, indeed,' Chupplejeep said.

~

It had been almost a month since his birthday, a month since he had taken Christabel on a palm-leaf thatched houseboat along the backwaters of Kerala. The wooden boat had been an unforgettable experience. They had breakfasted daily on bowls of fresh fruit and dined on spicy *Theeyal* of fat, juicy mussels and succulent crab scooped up straight from the riverbed. And they had slept peacefully too, to the sound of the waters of the Punnamada Lake lapping against the hull.

But it hadn't been plain sailing from the start. Christabel had been in a miserable mood from the time they stepped onto the houseboat. 'Why couldn't you just have a party in Goa?' she grumbled. 'Venice of the East, my foot! It would have been much cheaper and more fun to stay in Goa with our friends.'

Chupplejeep could tell that his girlfriend's irritation would take time to dissipate and he was determined to make Kerala memorable for the right reasons. So as she was unpacking and complaining about this expensive holiday, despite his sweaty palms and rapid heartbeat, he retrieved the small red velvet box from his pocket and got down on one knee. 'What are you…' she started and then Chupplejeep saw the realisation in her eyes. The day had finally come – the day she thought would never happen.

'Christu,' Chupplejeep said, his voice catching slightly. 'You're everything to me. I can't imagine my life without you.' He paused. 'Christabel, would you do me the honour of becoming my wife?'

Even now, just thinking about his proposal made his hands go cold. He had done it. He had asked the question, now all he had to do was go through with it.

'Yes,' Christabel said, her eyes brimming. Chupplejeep had stood up and slipped the ring on her finger.

'A ruby, how did you know?'

Chupplejeep wanted to say that she had given him enough clues by leaving magazines around the house with strategically folded pages, but he refrained. Despite his apprehension, he hadn't wanted to spoil the moment. And from that point in their trip, Christabel was all smiles. He could have pushed her off the boat and she would have still been smiling. He had to laugh to himself when on the last evening she said, 'Oh, I can see why everyone raves about Kerala,' as the boat gently glided past a small fishing village littered with stone and wooden huts. She didn't mention that four other houseboats, in line behind them, were making the exact same trip.

Yes, the holiday had certainly been a success for Christabel, but ever since their arrival back in Goa, Chupplejeep hadn't had a single conversation with his new fiancée that didn't involve the wedding in some way or another. And with each day that passed, he found himself wondering whether he actually wanted to go through with it. But he hadn't said anything yet and the wedding plans were snowballing. This wedding was going to happen with or without him.

Should they have an engagement party? When should they start looking at venues? What time of year should they marry? What flowers were most appropriate? These were all questions that Christabel wanted responses to and he didn't have the answers. It was a sorry state indeed.

When he did contribute to the conversation, Christabel ignored him. It seemed that whatever he said, she decided to do the exact opposite. He had considered pointing this out, but she was so happy, he let her be. Plus, it was better that he stayed out of the wedding business. It only made him break out in a cold sweat.

'Sir,' Pankaj said, pulling him out of his memory.

Chupplejeep looked up and gathered his thoughts. 'We need to clear the room. Kulkarni and his team need to take samples of the bath water and move the body to the lab for the autopsy to confirm the cause of death. We need to get the body identified and get the family's permission for autopsy.'

'Of course,' Pankaj said.

'But first let's go and speak to the woman who found the body.'

CHAPTER FOUR

Pankaj followed Chupplejeep towards the balcony of room 13. As he passed through the room, he noticed several medicine bottles on the bedside table. He saw Chupplejeep point them out to one of the sub-police officers and motion to them to bag them up. Pankaj had only ever been involved in one previous homicide, and in that case the victim was found in the nude. Now on his second case, the body was also found naked. He had to ask himself, was the probability of death higher when one was naked?

Stepping out onto the balcony, Pankaj took a deep breath and marvelled at the picturesque view. Dhesera was a large village on a hill overlooking miles of lush green trees and vegetation. And even though the village was only a few metres higher than Little Larara, the air seemed cleaner.

Dhesera had been a sleepy village until a developer snapped up an old and run-down colonial house, paying a hefty bribe to a local minister to turn it into a fifteen-bed boutique hotel. The Golden Orchid promised peace and tranquillity to its guests and the gardens were full of *objets d'art.* For some time now, Goa had been moving away from the beach parties and raves to rural retreats where illicit drug indulgence could take place in the comfort of beautiful hotels, amidst tranquil gardens. The super rich of India escaped the rat race of Mumbai and Delhi just for this, and the Golden Orchid was raking it in.

Pankaj wondered how locals would react to a suspicious death in their village. Would they panic? Or, like most villagers these days, would they take it in their stride?

What Kulkarni had said about the victim being unable to slash both her wrists with such precision made sense, but he could also understand why Subrina Basi would want to take her life. Last year *Icon Bites* published an article titled *Subrina Basi – Lost not Found* telling readers that despite the actress being born into wealth and attending the best acting schools in India, she never made it to Bollywood. Instead, she stuck to Dollywood. After a string of failed movies and relationships, she turned to her life-long friends – whiskey and cocaine. Pankaj knew that it was inevitable that something like this would eventually happen to the troubled star.

'Pankaj, get your head out of the clouds and get some sugary tea for Indu,' Chupplejeep said.

'Yes, sir.' Only now did Pankaj notice the woman sitting on the balcony floor. He looked for rope marks or scuffs on the paintwork to indicate that someone had scaled the side of the building to gain access to the room from the balcony, but there was nothing.

Chupplejeep pulled Pankaj to one side and whispered, 'The maid is clearly shaken up. Her colleague, Rosie, has gone to tell their families what has happened.'

The detective sighed. 'Look at those guests loitering down there,' he said, pointing to a young couple at the front of the hotel. Their newlywed status was displayed by the *mehndi* work of intricate designs on the bride's hands, and *choora*, a set of red and white bangles on the girl's wrists. There was also a group of girls lingering. He turned to one of the sub-officers. 'Tell them to clear off,' Chupplejeep instructed. 'News like this will travel fast. If Kulkarni thinks this death is suspicious then we could have a media circus on our hands. She may have been a D-list celebrity, but these journalists will make out like she was A-list for a story. As soon as I report this to the Inspector General, he'll want to know everything.'

Chupplejeep looked back at Pankaj. 'So when you go to the kitchen to make the tea, I want you to talk to the staff and see what you can find out. You know better than me that the staff will know all the secrets of the hotel's residents.'

'Yes, sir.'

'Pankaj.'

Pankaj turned to look at his boss.

'When I say the Inspector General will want to know everything, I mean everything. If Subrina Basi had biryani for breakfast, he'll want to know about it. Now stop dawdling and go.'

CHAPTER FIVE

Indu was slumped on the tiled floor, her head in her hands. 'It must have been a big shock to see Ms Basi like that, no?' Chupplejeep tried.

The girl whimpered.

'It's not a pleasant sight for a young lady to see.'

'It was terrible. I'll never forget it for the rest of my life.'

'Did you know Ms Basi?'

'I cleaned her room daily.'

'You liked her?'

Indu was silent. She dried her tears with the hem of her apron and looked at the detective. 'It's wrong to speak ill of the dead.'

'But I'm a detective. It's my job to know everything about Ms Basi and I can only find out about her from speaking to the people who met her.'

'She was murdered?' Indu asked, her tears falling afresh. 'I don't think I'll be able to sleep or use a bath ever again.'

'We don't know if it's murder yet. We have to do some tests first to find out.'

Indu looked at the detective out of the corner of her eye. 'I was just her maid whilst she was staying here. I didn't know her.'

'How many days did you clean her room?' Chupplejeep asked.

Indu looked back down towards her apron. 'I didn't count. She came here for IFFI.'

'*Haan*, the film festival. But that finished some weeks back.'

'She decided to stay on in Goa till after New Year's Eve. Her boyfriend arrived yesterday and also there was some art exhibition she wanted to see. She was best friends with the painter.'

'You know the name of the artist?'

'No, but you can find out, easily. The work is at a gallery in the village. They are running an art school there for one month.'

Chupplejeep nodded. There was only one gallery, accommodated in an old house in Dhesera, and he knew very well who had rented the space out. 'Madam told you this?'

'I overheard her,' she mumbled, 'when I was cleaning her room.'

'That's okay. It's not wrong. You can't help it if she was talking on the phone whilst you were cleaning. If she wanted to keep it private, she wouldn't have spoken of these things in front of you. I tell my officers the same thing. If they want to keep things private they shouldn't talk on their mobiles in front of other people.'

Indu nodded. 'She was always on her mobile. That's what I remember of Madam. A couple of days ago she was begging someone to meet her. Then yesterday on the telephone she was speaking to someone and she sounded so angry. She was cursing, saying that the truth must be told. She said it again and again. It must have had to do with her boyfriend. Everyone knows he likes to mess around with other women. Poor Madam, she sounded as if she was crying. But it's rude to look and she always wore her big dark glasses, so you couldn't see her eyes.' Indu smiled. 'She loved wearing big glasses, red lipstick and her gold chain and she always wore black. Everything in her wardrobe is black.'

'You looked in her wardrobe?'

Indu chewed the end of her hair. 'Maybe, just once or twice.'

'Does Madam have nice things?'

'Expensive things. She didn't care for them. She threw her bangles on the bedside table, her necklaces were all knotted and in a heap on the dresser. I had to tidy them every day.'

'There are so many clothes lying on the floor. We'll need to check if anything is missing.' Chupplejeep watched Indu fidgeting with the end of her plait as he spoke. 'It looks like there may have also been a burglary.'

Indu sat up. 'Madam's room is always like this. It takes me a long time to clean up after her.'

'It sounds like you were very good to Ms Basi.'

Indu shrugged.

'What else do you remember of Madam?'

Indu looked at Chupplejeep for a moment before answering. 'One time she made me laugh. She asked me if she had eaten in the restaurant two nights back. I told her she hadn't. She laughed and said that she didn't trust her own mind anymore. Madam was rarely funny, and I wasn't sure if I was allowed to laugh. It was like she was daydreaming when she said it. But then she started laughing and so I too laughed, then she asked me if I had a sister. I told her no. Then she was lost again in another daydream. That was the only time she asked me anything about myself. The rest of the time she used to just whinge and scold. I hated cleaning her room when she was around. If she was passed out, it was okay, I could clean around her. When she was drunk, that too was okay because she was happy when she was drunk. But when she was sober, she had a mouth like *kachra,* dustbin.'

~

Pankaj passed a few guests wandering around the lobby, marvelling at the Christmas decorations, before he found the small clean kitchen at the rear of the hotel next to the staff entrance. In the kitchen, he started opening the cupboards one by one until he found a box of Brooke Bond tea bags. He was still pondering over the dead woman and why Chupplejeep was adamant that this was a homicide. The more he thought about it, the more he was certain that the troubled Ms Basi had taken her own life.

Then out of the corner of his eye, he saw a figure dart out from an inner kitchen office towards the back door that led into the garden. He dropped the box of tea and followed in pursuit. He realised he was running after a man – a tall, thin man who ran like a cheetah.

He followed the figure through the hotel garden, thick with shrubbery and littered with ponds, rock gardens and huge sculptures that Pankaj could only imagine were the *objets d'art*. He stopped to catch his breath at a small fountain and took the opportunity to splash his face with water. He looked back at the hotel, now just a small building in the distance. He didn't realise how far he had run and he wasn't sure how much farther he could go.

He started to give chase again – this fellow clearly had something to hide – but when the man reached the edge of the garden, he disappeared into an unruly wooded area, and Pankaj gave up. It was no use. He turned around and walked back to the hotel.

Once he was back in the kitchen, he retrieved the box of tea bags from the floor and started looking for the sugar.

'What the hell are you doing in my kitchen?' Pankaj heard an aggressive voice behind him. He spun around to face a short, stocky Nepalese man wearing a white chef shirt and black and white checked trousers. He held a flat frying pan poised and ready to hit someone with.

'I'm looking for some sugar to make tea.'

The Nepalese shook his head from side to side and lowered the pan. 'I'll make it for you. I'm Abhik, the chef here.' He looked at Pankaj's khaki uniform. 'You must be a policeman here investigating the death of the actress.'

'Yes,' Pankaj said, introducing himself. He noticed the man's eyes were cold and dark, like he was dead inside. Quickly, catching himself staring, he looked away. 'Did you see much of her?'

'Nah, she rarely came down to eat with the other guests. She ate out, mostly. Occasionally, she would order food up to her room.'

'What?' Pankaj said, remembering Chupplejeep's words. 'What did she eat?'

'You police want to know everything. Mostly she ate chilli cheese toast,' Abhik said, putting the pan on the work surface. He plucked a tea bag from the box and put it in a cup. He put the kettle on to boil then appeared to relax a little as his shoulders dropped. He smiled. 'I was a big fan of Subrina Basi. She was a good, no, a great actress. She could have done Bollywood if she had wanted. No problem.' His eyes instantly brightened.

'Are there many staff here at the hotel?'

'A few. Hari is the general manager. Rosie and Indu clean the rooms. Furtado mans the front desk, although he's a useless fellow. There's a gardener-cum-bellboy. He's the man who just gave you the run around, a barman-cum-waiter, a driver-cum-handyman, a watchman and then there's me, the chef or cook.'

'Oh, so you saw the chase,' Pankaj said, feeling a little inept.

Abhik laughed. 'They need to give cops here better fitness training. Although Nishok is a slippery fellow.'

'Why did he run?'

'You're a cop.'

'Has he done something wrong?'

'Not everyone wants to speak to the cops.'

Pankaj could see his point. Still, he didn't see why Nishok had to run. It instantly made him look suspicious. He made a note of the man's name and occupation in his black notebook. 'Does the owner ever visit?'

'Now and again.'

'Has he visited recently, while Ms Basi was here?' Pankaj asked as the kettle came to the boil.

'Nah, his mistress and his wife are both about to have his babies.'

'Oh,' Pankaj said, feeling his cheeks flush.

Abhik poured the water from the kettle into the cup and gave it a stir. 'Sugar?'

Pankaj nodded. 'You have a very neat and tidy kitchen.'

Abhik straightened his shoulders. 'Everything has its place here,' he said, spooning the sugar into the tea.

'Are there many other guests staying here at the moment?'

'Check with Furtado. I heard Ms Basi rented two floors for her and her people. There were various faces coming and going over IFFI, but this past week it's been quiet, just a few guests. Mostly people from out have been coming here to see the art, having a drink in the

26

bar. Like that couple your officer just scared off. In the next day or so we have more guests coming. But they may cancel now, after hearing the news.' He took the tea bag out of the cup, added some milk and passed it to Pankaj.

Pankaj thanked him, but as he was walking out of the kitchen, a shiver ran down his spine. He stopped. He hadn't thought the case was suspicious, but now he was beginning to wonder. Was it the gardener running away which made him suspicious, or was it the way Abhik's cold eyes came to life when he mentioned Ms Basi?

'Something wrong, Officer?'

'Can I ask you if any of your knives have gone missing?' he asked.

Abhik curled his bottom lip. His eyes flickered like a man trying to control his anger. He stood still.

'Could you take a look?' Pankaj encouraged, touching his baton with his free hand.

The chef walked over to the other side of the kitchen and opened a large drawer to the side of the cooker. 'Serrated, cleaver, carving, bread, two boning, four paring, four utility…wait…my straight-edge utility knife is missing!'

'Are you worried?'

Abhik hesitated. 'I'm pissed…N-no, Nishok could have needed it in the garden to save an animal tangled in the trees. It's happened before. That fellow prefers animals to humans, even though I make him pluck the chickens,' he said with a sinister smile. 'Or Furtado could have borrowed it to open a package.'

'Don't you keep track of your knives?'

'Normally…'

'You do?'

'Look, we're not in America, Officer. This is India, who cares if one knife goes missing.'

Pankaj thanked Abhik for the tea again and walked out. It was strange. For someone who kept such an orderly kitchen with nothing out of place, to be missing a knife was a sign that something was definitely not right.

CHAPTER SIX

'What took you so long with the tea? That poor girl needed something fast, not one hour later.' Chupplejeep took the cup of tea from Pankaj. He handed it to Indu who was now being comforted by Rosie.

Pankaj relayed to Chupplejeep what had happened. 'Suspicious, don't you think?'

Chupplejeep twisted the end of his moustache. 'Could be.'

'I think so, sir.'

'Neither of the maids were around yesterday evening. They clocked off at six and went home. Check their stories later.'

'If it turns into a murder investigation.'

'It will, you'll see. Anyway, whilst you were prancing around in the garden I spoke to Hari, the general manager of the hotel. He knows of nothing strange happening here yesterday, but he did say that the two ducks at the hotel were stolen last night.'

'Ducks?' Pankaj said, still feeling slightly embarrassed at his inability to catch the gardener.

'They have a small pond with two ducks. Well, they had a pond with two ducks. Now they just have a pond. No ducks.'

'Sir, are you saying that whilst Subrina Basi was dying, someone stole two ducks?' As Pankaj was running through the garden, he had seen a pond with some netting next to it. He wondered if this was the duck pond Chupplejeep was referring to.

'I'm not saying that at all. It's probably just a coincidence.' Even though they both knew that when it came to homicide, coincidences were rare. 'A fox probably took them or perhaps they flew away.'

'I see,' said Pankaj, scratching his head.

'Hari gave me Subrina Basi's check-in form, but it tells us nothing new. I need to liaise with the commissioner in Delhi and get the news to her family. We need to get formal identification of the body first, though. The maid says Subrina's boyfriend is staying here at the hotel. We need to find him.'

'That we'll do, sir. It's a good thing her family is in Delhi. I hate having to break the news to the family.'

'Inspector General Gosht wants the autopsy done quickly. He's hoping it's a suicide despite what I've told him. Kulkarni is going to be under pressure. We're in the height of peak tourist season and Goa can't afford to have a high-profile murder, or any murder for that matter.'

'What do we do in the meantime, sir? Whilst we wait for the autopsy results?'

'We interview the rest of the staff and guests. Hari tells me that Subrina had booked all the rooms on this floor for herself and the floor below for her guests. She checked in on the 3rd with a whole entourage just in time for IFFI.'

'That must have been expensive, sir. Prices are always double when IFFI is on and over the Christmas break.'

'She was due to check out on the 6th of January.'

'A nice long break in Goa.'

'Most of her guests left on the 10th December. Apparently, Ayesha Saxena was having a big party in Mumbai last night. Everyone who was invited left in time for the party.'

'I bet that hurt Subrina, sir. Ayesha Saxena and Subrina Basi were best friends at one time. They had a falling out when Ayesha got a big role that Subrina had also auditioned for. Maybe that's what pushed her over the edge.'

'Hurt her enough to commit suicide? I don't think so. These celebrities have thick skin. Yesterday Subrina's boyfriend, Dinesh, arrived. They had a party in the hotel. Get me the guest list. Start with the receptionist and find out where the boyfriend is. Also, see which other guests were here in the last twenty-four hours. Make sure nobody checks out before we've spoken to them.'

'What will you be doing, sir?'

Chupplejeep looked over the balcony. 'I'm going to deal with the press.'

31

~

Pankaj found Furtado in the back office behind the reception desk, playing solitaire on his computer. He knocked on the open door. 'Police Officer Pankaj,' he said, introducing himself and extending his right hand.

'Furtado,' the receptionist said, briefly looking away from his screen. He clumsily shook hands with Pankaj. His tongue protruded slightly from his lips as he concentrated on moving the five of spades onto the six of diamonds.

'Do you mind if I ask you a couple of questions about your guests?'

Furtado turned around and gave Pankaj his full attention. 'Shoot.'

'Firstly, can I ask who has access to the room keys?'

'Most of the staff have access.'

'Even the gardener and the watchman?'

'No *re*. Not people like that. The maids and the managers.'

'And the receptionist, of course.'

'Naturally.'

'Would it be difficult for anyone else to get access to a key?'

Furtado looked behind him at the little wooden pigeonholes. Keys were inside some of the boxes, others were empty. 'What do you think?'

'So there is no keeping track of keys here at the hotel?'

'If the manager asks, I never said that.'

'And are any keys missing for Ms Basi's room?'

Furtado peered again inside the wooden key boxes. 'No, no. She had the only key to her room.'

'How many guests were staying at the hotel last night?'

Furtado stood up and walked out to the front desk. Pankaj followed. The receptionist pulled out a ledger and opened it. He ran his finger down the page. 'Last night we had two guests.'

'Only two?' Pankaj asked, wondering how the receptionist couldn't remember that without consulting his log.

'Subrina Basi and Dinesh.'

'In this fifteen-room hotel? Only one room was taken?'

The receptionist shrugged. 'What to do? Her guests left. She was still paying for most of the rooms. The others are not booked till just before Christmas. What does it matter?'

'I just saw some guests in the lobby. Who were they?'

'Eh, they are locals. Come to see our decorations to see if they want to use the same designer for their shop.'

Pankaj nodded.

'Anyway, it was two rooms not one room.'

Pankaj leaned in closer. 'What?' he asked, wondering if he misheard.

'Ms Basi and Dinesh stayed in separate rooms.'

Pankaj took out his jotter from his shirt pocket to make a note of what Furtado was saying. 'Why was that?'

'They had the whole floor to themselves. These celebrities are funny people. There are two large rooms on the top floor. I don't know if they slept in the same room or what, but all his clothes are in one room, all hers are in the other. Rosie told me.'

'Hmm, I see. I heard there was a big party here last night. Who all were there?'

'Big party? No, no, no.' Furtado yawned. 'They made enough mess, but there were only a few people.'

'Who?'

'Dinesh, of course. That was why Subrina was hosting the party, to welcome him to Goa. But you see, most of her friends had gone. Gone to Ayesha Saxena's party in Mumbai no doubt. Madam was in a foul mood all day. Complaining on her cell to anyone who would listen.'

'What was she saying?'

'That Saxena was a cow and that she only got the big Bollywood roles because she was dropping her *chuddies* for all the big directors. You think it's true?'

Pankaj looked at Furtado. 'I don't know,' he said, but he thought that it was highly likely. Bollywood, in his opinion, was full of sleaze.

'She was also saying that people were spreading rumours that Saxena was sleeping with Dinesh but that he was going to be in Goa with her on the night of the big party. She was very happy about that. That's why she wanted to have a party for him that same night. But it was more of a gathering.'

'Who else came for this gathering?'

Furtado leaned in. 'That artist and his friend,' he said conspiratorially.

'Advani?'

'That's the one. He is so, what do they say, Officer? Over the top, yes. Calling everyone his darling, kissing everyone on both cheeks, even the men, can you believe it? And that man he was with, do you think that…' Furtado shook his head from side to side.

'What?' Pankaj asked, feeling a little hot under the collar.

'Do you think they are friendly?'

Pankaj felt his cheeks flush. 'No,' he said. But while Furtado was telling him about what the people at the gathering ate and drank, Pankaj began to wonder about Advani and Takshak. He had seen them together twice now, both times at the police station regarding the blackmail case.

Advani was, like Furtado had said, a little over the top but he showed no real affection for Takshak or vice versa. When Advani first reported the crime he had wept as he relayed his situation to Pankaj, but Takshak didn't put his arm around him like a lover or even a friend would. As far as Pankaj could see, Takshak was merely Advani's assistant and paid companion.

'Were there many staff around last night? I'll need a list of all the guests staying here from Subrina Basi's arrival on the third, as well as a full list of the staff here. In particular I want to talk to Nishok.'

Furtado laughed. 'Good luck! That fellow won't say anything! Anyway, *baba*, not many staff were still here by the time the party finished. I was here and so were the watchman and the waiter. I asked Madam if they wanted the driver to stay on to take Advani and his fellow back. But she said they were staying close so they would walk. "I want to see the stars and the moon on my stroll home," Advani had said to confirm. He was totally drunk by this point.'

'So Abhik the chef and Nishok the gardener were not here?'

'No, no.'

'What time did the party wind up?'

'At one in the morning Advani and Takshak left. Five minutes after that, Xavier said that Subrina Basi had excused him and went home. He didn't look too happy.'

'Xavier, the waiter? Do you know what was wrong?'

Furtado shook his head.

'Okay, so what time did Subrina Basi and Dinesh go up to their rooms?'

'Shortly after that. I heard them shouting at one another as they went. Perhaps that was why they had separate rooms.'

'What were they saying?'

Furtado looked around him with pursed lips. 'I didn't hear everything, but she was accusing him of sleeping with that Saxena woman. I can't say I blame him. She is much better looking. That Subrina Basi looked utterly haggard. Do you know she was forty-three? She looked at least fifty. No wonder she was stuck in Dollywood. After that, I heard a loud thud. I looked up. She had fallen on the stairs. Dinesh picked her up. Then after some time I saw him storm off.'

Perhaps that's what caused the bruising on the arms and legs, Pankaj thought. That must be what Kulkarni identified, presuming they were defensive wounds. 'Where did Dinesh go? Did he walk somewhere?'

'*Na re baba*. He had a driver. You think a big-shot hero like Dinesh roams around without a car and driver? You police are something else.'

Pankaj made a face. Dinesh, in his opinion, was not a hero. He had done two Palmolive commercials and had released a song, which flopped in the charts. The only things he had going for him were his looks and his grandmother's fortune which, as the only grandchild, he was due to inherit soon. Everyone knew that. *Icon Bites* had reported it just last month.

'Dinesh left with his driver at around two-thirty this morning,' Furtado said. 'I haven't seen either of them since.'

CHAPTER SEVEN

Chupplejeep watched the man wearing a blue and yellow checked shirt and black jeans leaning against a leafy gulmohar at the front of the hotel. The tree, with its feathery green leaves, was a perfect place for a cunning reporter to take shade from the afternoon sun.

'Bonaparte,' Chupplejeep said, walking towards the journalist. He raised a hand to greet the reporter and put on his most genuine smile.

'Ah! The great detective himshelf,' Bonaparte said.

'The same one.' Chupplejeep twisted one end of his moustache. Bonaparte still had his lisp even after all that speech therapy.

'I see you are recovering your reputation since all that business with that Panaji case. I must admit I was always on your side, even back then when everyone said you were a fool for not taking that bribe. We need pukka cops like you.'

'You were working for the *Tribune* then, no?'

Bonaparte nodded.

Chupplejeep said nothing. He remembered the headlines of the *Tribune*: *Detective Demoted!* and *Chupplejeep*

– *The Village Cop*. Yes, Bonaparte had commended him on his moral compass but he also had a good laugh at his expense when he was transferred out of the city.

'I'm at the *Express* now.'

'Oh, so you too are in the villages?' Chupplejeep said with a smile.

Bonaparte narrowed his eyes. 'Only on a secondment for a year. Getting back to my roots.'

'*Aacha,* anyway, enough of the chit-chat. Let's get on with this. I have things to do.'

'Fine. So tell me, can you confirm that the troubled actress, Subrina Basi, died here last night?'

Chupplejeep shook his head.

'You can't?'

'No.'

'Why not? I've heard from a reputable source that the actress was killed here last night.'

'Killed here?'

'You're a homicide detective, are you not?'

'Yes.'

'Then it must be a murder, if you're here.'

'I am the most senior member of staff in this area, that's why I am here. Remember, in the villages we cannot afford to differentiate between homicide detectives and others. We solve any crime in our area.'

'Sho, you're saying her death is not suspicious.'

Chupplejeep suppressed a smile, Bonaparte's inability to pronounce the word so was endearing and softened his otherwise Machiavellian character. 'I can say that we are dealing with a body. Details to be confirmed when we have more information.'

'That's it? Why can't you tell me? I already know.'

'Know what?'

'Her boyfriend did it.'

'And how do you know this?' Chupplejeep asked. 'Journalist playing detective, are you?'

'In most cases, victims are killed by someone they know. The whole world and his wife know that her boyfriend has hit women before. A punch to the arm, a slap to the face. He doesn't care. This time he took it too far.'

Chupplejeep nodded. So this was why Dinesh was nowhere to be seen. Had the boyfriend done it? Was it that simple? He had seen cases like this. The boyfriend, jealous or angry because his girl was getting attention from other men or had said something to bring out his insecurities, throttled or punched her into a coma. It had happened before, it would happen again.

He took a breath. 'Listen, Bonaparte, if you print what you think, you know it won't benefit anyone.'

'The readers will benefit. If there is a murderer running on the loose in Goa, the people have the right to know. And if it is one of our movie icons then we must know. Goans take their *filmi* love very seriously.'

'You hold off printing any story about what happened here until we identify the body at least. Give the family some respect.'

Bonaparte seemed to mull this over. 'What if I had some information on the actress? I just told you about her violent boyfriend, but I have something even better.'

'If it is Ms Basi we end up talking about, I would expect you to tell the police what you know like the model citizen that you are.' Chupplejeep turned around and started walking back towards the entrance of the hotel.

Bonaparte started following him. 'We could make a deal. You give me an exclusive, I'll give you information you can't get anywhere else. Invaluable information.'

At the entrance of the hotel, Chupplejeep stopped. He turned, looked at Bonaparte and opened his mouth to say something, but then stopped himself. Instead, he turned to the man with the stick who was dawdling outside the main door of the hotel. 'Watchman,' he said, 'make sure this man doesn't come in.'

~

Chupplejeep found Pankaj talking to the waiter in Firefly, the restaurant at the Golden Orchid.

'You should see this place at night. There are hundreds of small green and white lights in the trees so when it's dark, it's truly magical,' the barman was saying to Pankaj.

Chupplejeep introduced himself. Pankaj said, 'Xavier here was just telling me what time Ms Basi retired to her room.'

'Yes. At around one in the morning, when the artist left, Dinesh produced a bag of white powder. And I did something terrible. If boss finds out, God only knows what will happen,' Xavier said, shaking his head.

'What did you do?' Pankaj asked.

'I knew what this white powder was. Of course, these days everybody is knowing what this is. I know you are cops, but what to say. It happens.'

'It's okay,' Chupplejeep said. 'You can tell us.'

'Usually, I see this white powder and I mind my own business. I know they line it up on a tray and snort it through a thousand rupee note. I don't usually bat an eyelid. But I was feeling so sleepy. I was tired from a late night the day before. It was already one, and I knew that my shift today began at seven, for breakfast. I don't know what came over me but I made a disapproving sound and I think I shook my head when I saw this bag of powder.'

'That's not so bad,' Pankaj said. 'Your boss should be glad you are discouraging this sort of behaviour. We wouldn't like to think that drug taking was happening here regularly. If that is the case we may need to investigate this further.'

Chupplejeep nodded in agreement.

'Please don't tell my boss. He'll fire me.'

'We have more pressing things to deal with at the moment,' Chupplejeep said.

'Boss does not like drugs at all at the hotel.'

'So why would he be angry at you for letting your feelings on drugs be known to Dinesh and Subrina Basi?'

'Because I'm just a waiter. It's not my job to tell customers how to behave. Hari can do so if he wishes. Not me. Guests don't like it at all. They won't come back if they think a barman or waiter is judging them.'

Chupplejeep nodded. 'Perhaps you don't want guests like that in your hotel?'

'When word got out that Dinesh and Subrina were staying here, rooms started to get booked fast. We are now fully booked from New Year till the monsoons.'

'So what happened when Dinesh saw your disappointment?'

'I held my breath. I knew what I had done. I thought Dinesh was going to give me a tight slap.'

'Do guests normally hit you?' Pankaj asked, his mouth gaping open.

Xavier looked at his shoes. 'No, but you never know. And I'd rather a slap than my manager finding out. I need this job to support my family. Dinesh just told me to leave. He said, "Boy, you must be tired working such long hours. Tomorrow morning make sure my baby gets whatever she wants for breakfast. Now, you go to sleep."'

'So you left?'

'Of course. I could see he didn't want me around. I was getting my things from behind the bar when Madam Basi said not to disturb her for breakfast. She was slurring her words. Dinesh laughed at her and then kissed her on the mouth. They both laughed.'

This didn't tie in to what Furtado had said. According to the receptionist, minutes later they were shouting at one another. He pressed Xavier further. 'So they were both in a good mood when you left?'

'Yes. But as I was leaving I heard Subrina Basi ask where Dinesh was going? She didn't sound too pleased with his answer.'

'Which was?'

'I didn't hear. I quickly scurried out of the room then and out the back door. I didn't really care to listen to their argument. I just wanted my bed.'

'I see,' Pankaj said. It was all slowly falling into place.

CHAPTER EIGHT

The convent was situated midway between Margao and Panaji in a small town where little happened. It was shaded from the sun by towering ashoka trees. Men sat drinking *feni* and playing carrom at the village taverna. Rickety buses, dangerously full and leaning to one side, stopped at a makeshift bus stand for the engineering college close by.

Suki sat in the corner of the room, contemplating her fate. The other sisters always said that whatever happened, good or bad, it was God's wish. Suki had believed that at first, because she had no choice. It was easier to accept God's wish than reality – a family's rejection and a murdered child. There was no reason for such atrocities so it had to be God's doing. And her calling? That too would have been God's desire. The church had been her salvation when life had not been worth living. That had been twenty years ago. Twenty years had passed since she had surrendered herself to God.

Suki couldn't say that she enjoyed her existence. She rose at four in the morning, said her prayers in the adjacent church and did her chores around the convent. There was always silver to polish or rosaries to sell at the church. Then after a simple lunch of rice and vegetables, she would do some needlework to sell in the market. She often worked on her crochet in the courtyard. It was peaceful out there, and crochet always took her mind off the real world and the events from her past.

Lately though, she felt an increasing dissatisfaction. A gnawing thought deep inside, telling her that she still had a chance to live a full life – a more satisfactory life outside the protective walls of the convent. Recently, when she looked around her bedroom, she only felt disappointment. The off-white walls had turned yellow over the years, the floor and the door were a dull brown, and they all evoked a feeling of sorrow in her. There was only a bed and a dresser in her room. She had endured the same mattress, as hard as stone, for as long as she could remember and wanted desperately to complain out loud. She couldn't. She had willingly signed up to this and it became her duty to live this way.

But now everything was about to change. She had met someone and he had found a way out for her. When he looked at her with those brown eyes and soft lips, full of warmth and compassion, she felt lighter. But this lightness often preceded the feeling of guilt. She tried to push the image of his kind face out of her mind by thinking about God. It usually worked, but lately this little trick had failed her. She couldn't stop thinking about him and she was desperate to talk about him, but talking to one of the other nuns would be too much of a risk. Even Sister Carmina, who had taken a vow of silence, because she already knew too much. Perhaps she could just go to confession and take penance instead.

Suki put her hands together and looked at the cross on her bedroom wall. 'Why do I feel like this now, after being here for so long, and being grateful for your protection for all these years?' she asked God. Slowly she raised herself off her bed, tapped the headboard three times with the palm of her hand and checked under the bed for her box of letters. They were still there – safe. Then she lifted the mattress. She retrieved a newspaper cutting from the wooden base and looked at the picture.

Why had Subrina wanted to make contact again after all these years? Why couldn't she have left the past in the past? Suki should have been like the silent Sister Carmina. She should have joined the Carmel Cloister in Chicalim and stayed within the four walls of the cloister, never speaking to anyone. No, instead she was free to come and go as she pleased and that is exactly what she had done. It wouldn't be long now until her secrets came out. She could feel it in her bones.

The newspaper clipping was a picture of a well-known Bollywood starlet and there in the background was the image of Subrina. Suki didn't usually pick up newspapers left in the church, as they often were. She preferred not knowing what was happening in the real world. She got most of her information from the other nuns along with their bigoted opinions. Nuns were not supposed to gossip, but sometimes she could swear they did nothing but. Recently, they had been talking about

IFFI. She had remembered her love for Indian film all those years ago, so when she saw the newspaper in the church a few weeks ago, she picked it up.

Of course, she knew her sister had become a film star. On the rare occasion when her mother was over from Delhi unbeknownst to her father, she shared the family news with her. Suki's father had disowned her when she lost her belief in Guru Nanak and stepped away from Sikhism, embracing the Catholic faith. Her family had then moved to Delhi and in doing so they wiped away all traces of her from their lives. Now she wondered if finding forgiveness and salvation in the Catholic Church had really been worth losing her family over?

Her sister, Subrina, had used her change in religion and her ostracism from the family to rid herself from speaking to her. But Suki knew the events of that fateful night had more to do with it than her choice of religion. It wasn't as if Subrina was religious. Yes, she made a big show for their papa after the accident – helping out at the *Gudwara* serving the *langar* to the people worshipping or poor people, but Subrina never really believed in the religion itself. All the drinking, smoking and taking drugs were evidence of that in itself.

In a way, she supposed she could hardly blame Subrina for wanting to make contact. Enough time had passed and it was time for each of them to accept their own responsibilities. They had met in public. That had been a mistake. People would recognise her famous sister, known for her partying and free spirit, speaking with a veiled nun. They would think it odd and remember it.

Today she was certain that people were whispering about Subrina. She wanted to ask the gossiping nuns what they knew, but she was afraid of knowing. She was afraid of drawing any more attention to herself. Her compulsions had returned and she was already being talked about. She was sure. The other nuns didn't know she was related to the famous Subrina Basi and she wanted to keep it that way. Well, Sister Carmina knew, but her vow of silence ensured she kept Suki's secrets safe.

She tapped the headboard again and then clasped her hands together, squeezing them tight. She didn't know how much longer she would be able to hide behind her veil.

CHAPTER NINE

'So, you haven't been able to locate Dinesh?' Chupplejeep asked.

'No, sir. The receptionist, Furtado, said that at two-thirty in the morning he left with his driver.'

'We don't know where he went? He didn't come back to the hotel?'

'I asked Furtado. He was at the front desk all night. Usually, another fellow called Vinod mans the desk at night, but not last night. Apparently he got last-minute tickets to some rave at Hilltop and Furtado said he would cover for him. But he admitted that he fell asleep. He didn't wake up until dawn.'

'Useless.'

'I spoke to the watchman though. He walks around the property all night.'

'And?'

'Nothing. He says he saw nothing. I also checked with the airport authority. No record of the boyfriend leaving the state, so I doubt he went to Ayesha Saxena's party. So we don't know where Dinesh is. We checked his room and his case is there, unpacked. But no passport. He may have had it on him. Nothing out of the ordinary.'

'Hmm, sounds like the watchman works all day and all night. He was at the hotel this morning. Don't any of the staff get time to rest at home? No wonder they are all falling asleep when they should be working.'

'The general manager, Hari, called him back when they found the body. Just to keep any press or unwanted people out. You know, sir, I was thinking.'

'Were you?'

'Maybe it was suicide. Is there any point thinking up scenarios when we don't even know if this is a murder investigation yet?'

'Pankaj, you're letting your imagination run wild again. There are no signs of this being a suicide. It was made to look like a suicide, but not very well. You saw the perfect cuts on the wrist. I have seen suicides before and they don't often look like that. The way Subrina's body was found – she was positioned in that way, post-mortem. I am certain Kulkarni is right and when the autopsy confirms it, Inspector General Gosht will want to know everything. So we need to start collecting evidence now. We have to treat this as a murder inquiry. Plus, I'm sure that snake Bonaparte is going to print a full article on Subrina Basi in tomorrow's *Express*. Gosht won't be happy, he may even pay us a visit.'

'So what do we do in the meantime?' Pankaj asked. He had to admit he was excited at the prospect of investigating the suspicious death of a celebrity, even if she was D-list. How often would he have a high-profile case on his hands in Little Larara? It was as close as he was ever going to get to a star.

He had done some work with the Panaji police force during the film festival. Police from all areas of Goa were called upon due to the added security required. He had jumped at the chance, hoping to catch a glimpse of Aishwarya Rai Bachchan or a Kapoor or two, but nothing. He hadn't seen a single famous person, not even a D-list celebrity. Instead he got to see just how much Panaji was spending on electricity. Every night the whole city was lit up like a beacon. What about all those poor villagers in Goa who had no electricity at all? Goa sometimes got its priorities wrong. It was a sad state of affairs.

'Bonaparte mentioned that Subrina's boyfriend used to hit her. Call around, find out if it's true,' Chupplejeep said. 'But not before we get formal identification of the body and permission for autopsy. The family need to be made aware before we start asking sensitive questions. I was hoping Dinesh could identify Ms Basi for us.'

'If Ms Basi's family are in Delhi, they won't be able to identify the body quickly.'

'*Aacha* and we want it done fast. The longer that body hangs around, the less chance we have of finding out what really happened.'

'Why is that, sir?'

'Didn't you go to training college? Because the body and any toxins in the body will start to decay.'

'Even if it's stored at the right temperature.'

'Correct. Plus, you think Gosht is going to be happy if we keep Subrina Basi's body here, unidentified for more than twenty-four hours?'

Pankaj shook his head. That would be a terrible idea. When the Inspector General wanted answers, he wanted them fast.

'We need identification soon.'

'Who can we ask?'

Chupplejeep twisted one end of his moustache. 'Come with me,' he said, walking towards the main door of the hotel. 'I know just the person.'

~

Chupplejeep and Pankaj stood outside the old Goan home. It was mid-afternoon and the sun was beating down on their backs. It was warm for December, so warm even the crows had stopped their cawing and were sitting under a deodar tree. Chupplejeep wiped away the sweat from his brow with a handkerchief from his pocket. The village house was typical with colonial-style red and cream pillars at the front. The house had a terracotta-tiled roof with a matching terracotta cockerel perched on the top, similar to the one Chupplejeep had on his own home, and the stone floors were a deep red. There was a large veranda that ran around the outside of the house and an old wooden front door, which creaked as Chupplejeep pushed it open. Inside was a dark hallway with two rooms either side.

The hall led into a spacious open-plan room with a large balcony. This served as the art gallery. Bunty D'mello had opened it shortly after her father died, and soon after the Golden Orchid officially opened its doors. 'This gallery will serve the community for generations. Visitors will be able to view authentic Goan art and purchase pieces at affordable prices,' Bunty was quoted in the *Express* as saying, following her opening party. Christabel had been trying to get Chupplejeep to take her there for some time. Now he was here without her. She would be cross when she found out.

The detective and officer walked around the room. 'I don't get it,' Pankaj said.

'What do you not get?'

'All this red and black paint – the strokes going this way and that way. It looks so messy. And here in this one,' Pankaj said, stopping in front of a large canvas next to a plastic Christmas tree. 'Who would hang this in their house? What is it exactly?'

'Not your cup of tea, Officer?'

Pankaj swung around and came face to face with the artist, Advani.

Chupplejeep sighed. This was not what he had wanted. But Pankaj did have a point. The red and black painting was hideous. This was hardly the authentic Goan art Bunty had talked about. But Advani was famous all over India. He was running a workshop here in one of the studios and no doubt charging an arm and a leg for it. His paintings were certainly not affordable either, as Bunty had promised. Chupplejeep sneaked a look at the price tag of the painting behind Pankaj. He pursed his lips together. Thirty-five thousand rupees was too much for something Chupplejeep was sure a child could have done, given some paints and no direction. Advani must have been paying Bunty more than enough to allow her to visit her daughter in the UK as much as she wanted.

'Err,' Pankaj started.

Advani was dressed in a black and pink kimono with vibrant flowers and birds printed on the silk. He played with the edge of one of the sleeves. 'Don't worry, I wouldn't expect you cops to know about art. In all my years, I've never seen a policeman take interest in my work. This,' he said, pointing to the picture Pankaj had just criticised, 'is a masterpiece.'

Pankaj turned around and looked at the picture again.

'See this bow line here? It represents the human form…the form of a woman, a beautiful woman. Have you got a girlfriend?' Advani asked Pankaj.

Pankaj blushed. He shook his head.

'Doesn't surprise me,' Advani said. 'Well, think of a gorgeous woman. This is her. And this red here, this is her sex.'

Pankaj took a step back, nearly knocking over the gaudy green Christmas tree. 'What?'

'Her mutilated parts. The black represents her pubic hair. The red represents the blood. This is what we have to be aware of in society – mutilation of the genitals.'

Pankaj's jaw dropped. He stood there gaping at the canvas.

Chupplejeep swallowed but held his tongue. He couldn't upset Advani. They needed him.

Advani put his hand on Pankaj's shoulder. He pointed to another painting that stood out as distinctly average amongst the other pictures.

'Look at that picture, a nice green bungalow. That is more your cup of tea, is it not?' Advani smiled. 'My friend who's in Goa at the moment took me to see this house one evening. It was like she knew the owners, but she couldn't have because she nearly jumped out of her skin when I suggested we knock on the door. The house looked so quaint I thought I would paint it from memory. I must go back and look inside. Maybe I'll go without her,' he said with a mischievous smile. 'But it doesn't belong here. It's too mediocre. It was just an idea I was playing with. I'll get Takshak to remove it later.'

Pankaj studied the picture of the bungalow, but it was obvious he couldn't erase from his mind the image of the violent black and red brushstrokes that he had just seen.

'Why don't we go out on the balcony?' Chupplejeep said to Advani. 'We're not here to talk about art. We are here on business and we need to talk to you about a serious matter.'

'Finally, you lazy cops have started investigating my case. Look at my eyes. Look at the bags under my eyes. This is because I have not slept. I'm so fucking worried about this man who is terrorising me, oof.' Advani turned and walked out towards the balcony.

'So you know it's a man who has written the blackmail letter to you?' Chupplejeep looked at Pankaj who was still in shock from Advani's art.

'Of course it's a male. A fat, hairy, heterosexual male.'

'And how do you know this?'

'All you male heteros are the same. You're all haters.'

Chupplejeep clenched his teeth. He was sceptical of Advani and his secret. It didn't seem to add up to him, but he held back. This was Pankaj's case and it was up to him to solve it. Pankaj would never learn if he stuck his oar in every five minutes.

The detective cleared his throat. 'I understand that you are upset and concerned about the letter you received. And I can assure you we're taking this very seriously. But…'

'*Hai, hai*, I knew it. I knew there would be a but. A big hairy but, no doubt. Where is my assistant, *yaar*? Takshak, come out here. Save me from these Neanderthals.'

'I understand that you were good friends with Subrina Basi?'

'Of course. I knew her from when, for years I have known her. She is my muse, my love, my best fucking friend. She's here, you know. She's staying in the same village. She's so sexy. I said to her last night, I said, "Subby darling, let me paint you. Let me paint you naked again." Oh, I hope she agrees. But, you know, that boyfriend of hers, I don't think he will let her do it. He's no good for her. It's because of him that her career has stalled. He holds her back. I've told her to lose him. But she won't listen to me. Says she's too old to start looking for another man and she says he's good in bed. So I suppose I can't blame her.'

Chupplejeep didn't know what to say to Advani's monologue. When he saw his mouth open to carry on with his speech, he just said what he needed to say. 'Subrina Basi is dead.'

Advani leaned his head forward, shrieking. 'What! What are you saying?'

'Subrina Basi has been found dead at the Golden Orchid Hotel. We have been at the hotel for the best part of the afternoon. Her body has been taken to the morgue but we need someone to make the formal identification. We can't locate her boyfriend Dinesh and we know that you are friends with the actress. We were wondering if you would be able to accompany us back to the medical examiner's office to identify the body.'

Chupplejeep heard another high-pitched sound. It sounded half human, half animal. The noise was coming from Advani. And he wasn't quite sure how to react. Luckily, Takshak came running out of the gallery.

'What happened?' he asked, looking somewhat afraid. Chupplejeep couldn't blame him after hearing that scream. 'Did you find out who the blackmailer is? Did you tell him?'

Chupplejeep shook his head. 'Subrina Basi is dead,' he repeated.

'Oh, I see,' Takshak said coolly. Then he put his arms around Advani. 'It's okay,' he said to Advani, who was sobbing uncontrollably. 'It's okay.'

Chapter Ten

Four hours later, Advani had positively identified the body as that of Subrina Basi and the police in Delhi had notified her family. The Commissioner in Delhi told Chupplejeep that her parents were too old and unwell to fly, but they had no problem with the autopsy.

'I explained that because the death was so sudden, it is natural that an autopsy is required,' the Commissioner said over the phone. 'The parents were very much in favour of this. They didn't think their daughter would take her own life.'

'And what do you think?' Chupplejeep asked.

'Your pathologist has got it wrong. Want me to send one of my guys down there to help you? I know what facilities in Goa are like.'

Chupplejeep clenched his teeth. 'I have good enough reason to believe it is a suspicious death.'

'You're used to much more action than suicides, no? You were the detective who caught that serial killer, were you not?' the Commissioner asked.

'Yes, that was I.'

'I knew Subrina. She was troubled and delusional. Suicide is a possibility. A big possibility.'

'Delusional?'

'Just recently she called me in the dead of night, said she had once killed someone. I mean come on *men*, what more proof do you want? Something was wrong in her head.'

'It is a possibility that she did murder someone,' Chupplejeep said, feeling a little uneasy. This Delhi Commissioner was far too confident for his liking. 'Did you question her further?'

'Don't you think I would know about s-something like that?' Chupplejeep heard hesitation as the Commissioner stuttered. 'The woman was out of it half of the time. Drugs make you say things that are not necessarily true.'

There was a name for people like this commissioner, Chupplejeep thought. They had their heads so far up their own backsides they couldn't see reality, let alone sieve out the lies from the truth.

Chupplejeep looked at Pankaj, held his hand over the mouthpiece of the phone and rolled his eyes. '*Pisoso*, imbecile,' he said under his breath.

~

Pankaj buried his head in his hands. He still couldn't get over what Advani had said to him about that painting. Throughout Advani's identification of Subrina Basi, Pankaj could only think of one thing – why would anyone want to paint mutilated parts of the female body? And not just any parts, those parts so sensitive to a woman. He crossed his legs. He wanted to talk about it, but he couldn't muster up the courage to do so. His mother would have been mortified, his father would not want to hear such things and his friends, well, it was just too embarrassing to talk about with anyone. Who would buy a painting like that to hang in their house, he wondered? His mind drew a blank.

Now back at his desk, he decided it was best to concentrate on the task in front of him. He took a sip of his milky tea before looking at the threatening letter that Advani had received, which was protected in a clear plastic bag.

Advani

You have secret. I know. I will expose you if you dant live 40 lakhs in yellow garbage can outside your gallari on the eve of Christmas. Do not disregard this.

The letter was short and to the point, but something about it didn't seem right. He read it twice, before he realised what was bothering him. The author of the letter had written in English. These days, especially in Goa, everyone spoke English so it wasn't uncommon. But the grammar, spelling and vocabulary didn't ring true. The author could spell 'disregard', yet he couldn't spell 'don't'.

It was clear that the author was better educated than he wanted the reader to believe. The blackmailer had purposefully misspelled words and left out some words to give the impression that he was ignorant, when in fact he was very clever indeed. But not as clever as the police, Pankaj thought. Pankaj was no graphologist, but he had taken a module on handwriting at the Police Training College so he thought he would examine the handwriting himself. There was no need to send it to the expert all the way in Ponda because he knew it was rare these days that a court would give credence to the results. Besides, he was going to send the letter to Kulkarni for fingerprint analysis. The letter couldn't be in two places at once and he had already sent one of Kulkarni's men to the gallery to take Takshak and Advani's prints, so he could rule them out. Fingerprints, he decided, were more important than handwriting analysis.

He hoped the blackmailer wasn't smart enough to put gloves on when he wrote the note, because he desperately needed some more information. Pankaj felt like he was going around in circles and getting nowhere fast. The case was unsatisfactory, he thought, like a samosa without any filling.

Pankaj looked at the sheet of paper, at the curves of the letters, and tried to remember what he had learned. The writing slanted backwards. The letters were sometimes joined and sometimes not. Was this deliberate or was it just the author's style? It was difficult to tell. He studied the writing with a magnifying glass he retrieved from his drawer. The 'm' in 'Christmas' was curly and there were loops in the 'o's, telling Pankaj the author was secretive. The 'e' loops were fairly open so the blackmailer was a good listener too. Pankaj imagined that this person paid attention to everything and then used it to his or her advantage. No wonder he or she knew Advani's deep dark secret. The mixed connectivity and style of the writing made Pankaj think that the person who wrote the letter was creative as well.

The press had called Advani a creative genius. He wondered if Advani had sent the letter to himself. It was fair to say the man was an attention seeker. Pankaj thought of his hideous red and black paintings. He wondered if he would ever be able to get rid of that image from his mind. Advani had signed them. His handwriting was large with big loops and round letters, unlike the writing before him. But how easy would it be to change your handwriting? He took a closer look, keeping his eye out for an unsteady hand. Looking for something that would tell him if the writer was trying to change his or her natural writing style. Nothing.

Pankaj looked at the 'i's and the 't's. The i was dotted to the right of the stem and the t was a small upward slant. The person writing the letter rarely achieved what he or she set out to do, they needed to loosen up. Advani had achieved his goals, hadn't he? It was difficult to tell because one's ambitions were so varied. Perhaps Advani was a failure in his own eyes.

Could it be Takshak, Pankaj wondered? The assistant who at first didn't seem to care about his boss, but when he heard Advani's howling on hearing of Subrina's death, comforted him like a brother. Advani had been adamant, though, that his assistant didn't know his secret.

He turned the letter over. There was a partial visible fingerprint in ink. It wasn't a full print, but a partial nevertheless. Pankaj was certain that the lab could extract some latent prints as well. Once the prints came through, he could ask Chupplejeep to authorise running them here and in Mumbai. Advani lived in Mumbai so chances were the blackmailer could have followed him over to Goa. Pankaj wrote this down and then added Delhi to the list as well. With so many *Delhi-ites* having stayed with Subrina Basi at the Golden Orchid in the same village as the gallery, it was best to check Delhi as well.

Pankaj put the letter down and finished his tea. Looking at the handwriting wasn't going to get him far. He needed to know about the artist's early deception. Outside the morgue, he had questioned him at length about his stolen works. The four paintings Advani had stolen, by an artist called Vallabh, were simple scenes of trees and temples, but the artist was no longer alive so he wasn't the one doing the blackmailing.

'He died,' Advani said. 'Got hit by a bus, the fool. What a way to go.' Advani shrugged. 'When God calls you, you have to go, I guess.'

The paintings had been sold for a pittance, but that wasn't the point Advani had made. His reputation was at stake.

'Why did you do it?' Pankaj asked.

'Isn't it obvious, you oaf? I was having a crisis of confidence. I wasn't getting anywhere with my paintings and before Vallabh's death, he got some serious praise from our art teacher. He had left four paintings at my digs. I decided to use them as my own.'

'Even though you didn't get much money for them?'

Advani stared at Pankaj. 'Even.'

Pankaj heard him swear under his breath. 'Didn't you think your art teacher would notice?'

Advani lifted his cigarette to his lips. 'What is your problem? Am I the offender now? I'm the bloody victim.'

'Sir, I'm just trying to get the facts.'

'You should be out there finding the blackmailer, not crucifying me.'

'And can I ask, do you know who has these four paintings?'

Advani shrugged.

'Are they ever talked about in papers? Are people selling them?' Pankaj had asked, trying to remember what Chupplejeep had said.

'How should I know?'

'If you knew, you could buy them back. It's only four paintings and if you bought them back, you could destroy them and no one would know.'

Advani took a final drag from his cigarette and threw the butt on the floor. 'You cops, where do I start with you? You just want me to make it easy for you. Lazy is not the word.' But Pankaj observed that he looked noticeably irked by this line of questioning.

Pankaj had since carried out some background checks on Vallabh, this artist who Advani stole from, and so far had discovered very little. He found several Vallabhs and relations of dead Vallabhs but no one he had contacted yet had been remotely interested in art, let alone an artist. The college at which Advani studied art had been demolished and Pankaj was still trying to track down his art teacher.

Was Advani lying? No, Pankaj didn't think so. He had to find someone who knew this artist. This was the first case Chupplejeep had put him in charge of and he needed to prove himself if he was ever going to earn his stripes.

CHAPTER ELEVEN

Christabel looked at her guest list. It was a little one-sided. She had over one hundred and fifty guests who had to attend – Arthur only had thirty-five. She asked herself if this was fair or not, but then decided it was. The Chupplejeep family tree was non-existent and that wasn't her fault. Arthur had been orphaned as a child and Nana, who had taken him in at twelve, was long gone. God rest her soul. She too had no living relatives to speak of. So it wasn't her fault that Arthur's guest list was so short. She hoped he would also see it that way, especially when she added the extra twenty names to the list.

She had decided on a delicate shade of pink for the primary wedding colour. Pink with perhaps some peach thrown in. Some people said the two colours clashed, but this was her wedding and so she was going to do it her way. She cast her eyes towards her engagement ring. Arthur had done well choosing a small ruby with diamonds either side. It suited her perfectly. She doubted she could have chosen better herself, and that was saying something. Her friends, all married now, had made all the right noises when she showed it to them.

Only her mother had complained. 'It's a bit small, no,' she said. 'I would have thought at his age he would have enough money to get you something better. As it is, you have to take his name.' Her mother had looked at her sideways as she fidgeted with her satin blouse. 'I suppose you could be like the modern ones and keep your own name. That would give my friends something to talk about other than the size of the stone on your engagement ring.'

Christabel would definitely be taking her husband's name and the ring was a perfectly decent size, similar to what her friends had. And anyway, they couldn't go spending money on a bigger stone just to show off. They had a future together to think of. Just thinking about this brought a smile to Christabel's lips. Yes, they had a future filled with the pitter-patter of tiny feet, although time was running out. Before children, they had a wedding to plan and they hadn't even decided on a date. Since the proposal in Kerala, Arthur had been awkward when it came to talking about the wedding. And now with the death of Subrina Basi, Christabel wondered when they would get a chance to set a date. Perhaps she could set it without him.

Pulling out next year's calendar from the kitchen drawer, Christabel turned to her birthday month: July. She would be thirty-nine next July and she couldn't let another birthday go by without replacing her title of Miss to Mrs. She couldn't possibly be thirty-nine and still be called Miss. What would people think? Christmas was just around the corner, which meant that between her birthday and Christmas, they only had six months in which they could marry. And if she really thought about it, one couldn't get married in the summer, from March to June. It was far too hot – guests would faint in the church. It quickly became clear in Christabel's mind what she had to do – she had all of two months to fix a plausible date. A date had to be set soon, in January or February. And she would give Arthur the choice so he couldn't complain.

With one less burden on her mind, she turned her attention to Christmas. They were already halfway through December and she and Arthur had decided that they would spend this Christmas at his house. It was bigger, with three bedrooms, a large kitchen, a lounge and a big garden. Plus, it was better located. And it was for this reason also that she had come to the conclusion that they would live in his house after they married.

She wondered what it would be like to live day in and day out with the same man. Things would certainly be easier. She could talk to him whenever she wanted. She wouldn't need to call him at the office or wait for him to visit her. No, she could just ask him whatever she wanted when they were at home together. If a question came to her in the middle of the night, or first thing in the morning, she could poke him in the ribs and ask him without having to lose any sleep over it. She smiled. She couldn't wait!

Perhaps she would take some extended leave from work and decorate his house just how she liked it. He needed new chairs in the lounge. The wicker ones were uncomfortable, and she would need a dresser in their bedroom. And the garden! Oh, the fun she could have planting shrubs and trees in his barren back yard. Perhaps they could invest in some grass too. Children loved grass.

Christabel put next year's calendar away and looked at the current one. A festive table of edible treats illustrated the month of December. Her mouth started to water looking at the *San Rival* cake. She imagined the taste of the sweet buttercream, meringue and cashews. Then she caught a glimpse of the *nureos, bebinca* and *perad*. She turned away. It was too much temptation for her. She had been on a strict diet since their return from Kerala and not a single piece of fried or sweet food had entered her mouth. It would be terrible if she were fatter than her bridesmaids on the big day. But it was increasingly difficult to avoid temptations with all the festivities and Christmas parties around. And just because she was on a diet, she couldn't deprive their guests should anyone happen to drop in, as people did at this time of year. Perhaps, she reasoned, if she only bought two-thirds of everything she normally purchased then there would not be as many leftovers and she wouldn't be so tempted.

Christabel took a pen and her Christmas list from the kitchen drawer. She added some sweet treats to her list of tinsel and Christmas presents before picking up her shopping bag and leaving the house.

CHAPTER TWELVE

Indu walked into the kitchen. 'Abhik,' she called.

'What's the matter?' he asked, walking out of the pantry. He was carrying two bulbs of garlic and some flour, which he put down on the worktop.

'Oh nothing, I just came to see what you're doing. It's so quiet without Madam in the hotel. None of her guests coming and going, no shouting. The hotel is still not busy.'

'There are some day guests. There are some people right now in the restaurant.'

Indu exhaled. She wanted to confide in Abhik, tell him her real reason for visiting him. But could she trust him? Not with something as serious as this. She was sure the police were already suspicious of her.

She had done a terrible thing. One the gods would never forgive her for. She had never meant to, but she had done it and now there was no going back. She would end up paying for her crime. Already she was suffering the consequences of a guilty conscience – jumping at the slightest sound, turning as she walked to see if anyone was watching her. She was certain that she would be reincarnated as a cockroach in her next life, and someone like Madam would stamp on her.

'You're worried?' the Nepalese cook teased. He picked a knife out of the drawer and examined the blade, testing it with his thumb. 'Don't worry, they won't come after you. You're quite safe here.'

Indu stared at him.

'I'm joking,' he said.

'The police say that they have to look into all Madam Basi's affairs,' she said. Abhik had no right to tease her.

'I suppose they do. You don't need to worry. It's only people like me and Nishok who have to worry.' Abhik smashed open a head of garlic with the flat of the knife.

'Why you two?'

'When you're different or if you have a past then the cops try and pin things on you.'

Indu considered this as she twisted her hair around her index finger. 'What if you did something bad but you regretted it, what then? Would the cops still come after you?'

'It depends on what you've done,' Abhik said, his dark, empty eyes looking into the distance. 'Sometimes if they don't catch you the first time and you're stupid enough to make the same mistake again, you'll get caught.' He began to chop a clove of garlic.

'But what if the police catch you the first time? What do you think they will do?'

Abhik looked up at her. 'What have you done?'

'Who, me?' she asked, picking at her fingernails. 'Nothing. I'm just curious. You're always watching movies. And this is like a movie, isn't it? You know what happens.'

'What happens in movies is not the same as real life. Back in Nepal I did something I shouldn't have. It was an accident, but others didn't see it that way so I ended up moving here. It wasn't just what the police wanted in the end, it was what people thought about me that ruined my life there.'

Indu swallowed hard. 'I didn't think about that. I didn't think about what other people would think,' she said. Her boyfriend would certainly ditch her.

'That's the most important thing in a community such as ours, although Goa is different from Nepal. I think here people would eventually forgive your mistakes. Of course, it depends on what you've done and why you've done it.'

'So if you do something with good intentions then people will look kindly on you?'

'Maybe. But what you think is reasonable, others may not.'

'I see,' Indu said. The knot in her stomach tightened.

'Let's leave the police to their detective work. There's nothing we can do now. Well, you could run, but where would you run? It's not that easy setting up a new life in a new place. And besides, you've done nothing wrong, have you?'

Indu bit her lower lip. She shook her head. Running was not an option, not when her father was so sick. How would he feel when he found out what she did? Silently she prayed that it wouldn't kill him off. Abhik was right, there was nothing she could do now. The police had cordoned off Madam Basi's room and stationed a cop outside the front door, twenty-four hours a day. There was no way she could sneak back in there.

'Good, then I'll make your favourite chicken *momos*. They'll definitely put a smile back on your face.'

Indu was too scared to tell Abhik that the thought of chicken dumplings made her feel even worse. She had never once refused a chicken *momo* before and often had to plead with Abhik to make the Nepalese dish for her. If she told him she didn't want any now, it would definitely give her away. So Indu pulled up a stool and sat down in the kitchen, watching Abhik as he cooked, waiting to be served.

~

Advani sat on the balcony in his gallery, smoking. He alternated taking a drag on his cigarette with sipping a glass of cold white wine. His nerves were frayed. The life he had spent the last ten years carving out for himself was beginning to crumble. And how could his muse, Subrina, be dead? It wasn't just the useless cops getting it wrong, as usual. He had seen her lifeless body with his own eyes. Her long, black glossy hair limp and dull…her glowing complexion now just a distant memory. Even her generous bosom seemed deflated. Subrina would never have killed herself. Yes, she had problems, who didn't? But to take her own life. He had seen the dried-out cuts on Subrina's wrists, though, and he couldn't deny they were there.

He stubbed out his cigarette in a black ashtray and drained his glass of wine. 'Takshak,' he shouted. 'Fetch me my wine. My glass is empty.'

No, Advani could not accept that Subrina had committed suicide. He would tell that to the cops. He should have told them there and then in that stinking morgue, but he had been distressed and his good-for-nothing assistant had forgotten his tablets – the ones that made him feel like he was floating above all the pain and suffering in the world. Instead that useless article, Pankaj, had questioned him about his secret outside the morgue. Needling him in that way was not professional, given the circumstances.

Takshak arrived carrying the half-empty bottle of wine.

'Subrina was in good spirits when we partied with her last, wasn't she?' Advani said.

Takshak nodded. 'I can't believe she's no longer with us. You remember when she came to stay with you in Mumbai? She had all your friends captivated with her stories from the *filmi* scene. And remember the dance she put on? How we laughed.'

'She was so drunk that night – on VAT 69 or Black Dog, remember we had no other alcohol in the house and it was one of those fucking dry days for the election. Not a single bar open in town. Remember how she shouted at that peon I had working for me. I had to beg him to come back to work the next day. I think he thought she was going to give him a tight slap at one point. For what?'

'Because he didn't put enough ice in her drink,' Takshak said with a look of contempt.

'She had a short temper, so feisty. I knew then she would inspire my works. Ooh, she was so yummy. And now Takshak, what will we do without her?'

Takshak exhaled. 'Everything happens for a reason.'

'Takshak! How can you say that?'

'No, what I mean is that I suppose we should look at it that way. It will make the pain less.'

'Will it? I don't think so. I feel like someone has fucking ripped my heart out.'

Takshak filled up Advani's glass and left the bottle on the table before disappearing back into the gallery. Advani watched his assistant slowly disappear. He couldn't blame him for walking away. Subrina's death had troubled everyone and even if it was suicide, someone was to blame.

When Subrina first introduced him to Dinesh, he knew no good would come of their relationship. Dinesh and his father were both horrible human beings who should never have been allowed to walk the earth. The world was an uglier place because of people like them. They used people and discarded them ruthlessly after they were done. Advani had first-hand experience of that. Dinesh was selfish, there was no doubt about it, but was he evil enough to cause her so much suffering that she would take her own life? And if it wasn't suicide, if it was murder, could he have been the one to take such a beauty away from the world? Where the hell was Dinesh now?

Would the useless cops be able to solve the crime? He doubted it. Most probably they would just accept suicide to avoid doing any work. Villagers were like that – lazy, fat oafs. They hadn't even figured out who was blackmailing him.

CHAPTER THIRTEEN

'She had buttocks,' Kulkarni said.

'Well, of course she had buttocks. Only some skinny people don't have buttocks and they are very unfortunate.' Pankaj shook his head. Sometimes, Kulkarni didn't make any sense.

'What are you saying, eh? I'm saying the woman had buttocks. Can't you understand?'

'And I'm saying most people do. What sense does that make to a sudden death?'

'Kulkarni means that Subrina Basi had Botox, not buttocks,' Chupplejeep said.

Pankaj looked at his boss and then at the medical examiner, who was grinning. 'Oh, I see, sir,' he said, as his cheeks coloured. 'That makes sense.'

Kulkarni pointed towards the victim's lips with a scalpel. 'They were done recently, probably during her stay in Goa.'

'I didn't know they were doing such procedures here.'

Kulkarni sucked his teeth. 'Of course, they call them 'medical tourists'. They come here for cheap operations and get a holiday out of it also. It was probably the reason why Subrina Basi stayed here after IFFI. She wanted to go back to Delhi looking super-hot and land a new role. Especially after all the criticism she got for her last film, this would be a nice boost for her confidence, eh.'

'So Kulkarni, now you're turning into Freud?'

'Just my thoughts, Detective.'

'You have a point.'

'Why would she have an operation carried out here, in Goa?' said Pankaj. 'If I needed an operation, I would want to return to my own bed after it was over.'

'Botox is not an operation, it's just an injection,' Chupplejeep said.

Pankaj made a face.

'Am I right, Kulkarni?'

''Es. One hundred per cent correct. But I didn't call you here to talk about body enhancements.'

'No.'

'Would you pay for a procedure like this if you were going to kill yourself?' Pankaj asked.

Chupplejeep looked at Pankaj. 'I don't think she did kill herself. And in any case, it doesn't work like that when you suffer from depression.' Then he looked at Kulkarni. 'What does the autopsy tell us?'

'That's the thing, the toxicology report isn't back yet, but the autopsy didn't throw up anything suspicious.'

'Suicide?' Pankaj asked eagerly. 'I knew it!'

'Like I said at the hotel, the wrists are cut too precisely for that. So I kept looking. I searched her body entirely.'

'And?'

'Finally, just one hour ago I found something on her behind. Something I only thought of after seeing the injection marks on her upper lip. So I called you. Pankaj, help me turn the body.'

Pankaj stepped forward. He winced as he helped Kulkarni. 'I think looking at a dead body is worse when it has been opened and stitched back up again. There should be some windows in this cupboard of yours that you can open.'

'This may be a cupboard to you fancy officers, but this is my lab. Don't criticise it, eh. You're lucky there is a facility here. Otherwise you'd have to go all the way to Panaji whenever you needed to visit a medical examiner.' Kulkarni narrowed his eyes until Pankaj apologised. 'Anyway, we can't have windows to open. The room has to stay at this temperature. It's hot enough to cook an egg outside.'

'Enough, you two,' Chupplejeep said. 'We don't have all day. Inspector General Gosht is on my case. I need to give him an update.'

'See here,' Kulkarni said, giving a magnifying glass to Chupplejeep. He pointed at the victim's posterior. 'There is a beauty mark on her left butt cheek.'

Pankaj strained to get a better look.

'I see it,' Chupplejeep said. 'There is a small puncture wound right in the middle of the spot.'

''Es. My guess is that someone injected Subrina Basi with poison and tried to make it look like a suicide.'

'How would they inject her in the bottom without her knowing?' Pankaj asked.

'Easily,' Kulkarni said. 'If the victim had been on a cocktail of drugs and alcohol like I suspect, then she may well have passed out. Then she could be injected with a poison.'

'This is truly sinister,' Pankaj said. 'Is it possible that someone could have done that?'

Chupplejeep smiled, remembering an old Poirot quote: 'The impossible could not have happened, therefore the impossible must be possible in spite of appearances.'

Kulkarni and Pankaj looked at Chupplejeep. 'Detective, what are you saying?' Kulkarni asked.

'Never mind, you wouldn't understand.' No one in Goa understood his favourite on-screen detective. Chupplejeep twisted one end of his moustache, he felt more like Poirot when he did that. 'Don't you read the news, Pankaj? This kind of thing happens.'

'But not in Goa. You read about foreigners getting killed, but usually that is by asphyxiation. Then there is the hardened local criminal who beats someone up or takes a knife to their throat. But this element of cunning, I'm not sure I've seen that happen, especially here in our Goa.'

'There is a first time for everything.' Chupplejeep turned to Kulkarni. 'Wouldn't she have woken up whilst the murderer was slitting her wrists?'

'It depends what drug was used, eh. There is ricin, derived from castor beans, and there are castor oil factories in India so it's not hard to obtain without anyone knowing. They have been using that one a lot in television shows recently because it's almost undetectable during autopsy. But I think the victim would have woken up if they had used that drug. Plus it takes longer to work. Then there is succinyl choline. With this poison you can paralyse your victim so they can't move and then you can slit their wrists if you like. The list of poisons is endless and these toxins break down after time. So sometimes by the time the autopsy is done, the poison is no longer detectable in the body.'

'You really think that Subrina Basi was poisoned?' Chupplejeep asked, somewhat surprised by Kulkarni's knowledge. Pankaj was right, murder like this was rare in the villages.

'What other reason is there for her to have a puncture wound on her bottom? And that the wound is cleverly concealed too. Plus, there was not enough blood loss for death to be caused by the slashing of the wrists.'

'We are dealing with someone smart,' Chupplejeep said.

'Perhaps,' Kulkarni said. 'Perhaps not. Remember what I told you at the hotel? A true suicide would have some telltale marks like hesitation wounds – jagged cuts which were not so precise, eh.'

'And she would have left a note,' Pankaj said, taking a step away from the body. 'Even if someone else wrote it.'

'When will the tox report come back?' Chupplejeep asked.

'I've sent some urine from the bladder as well as blood and tissue samples from a number of sites around the body to the toxicology lab in Margao. I've asked them to do some screening for poisons.'

'We should know by tomorrow?'

'Detective, this is not *CSI*! But I've asked for the results to be fast tracked. I'll call you as soon as I know.'

'Anything else we need to know?'

'I mentioned defensive bruises back at the hotel, but on further inspection these bruises are not what I had first thought. A couple of bruises on the arms suggest that she must have been grabbed like this several hours, a day even, before her death.' Kulkarni grabbed Chupplejeep's biceps. 'The bruises on her legs are consistent with a fall closer to her death.'

Chupplejeep made a note. 'So, no signs that there was a struggle on the night of her death?'

'No. From the rate of decay of the body coupled with the conditions in the room, I would suggest she died between one-thirty and five am.'

'She was last seen just after one in the morning. She was heard arguing with Dinesh shortly after. So she must have been murdered soon after that,' Pankaj offered.

'Dinesh was seen leaving at two-thirty in the morning. That's enough time,' Chupplejeep said.

''Es, enough time to kill her, slit her wrists and dress her body with her sunglasses and lipstick, if he was quick.

I did some vaginal swabs for semen, but nothing came up.'

'Is that so? It surprises me, considering her boyfriend just arrived in Goa.'

'No evidence of sexual activity was found in the room or that of Dinesh,' Pankaj said, his cheeks turning pink again.

'But they must have been intimate at some time previously, so Dinesh would have known about her beauty mark on her behind,' Chupplejeep said. 'Any news on his whereabouts?' he asked Pankaj.

Pankaj shook his head.

'I've sent for copies of her medical records from her physician in Delhi,' Kulkarni continued. 'It took a little persuading, but eventually I threatened him with the Director General.'

'Good.'

'The bathwater, as we know, was contaminated by the maid. Along with the vomit there was also presence of faeces and urine – Subrina's. No other trace evidence was found at the scene. Her bedroom was another matter. There was so much stuff in the room – broken jewellery, clothes and electronics. I am getting the prints done as we speak.'

'A phone?'

'A mobile phone was recovered. We charged it up.'

'Anything suspicious?'

'She used it for her emails, to make calls, messaging, the usual. I'll leave it for you two to have a good look. There was one thing though.'

'What's that?'

'In the notes section on her phone she had written: Be careful of the Cobra! I got the impression that it wasn't sinister. It was something that made her laugh.'

'Sometimes the things that make us laugh are the same things that can make us cry,' Chupplejeep said.

'True,' Pankaj said. 'One minute a girl can make you smile with kind words, the next she tells you it's over and then you're crying.'

Kulkarni frowned. 'What is that fellow on? I'll give her phone to you before you go, Detective. I've scraped the victim's fingernails, but apart from her own makeup and a few strands of hair, which looked very much like hers, nothing suspicious was found. I sent the victim's hair samples to the lab. I've asked them to do an analysis to show any acute or chronic drug patterns. The knife used to slash the victim's wrists was also found in the bath, under the body. There was a small fish scale on the knife. I sent it on to the lab for fingerprint analysis and all that stuff.'

'A fish scale?'

''Es, that's what I said.'

'Okay, good work, Kulkarni. We'll be in touch.' Chupplejeep started towards the door. Then he turned. 'The mobile?'

Kulkarni delved into a drawer and passed a plastic bag containing the phone to Chupplejeep.

'What do we do now?' Pankaj asked as they walked out of the lab together.

'Usually we would wait until Kulkarni gets confirmation of the cause of death, but I want to be the one to call Gosht, not the other way around. And that article Bonaparte is working on is going to hit the newspaper stands soon.'

'I would hate for Gosht to think we are no good at our jobs, sir.' Pankaj kicked at the red mud as he walked past an ice cream *gado* to the old blue Maruti.

'I would hate for him not to give us a portion of the ten-lakh budget he has just been awarded for the North Goa police division.'

'I don't understand, sir.'

'Before we were called to the Golden Orchid, I heard from a superintendent in Greater Larara there is a ten-lakh budget allocated to improve police departments north of the Zuari Bridge at Cortalim, and Gosht wants to divide it amongst the best teams. I don't want to give Gosht any reason to withhold it from us. Just think of how we could improve our station.'

'New computers, sir.'

'Yes, new computers. Maybe, someone to help us with administration in the mornings.'

'Someone to help with filing, that would be super.'

'So lets make sure we keep on top of this case.'

'Of course, sir.'

Chupplejeep opened the door of his four by four. 'So, Pankaj.'

'Sir?'

'Let's go solve this homicide.'

Chapter Fourteen

Pankaj and Detective Chupplejeep arrived at Advani's gallery early the next morning, shortly after the detective updated the Inspector General. Gosht had demanded daily updates on the case, given the predicted media interest. Apparently he was in the running for a promotion, and failing to solve the case fast would have all sorts of implications for him.

As they walked into Bunty D'mello's converted house, Pankaj averted his eyes from the black and red canvasses that littered the gallery walls. He wished Advani hadn't told him what the paintings represented. Now he finally understood why people said ignorance was bliss.

'*Hai*, so the cops are back. Why are you here now? Working on my case or that of my dearest friend?' the artist asked.

'We need to talk about Subrina Basi,' Chupplejeep said.

Advani grimaced.

'Of course we're keen to get to the bottom of your case also.'

'This is a murder investigation, isn't it? Yes, I think it is. Let me guess, you want to know my whereabouts for the night of the 15th?'

'We know you were with Ms Basi and Dinesh.'

'I left after midnight or thereabouts, ask Takshak. We walked back to the gallery together. You see, Detective, I don't like walking alone in the dark. Don't want to end up in a *naala,* ditch, and I always lose time when I drink. My memory turns to shit after four glasses.'

'It's true,' Takshak said, stepping out of the shadows. 'He doesn't like doing anything alone. We left just before one.'

Chupplejeep turned to look at Takshak. He had dark circles under his eyes and his face was drawn. Takshak yawned, confirming Chupplejeep's suspicions. He turned back to Advani. 'And you stayed here after that?'

'*Yaar*, I went to bed. Are you really accusing me of murder, you oaf?'

'We have to get the details of everyone's whereabouts.'

'Well, we were both here,' Advani said, answering Chupplejeep's next question. 'Takshak's a light sleeper, he would know if I went on walkabouts, wouldn't you?'

Chupplejeep looked back at Advani's assistant. 'I'm afraid I would. I get good sleep here in the village. It's so quiet, unlike Bandra.'

'You do, do you?' Chupplejeep said. The man was clearly lying. Why? He looked like he hadn't slept in days.

'Detective,' Advani began, 'tell me if I'm wrong, but don't you need to have a motive to kill someone? Subrina Basi was a friend, one of my best friends. I knew her since forever. She knows so many things about me that no one else knows. Knew, she knew,' he corrected himself, wiping a tear from his eye with his yellow scarf.

'Like secrets you didn't want her to tell?' Chupplejeep asked.

Pankaj had to smile. This was why he admired his boss so much. One minute he was casually asking questions, the next he was making accusations, *phataak*!

'Subrina knew a lot about me, but nothing that she could blackmail me with. Nobody knows *that* secret. Not even him.' Advani looked over at Takshak.

Chupplejeep followed his gaze but Takshak didn't seem in the least bit interested. Instead he was carefully mixing blue and green paints.

'Takshak, fetch me my tablets. These officers get my blood pressure so high.'

Takshak put his paints down, sighed and then left the room.

'And Dinesh, you didn't have anything nice to say about him the last time we met,' Chupplejeep said.

Advani raised an eyebrow. 'Why don't you ask him? Oh yes, I know why you can't ask him. You've lost him.'

'He wasn't ours to lose. He could be missing for a number of reasons.'

'Ya, ya, ya.'

'Did Dinesh know your secret? Is that why you had nothing nice to say about him?'

'*Hai!*' Advani shook his head. 'What the hell are you cops on? Do you want me to call my solicitor? I'll sue you. I'll sue your entire department. I'm grieving for my friend and you're accusing me like a bear with his paw stuck in the honey pot. I'm a fucking artist, gracing this *faltu*, useless, village with my presence. Show me some respect.'

'Advani, you were one of the last people to see Ms Basi alive. We wouldn't be doing our job if we didn't ask you these questions. Like you pointed out, Dhesera is a sleepy village. It's rare we get one case here, let alone two. You have to wonder if there is a connection.'

Advani took a step back as he considered this. 'Fine, have it your way. But let me tell you, if – and it's a massive if – Dinesh knew my secret, he wouldn't tell anyone. I have something just as big on him.'

'Like what?' Pankaj asked a little too eagerly.

'Well, I'm not going to tell you hairy oafs. Once I tell his secret, he could tell mine.'

'You just said there is no way he knows your secret.'

'Yes, I suppose.'

'And we're police. We are not going to idly gossip.'

'In my experience of cops that's all you do, gossip.'

'Well, not us,' Chupplejeep said.

'Dinesh's father is one of the big-shot MLAs in Goa.'

'A Member of the Legislative Assembly?'

'That's the one. He has a wife and two kids. One child is Dinesh, the other is much younger. You know this MLA lives here in Goa – in this village. How do you think that hotel got permission? Someone gave him a bribe. His con-artist father is why Dinesh agreed to come to Goa to meet Subby. He was going to spend some time with his dad whilst he was here. But he isn't here now, is he? He ran away.'

'What has his father got to do with this?'

'Four years back, I was having an affair with his father.'

Pankaj's jaw dropped.

'Don't stare at me like a monkey,' Advani said. 'I'm not proud of what I've done. Politicians are dirty but they have their advantages. Dinesh knew about it.'

'But how did he know?' Pankaj asked with an incredulous look. This was juicier than *Icon Bites*.

'Let's just say he caught his father with his pants down.' Advani pressed his lips together to suppress a smile.

'And let me guess,' Chupplejeep said. 'You haven't seen eye to eye since?'

'Dinesh is scared of his sexuality. What can I do? I've heard him call me a fag and other shit before. I'm not worried about him. He hates that I actually care, cared for Subrina. He hated that I was still around and that I was his father's sordid little secret.'

'He could blackmail you for revenge. It's not so hard to hire a private investigator these days and dig some dirt on people.'

Advani pursed his lips. 'And risk me telling everyone what his father likes in the sack? You've got to be kidding me. And if it was him, he wouldn't ask for a measly forty lakhs. Everyone knows he has stacks of cash from his grandmom. When she dies, he'll get the lot. See, you cops know shit.'

~

Pankaj left Chupplejeep and Advani and headed into the back room. What Advani said made sense, but all this talk of blackmail reminded him that he didn't have long to solve the case of Advani's blackmail. 'Ah, there you are,' he said to Takshak who was searching through the drawers of a dressing table.

'He never looks after his meds and he just expects me to put everything down and search for them when he needs them. Sometimes he's like a toddler.'

Pankaj was silent.

'Sorry, I shouldn't have said that. Don't tell him I said anything. He has a short fuse.'

'How do you feel about the death of Subrina Basi?'

'Subrina, she was okay.' Takshak stopped looking through the drawer momentarily as if he had remembered something, but then quickly commenced his search again. Pankaj noticed that his top lip curled in a snarl just before he said Subrina's name. Did Takshak know something about the death of the actress?

But the death of Subrina Basi wasn't why he had followed Takshak. The blackmail case was his responsibility. He needed to get somewhere with it if he was to prove his worth to Chupplejeep, especially now that they had a homicide to deal with as well. How could he get Takshak to open up and tell him a little more about this great artist, whose latest collection seemed so violent and unnecessary?

He remembered Chupplejeep saying that in order to get someone to talk, you had to reveal something about yourself first. The best thing to do in this situation was to lie. Well, not exactly lie, but stretch the truth a little. Pankaj cleared his throat. 'I once had a boss who was very demanding,' he said, the words tripping off his tongue. He found that stretching the truth came quite easily when there was a reason behind it. 'But it's hard to be so attentive all the time.'

'You know,' Takshak said, closing one drawer and opening another, 'when I first started hanging out with Advani, he was a nobody and he treated me so well. Sometimes I wish he was a nobody again. He didn't have any money so we used to eat *daal* and chapattis for dinner most nights, two *charpoys* for our beds. We only had each other as our entertainment. We used to paint together and laugh and joke. You know, we went to college together – we went through everything together. He saved me more than once from my tyrant of a father. He was my closest and dearest friend.'

Pankaj swallowed. He would never have expected that. Advani looked older, but now that Takshak had mentioned it, he could see that perhaps they were closer in age than he first thought.

'All that changed when Advani found fame. He turned into this person I didn't recognise. Our meals of *daal* were replaced with legs of mutton. Our water was replaced with wine.' Takshak shook his head. 'It'll never be the same again.'

'Why do you stay with him then?' Pankaj asked, wondering if Takshak could be behind the letter. He knew Advani before he was famous. It would make sense.

Takshak was silent.

'Did you know an artist, a classmate, who died when you and Advani were in college?'

'One. I wouldn't call Vallabh an artist. He wore a white *dhoti* all the time. Thought he was going to be famous then one day a bus hit him when he was crossing the road. Bad trip.'

'What happened to his possessions?'

'His Marwari people came and collected them.'

Pankaj nodded. So far Takshak's story matched what Advani had told him.

'Did he leave any paintings behind?'

Takshak shrugged. 'Not that I remember. His paintings were hopeless.'

Pankaj raised his eyebrows. 'Hopeless? Would you be able to tell if you saw one?'

'Why are you asking all this?'

'Advani mentioned being affected by the death of a classmate – mentioned about doing something in his honour,' Pankaj said, thinking on the spot.

'That fellow's paintings were garish. Large brushstrokes – no finesse. Advani could paint better than that fellow with his eyes closed. Fuck it. I could paint better with my eyes closed. Why would Advani want to honour that fool? It would be like honouring some *faltu* singer on *Indian Idol*.'

Pankaj watched Takshak as he spoke, waiting for a reaction, something that would give his game away, but the man answered calmly. He could see that Takshak had nothing to do with the blackmail. Pankaj sighed. He felt he was even further away from solving the case than before he spoke to Takshak. He had spent hours yesterday evening calling Advani's classmates to find out about this artist, Vallabh. Most of them were no longer artists, but teachers and businessmen. It had been a job and a half trying to track them down. And still he hadn't uncovered any new leads.

Takshak opened a drawer, pulled out a small white bottle and rattled the contents, waking Pankaj from his thoughts. 'But why do I stay with Advani? I told you. Without him I wouldn't be here. I wouldn't be the man I am. He taught me not to care about what my father said. My father broke my spirit with his words. He could never accept me for who I was. He constantly belittled me, telling me my paintings were ugly, that a baboon could paint better. He said it so often I started believing him. "Who will buy your paintings?" he would ask, laughing like a drain. He didn't even accept that I wanted to paint. If I didn't paint I would die. That's what artists are like. When I was still living at home Advani would visit me daily, encourage me out of the house, take me to a local bar or gallery, tell me that my paintings were worth something. He said they were beautiful. He gave me the courage to pursue my dreams. Eventually he offered me a job as his assistant so I would have my own money. He has even sold one or two of them, and here with Advani I can paint every day.'

'But he treats you so...You said it yourself.' Pankaj noticed that the drawer Takshak had just retrieved the bottle from was full of other medicines and syringes. He immediately thought of Subrina Basi and her unfortunate demise. 'You have a lot of medicine there.'

Takshak made a face. 'For headaches, allergies. And I'm diabetic. Anyway, forget what I said. I nearly had a breakdown with my father breathing down my neck at that time in my life. If it wasn't for Advani...I owe Advani my life.'

Pankaj found himself thinking about the syringe he had just seen and the puncture mark in Subrina Basi's bottom. 'Enough to lie for him?'

'Advani is right. Cops are useless and in Goa they are even worse,' Takshak said, closing the drawer. Holding the bottle of pills in his fist, he pushed past Pankaj and marched out of the room, leaving the police officer alone with his thoughts.

CHAPTER FIFTEEN

Chupplejeep stared at the chopped papaya in front of him. It wasn't what he wanted for a late-morning snack but Christabel was adamant that he had to lose weight for the wedding.

'We can't be like two fatties walking down the aisle,' she had said to him this morning as she shoved a small papaya in his hand. 'Eat this instead of *bhajias* and you'll look nice and trim soon. And if you're not busy, rub the skin of the papaya on your face. It'll keep you looking young.'

Chupplejeep touched his cheek. He didn't look old, just yesterday his neighbour commented on his bright eyes. There was no way he was going to rub papaya on his face. A gentle aroma of lightly spiced potato filled his nostrils. 'What's that you've got there?' he asked, looking over at Pankaj.

'*Batata vadas*, you want one, sir? My mother made them fresh this morning.'

Chupplejeep took in the fragrance once more then he shook his head. 'No, no I mustn't.'

'Christabel's got you on another diet, sir?' Pankaj grinned.

'You wait till you reach my age then we'll see who is laughing. Enjoy your *vadas* now whilst you are young.' Chupplejeep turned away. Pankaj's mother, Jyotsana, was quite possibly the best cook in Larara – perhaps the best cook in Goa. 'I hope you are doing research like I asked,' he said.

'I'm typing Subrina Basi into the search engine right now.'

'Good, good.' It had been a busy twenty-four hours and they still had so much to do. It was one thing investigating the death of a Goan citizen, but it was much harder when the victim was from out of town. Usually this would fall to the tourist police, but given the locality of the crime, Inspector General Gosht had expected him to solve it and he was happy about that. Not only was it an intriguing case, it took his mind of his impending marriage. Just the thought of standing in a church making vows to Christabel made his hands go cold.

Yes, this was an interesting case indeed. The killer was unlike any he had caught before. Using poison administered via an injection through a beauty mark and then making up the body with red lipstick, a gold chain and sunglasses. The body had been staged. Why? Because Subrina was an actress and loved the stage? Was this a crime motivated by something she had done in her career? Perhaps she had won a part meant for another or didn't complete a film she was supposed to. Or was it something else, something he could not yet see?

Chupplejeep picked up the copy of the *Larara Express* he hadn't had time to read before visiting Advani. He stabbed a piece of papaya with his fork and popped it into his mouth as he opened the first page. Chupplejeep coughed and spluttered. A piece of papaya shot out though his nose.

'Sir, are you alright?' Pankaj said, hastily getting up from his desk and running over to his boss.

Chupplejeep's face was red. 'Water,' he gasped, his hand around his throat. Pankaj ran to the kitchenette, poured a glass of water from the bottle in the fridge and gave it to his boss. After Chupplejeep had gained control of his breathing, he showed Pankaj the cause of his distress.

On the second page of the *Larara Express* was a picture of the late Subrina Basi. The headline above the picture read *Dhesera Death Mystery*. The article written by Bonaparte suggested that there was an air of mystery surrounding the actress's death and that her body was found in not too dissimilar a situation as that of Whitney Houston.

'He's comparing Subrina Basi to the great Whitney Houston. Some Dollywood has-been cannot be compared to the woman who gave us *I Will Always Love You*,' Pankaj said.

'Bonaparte is comparing the way the body was found to that of the late singer. He's not comparing the two generally.'

'I suppose the staff must have talked to him after we left the hotel,' Pankaj said, examining the grainy black and white picture of Subrina Basi at a movie premiere in 2004, which accompanied the article.

'Can you blame them? All he would need to do is slip them a one hundred rupee note. Anyway, that's not the problem.'

'What is, sir?'

'This bit here.' Chupplejeep pointed to a line three-quarters down the page. 'It says that Subrina Basi was here getting back to her roots.'

'I thought she was from Delhi through and through. Nothing else has ever been reported in the press.'

'Nothing online?' Chupplejeep said, taking the paper from Pankaj and placing it on his desk.

'Sir, I checked.'

'Well check again. Because this article says she has a sister who lives in Goa – a local here.'

'I would never have guessed.'

'I didn't ask you to guess. That's what Bonaparte must have meant when he said if I gave him an exclusive on the case that he would give me some invaluable information.'

The green telephone on Chupplejeep's desk rang. He answered it.

'Detective Chupplejeep!' a voice boomed from the other end of the phone.

Pankaj stood back.

'Yes…yes…Sorry, sir. Of course, it must have been terrible to find out from a sub-officer…No, no need for that. We are looking into it as we speak. No, we won't wait for the full autopsy results. We'll get on it now. No, it's not too much,' he said, rubbing his forehead. 'We can manage. Yes, sir. It must be hard for the family. No…Yes…I'm going to visit her myself. Oh.' Chupplejeep put the receiver down.

'Inspector General Gosht?'

Chupplejeep twisted the end of his moustache. 'He's in a terrible mood. How the hell did we not know this? That bloody Bonaparte. This makes us look bad, Pankaj, very bad. Gosht's not happy. He has to report to the Director General of police by the end of the week.'

Pankaj returned to his desk. 'I'll search for Subrina's family online now.'

Chupplejeep pushed the plate of papaya away from him. 'Why didn't her family mention her sister when the Commissioner in Delhi gave them the news?'

Pankaj shrugged.

'And her best friend Advani never mentioned a sister either. We asked him outright if she had any other relations.'

'Maybe the family don't speak to the sister anymore.'

Chupplejeep made a face. 'Brothers fall out often, sisters rarely do. Something big must have happened.'

'Sisters fall out, sir. My mother and her sister didn't speak for years. Eventually, my mother couldn't remember what they had fought about but still she wouldn't talk to her sister. Then an uncle of theirs died and they realised how foolish they had been. They quickly made up after that.'

'But if the sisters fell out, why would Subrina's parents not mention her?'

Pankaj looked up from his computer screen. 'There is nothing online about her having a sister. In one article it says Subrina Basi was an only child. But *Filmi Today* is not a reliable source. They also said that Cameron Diaz was half-Goan.'

'What nonsense.'

'Exactly. Some fellow at the magazine mixed up Diaz for Dias.'

Chupplejeep shook his head.

'The blond hair and blue eyes should have given him a clue, sir.'

'Enough of Cameron Diaz. Give me Subrina's cell.'

Pankaj retrieved the phone Kulkarni had given him from his drawer. 'It's an expensive model. It's the latest Apple phone, sir. I've not seen many of these.' He passed the phone to Chupplejeep. 'The fingerprints have already been taken and wiped for trace evidence. It's fine to take out of the bag.'

Chupplejeep switched the phone on and swiped his finger across the screen to unlock it. It looked much better than his old Nokia. An Apple was too expensive for him though, he would have to settle for an LG or a Sony when he changed his phone next. He pulled up Subrina's list of contacts and scrolled through them. There were hundreds of names and numbers.

'Any sister in there?'

'Pankaj, if you had a sister, would you store her name in your phone as 'sister'?'

Pankaj shook his head.

Chupplejeep found Dinesh's mobile number in Subrina Basi's phone and dialled it. It started to ring.

'This is the Idea cellular service for telephone number...'

Chupplejeep rang off. 'Is Dinesh not answering because he killed Ms Basi and is hiding or is he in some kind of drug-induced coma in some hippie joint in Anjuna? Phone Panaji and put a trace on this number.'

'But it's out of range, sir. You can't trace a phone out of range.'

Chupplejeep sighed. 'But you can when it's back in range, *baba*. Unless he is also dead!' Chupplejeep switched the phone off. He stood up and put it in his pocket. 'Come on, let's go.'

Pankaj stood up. 'Where are we going, sir?'

'We're going to get some answers.'

CHAPTER SIXTEEN

Chaaya ran a brush through her long grey hair. She took a bottle of *Parachute* coconut oil out from the cupboard and poured a little into the palm of her hand. Carefully, she applied it to the roots of her hair and took her usual seat on the veranda. Her son had carved the rocking chair she sat on and in thirty years she was the only one to have used it. The wicker seat had been replaced several times over the years, but it was still as comfortable as ever.

She looked out into the garden. The sun was setting and she could hear Balbir singing to himself as he watered the jasmine and red hibiscus. Her eyes turned to the barren drumstick tree, swaying slightly in the gentle evening breeze. She licked her lips. She would have to wait till April before she could make *sangacho ross* with coconut and *daal* and this long, spindly green vegetable that grew on the tree she was eyeing.

A young boy with a large bag around his shoulders started walking up the path of the house towards her, kicking up clouds of red dust as he went.

'Boy, you have the evening paper?'

'Yes!' said the boy, eager to please this old woman as he climbed the red stone stairs up to the veranda. 'Today, there is some exciting news.'

'Exciting news in Dhesera? You must be telling lies. You know what happens to little children who tell lies.'

The young boy looked at his feet. '*Mataji,* I'm not lying. A lady has died.'

'Well, if this is true this is not exciting. You should be sorry. She was someone's daughter, perhaps someone's mother also.'

'She was famous.'

'Someone famous in Dhesera died? Give me that paper, boy,' Chaaya said. The boy was right. If he was telling the truth then this was exciting news, indeed. Nothing like this ever happened in sleepy Dhesera. Finally, she would have some gossip to tell her sister in Bihar.

Chaaya took the newspaper from the boy, pulled a five rupee note from her pocket and shoved it into his hand. The boy squealed with delight and bounded down the polished stone steps to deliver his news to his next customer.

She licked her lips as she opened the paper. As soon as she saw the picture she gasped. Her hand flew to her chest. It couldn't be, could it? Could this really be?

~

Nishok, the hotel gardener, sat in the corner of the kitchen on a low wooden stool, plucking a chicken. Just twenty minutes earlier he had chased it around the coop and wrung its neck. The bird was still warm. He was sad that he had to capture the bird like that and that he had to kill it. It would have been better for both of them if the bird had surrendered to begin with. But he understood the chicken. It was scared, so it ran. He knew he shouldn't have run away from the policeman either. But he too was scared. They had taken him by surprise, he hadn't expected them so soon. Now time was running out. It wouldn't be long till the police caught up with him again. They knew where he worked and they could easily find out where he lived.

If the circumstances were different then he would escape. He had done it before. But he couldn't do it again. Not with his frail mother at home. And what would she think when she found out his shame? What would she say to him when the police…what would they do? Would they publicly shame him? What about his wife and children, would they turn away from him in disgust? Then he would end up taking his own life. That would be the best thing to do. The honourable thing to do.

Abhik walked into the kitchen with a steel bowl of *bimblies*. 'Why do you have to do that in here? Can't you do it in the yard?' he asked Nishok. 'I suppose you may offend the guests. But such few guests. It's like a haunted house since that woman died. No one is staying here, just a handful of day-trippers and restaurant guests, and the staff look miserable. A bit like you, Nishok. Your name means happy, no? Your mother got that wrong, didn't she? With your crooked nose and your lopsided smile, I'm not sure if you're really happy.'

Nishok shrugged.

'You know you shouldn't have run away from that policeman like that. What do guilty people do? They run. You must have seen it first-hand in the last village you came from. That village was nicknamed *tsoor,* thief village, was it not?' Abhik rinsed the small green *bimblie* fruit under the tap, then pulled out a chopping board and a knife from one of the kitchen drawers. 'You think I don't know anything, but I know your secret. What a terrible shame if you were put away and missed the festive period with your children.'

Nishok took a fistful of white feathers and yanked them out of the limp bird.

'There is no use pretending with me. I run this kitchen, I know exactly what happens here, even when I'm not around. I know you took that knife. I know what you did.'

Nishok looked up and caught Abhik's stare. He shook his head.

'You didn't take the knife? I see. You would never say that though, would you?' Abhik let out a low chuckle. 'What else didn't you take?' He started cutting the small, green sour fruits in half.

Nishok went back to pulling feathers. Some chefs scalded the chicken with boiling water to make removing the feathers easier, but he chose not to. He found that if he plucked the feathers soon after death, they came away easily. Usually he didn't like this task one bit, but today there was something calming about removing the feathers this way.

'The police will come back,' Abhik said. This time his voice was soft, but Nishok knew he didn't care. The only person Abhik cared about was himself. He was an angry man with a terrible temper. A man who would sell his mother to save himself.

Abhik put his knife and fruit down and wiped his hands on his apron. He walked over to Nishok, squatting next to him. The gardener could feel his breath on his face as he spoke, making the fine hairs on the back of his neck stand on end. 'Next time don't run. Trust me, I've been there before. I can see from your sunken eyes that you didn't sleep last night. If I've noticed it, who else will notice? It will only get worse if you don't admit to your crimes.'

Nishok stopped plucking the bird. He looked into Abhik's large, vacant eyes.

'Next time when the police come, you must stay calm. Listen to what they have to say and then you must find a way to answer them. You must tell them exactly what you have done. It's the only way out of this mess.'

Nishok opened his mouth as if to say something, but then closed it again. Some things were better left unsaid.

Chapter Seventeen

Chupplejeep knocked on the small door of the maroon and yellow villa at the edge of the village of Suuj. It was one of the villages in Goa where the houses were reminiscent of the Portuguese rule with their large arched white windows, wooden shutters, street-facing verandas and terracotta tiles. The houses in the village were well looked-after. All except one, a derelict shell of a house at the far end of the village where only the walls remained, shrouded by money plant creepers and black pepper vines. A neem tree grew in the middle. The branches, good for cleaning one's teeth, thought Chupplejeep.

A butterfly landed on Pankaj's shoulder. 'Sir,' he whispered. Chupplejeep turned around and in doing so, scared the butterfly away.

'What's wrong? Why are you whispering?'

Pankaj sighed. 'Never mind, sir.'

'One day you should see a doctor about your attention span.' Chupplejeep turned back to the front door just as it opened.

'Ah, Detective. I was expecting you.'

Chupplejeep smiled. 'You were, were you?'

'Detective, Officer, come in.' Bonaparte turned and walked back into the house. It was dark inside with little natural light. They walked through the house and stopped on the veranda facing the small rear garden. Bonaparte excused himself to get some drinks. Chupplejeep noted that the outside space was as barren as his own garden, with just a peach bougainvillea and an arjuna tree. A green pigeon sat atop one of its branches. Bonaparte returned with two glasses of water and a bowl of cashew nuts, and the bird took flight.

'You don't see many green pigeons these days,' Pankaj said. 'They only come out in the evenings. Lucky man, having all this wildlife around you.'

Chupplejeep smiled but he wasn't really paying attention to what Pankaj was saying, instead he was wondering why the boy hadn't studied agriculture at college instead of training to be a policeman. He was forever examining the local flora and fauna in every new village they happened to stop at. 'I read your article, Bonaparte,' Chupplejeep said when Pankaj had finished telling the story of a green pigeon he had once saved from the jaws of a snake.

'Of course you did. And what did you think?'

'It was interesting. Especially the part about Subrina Basi's sister.'

'I thought you'd be intrigued. Please sit down.'

Chupplejeep and Pankaj sat on the wicker chairs. Bonaparte did the same. 'So?'

'Sho what?' he said, his lisp evident.

'You know that's why I'm here. I want to know more about her family.'

'Is this now a murder investigation?'

'I can't tell you that.'

'The death is suspicious.'

'I can't say anything else right now. We are waiting on the autopsy results.'

'Well then, I can't tell you about her sister or what happened to Subrina when she was growing up here. If it's not a murder inquiry then I'm not withholding information, that's correct, isn't it?'

Chupplejeep made a face. He looked over at Pankaj and then back to Bonaparte. 'Okay. I'll make you a deal.'

Pankaj took out his notebook. His pencil poised above a blank page.

Chupplejeep shot Pankaj a look telling him not to write anything down yet. He turned to Bonaparte. 'Listen, you tell me all you know about Subrina's sister and her upbringing here and I'll give you an exclusive piece as soon as we have wrapped up the case.'

Bonaparte laughed. 'You think I'm stupid, *awhat*? What if you never solve the case? And that is a high probability. After all, you are coming to me for information. I want to know whether it's a murder or not as soon as you find out.'

Chupplejeep clenched his teeth, took a breath and then spoke. 'You've followed my career, haven't you?'

The journalist nodded.

'So you know I always get to the bottom of things.'

'But you've never dealt with a celebrity before.'

'Minor celebrity,' Pankaj said.

'No deal,' Bonaparte said.

'Okay.' Chupplejeep knew that the death was suspicious. But it was police procedure to wait for confirmation from the forensic pathologist before he could officially state that it was the case, and Kulkarni was still waiting for the toxicology reports. 'What if I tell you what the medical examiner is leaning towards from his findings at present? That will give you something to work on.'

'I already know it's murder, by the fact that you are being so cagey. If Basi's death wasn't suspicious, you wouldn't even be here.'

Chupplejeep shrugged. 'What if I guarantee I will tell you everything the minute we get to the bottom of this. Deal?'

Bonaparte rubbed his chin. 'Hmm, let me think about it.'

Chupplejeep stood up. 'We don't have time for this. Either you tell us now and take the deal or forget it. There are many other up-and-coming journalists who are waiting for their big break. You, keep your eye out for a subpoena.' Chupplejeep started towards the front of the house.

'Okay, okay,' Bonaparte said, as Pankaj stood up to follow his boss.

Chupplejeep returned to the veranda and offered his hand.

Bonaparte shook it. 'Where do you want me to start?'

'At the beginning.'

CHAPTER EIGHTEEN

Chaaya read the article in the *Larara Express* for the third time. 'So the *dukkar* came back.'

'Who are you calling a pig, ma?' asked Balbir.

'That woman, that woman who ruined our lives, was here in Dhesera. I used to read about her in the cheap magazines. That's all she was good for. I never once paid to see her films. I wouldn't give my money to that *chedi*. Never.'

'*Mamaji*, don't use such language. A whore! I've not heard you talk like this in some time. Who is the woman you are talking about?'

Chaaya showed Balbir the picture in the newspaper. 'Who's she?'

She studied Balbir's eyes, looking for recognition, then her face softened. It was better when he didn't remember. 'Doesn't matter now. It was a long time ago. Don't you worry about it.'

'Was it someone you knew before I was born?'

'Something like that.' She leaned over in her rocking chair and stroked her son's face. At times like this it was better not to remind him of the pain.

'Tell me, *mamaji*. You haven't told me a good story in so long.'

'This woman, she caused me a lot of pain. Pain that I'll carry with me in my heart till the day I die. Now, finally, she has got her comeuppance.'

'Is she dead?'

Chaaya nodded.

'How did she die?'

'Painfully, I hope. The article is vague. It doesn't say that she took her own life or if it was murder. I wouldn't blame her if she killed herself, she must have carried that guilt of what she did everywhere she went. She left Goa to forget, but you can't forget something like that so easily. I read in the papers that she was dependent on drugs. She was never happy – two divorces behind her. But it's good. Because someone like that does not deserve happiness.'

'Maybe she was killed.'

'I wouldn't blame someone for taking her life either. Perhaps Kali, the goddess of death, wanted her and sent some poor soul to do her dirty work. Perhaps it was time. In this great land we must trust in the gods to bring justice and retribution.'

'*Maa*, these are big words you are using. Tell me what this woman did?'

'She took someone away from us, Balbir. She took him away forever.'

CHAPTER NINETEEN

'So basically you're saying that Subrina's full family lived here in Suuj until she was twenty-three,' said Chupplejeep.

'Yes,' Bonaparte said, 'her mother, father and her sister. There were only two children.'

'And you say her sister still lives in Goa.'

'Yes.'

'Why did they move away from Goa?' Pankaj asked. 'Was it because Subrina Basi wanted to further her acting career?'

Bonaparte smiled. 'That is what all the magazines say, is it not? Tell me, did you read that in *Icon Bites*?'

Pankaj nodded. 'There was no mention of Goa. But they mentioned the family wanted to be in Delhi for acting classes.'

'Because that is what the family wanted everyone to believe. But let me guess, that's not the real reason why they moved away and you know why she moved,' Chupplejeep said.

'Most of the people in Suuj, well those that remain, know why the family moved. The trouble is, not many people who were here twenty years ago are still here now. Things have changed in these parts. Very few Dhesera residents remain. First the new hotel, then the gallery. Some of the older folk didn't like it, so they went.'

'I see,' Chupplejeep said encouragingly, although he knew this. It was the same in every village.

'Plus, there are educational benefits of moving out of the villages like Dhesera. The cities have better schools. And here in India where education is king, parents want to give their children the best start – especially in the villages. They are all scared their kids will be poor like them. Nobody wants that.'

'Why are you talking of Dhesera if they lived here in Suuj?'

'Because Subrina, our beloved movie star, killed someone in Dhesera.'

Pankaj coughed.

'Can I get you some more water?' Bonaparte asked.

'Cashew nut,' Pankaj managed to say in between trying to breathe. He shook his head.

'She killed someone?' Chupplejeep asked. 'Who did she kill? And was she tried for this murder?' He remembered the conversation he had with the Commissioner of Police in Delhi. The Commissioner had been confident there was no truth in her confession, thinking that Subrina was deluded. But perhaps the actress was telling the truth all along.

'She killed a small boy. He must have been one, perhaps two at the time. I myself was only about ten.

119

Subrina was just twenty-three – young but still with some sense about her. Back then, my classmates and teachers were talking about her all the time after the incident. They said she had a bright future ahead of her. She achieved a distinction for her tenth and twelfth standard, even after all her partying – apparently with different boys every night. What shame for her family. Her parents wanted her to become a doctor, you know. They forced her to take science at college. But Subrina had her own plans. My mother used to shake her head every time she spoke of Subrina and her family. Indira Gandhi said that you cannot shake hands with a clenched fist – well, Subrina was the clenched fist.'

Pankaj, now fully recovered, asked how Subrina killed the child.

'It was an accident. After all, she was only in her twenties. And the kid, well he was just a child – too small for people to want him dead. Subrina and her sister were going to a late-night party. They had been drinking. If Subrina was the same then as she was later in her life in Delhi, well then she was probably on some *bhang*, hashish, too. Her sister, though, was the complete opposite – quiet and reserved – but Subrina dragged her along for company. You know how it is around here…if you're the only girl going out all the time, you get a bad reputation. Rumour had it that Subrina forced her little sister to go out with her as soon as she turned seventeen.'

'So they were out together and drunk too. I get the picture,' Chupplejeep said, trying to hurry the journalist along. He could tell that Bonaparte was enjoying recounting the story. Of course he was, he had a captive audience.

Bonaparte popped a cashew in his mouth and chewed.

'It must have been around midnight. Late for a child to be out playing near the road, but nevertheless that was where the child was. Later, his mother said that the boy wanted to go to make *su-su* and he was awake and happy to go outside so they let him. You know how it is.'

Chupplejeep didn't know how it was, but he didn't want to interrupt Bonaparte and slow him down even more. So he nodded as if he knew exactly what the journalist was saying to be true. In the orphanage where Chupplejeep had grown up, there were three toilets in a make-do shack within the compound of the home. No one would dream of going to the toilet on the roadside, but then again one of the mamas at the orphanage would have twisted his ears had he been caught doing such things on the road.

'Subrina had been driving her father's car. The family were quite well off.'

'I would have expected that. It's rare to get into Bollywood or Dollywood without wealth and good contacts, especially at twenty-three,' Chupplejeep said. Pankaj agreed. It was either wealth or the casting couch that gave these starlets their fifteen minutes of fame.

'She was supposed to slow down at the corner where the boy had been playing or shitting or whatever he was doing. But she didn't. A cat ran out from one side of the road, she swerved to avoid it. She lost control of the car and she ended up killing the poor child. I think the child's name was Nitin. Such a shame, such a shame.'

'What happened after that?'

'What normally happens in such cases?'

'The family got a big payoff to keep quiet and not to press charges,' Pankaj suggested.

Bonaparte nodded. 'That's exactly what happened. The family put up the usual fight. Eventually, Subrina's father offered more than they would earn in a lifetime. Which is probably not much, you know.'

'I know,' said Chupplejeep. He was fed up of these rich families getting away with murder, literally. It wasn't just a problem in Goa. It happened all over India.

'The family took the bribe and kept quiet. They managed to move from their little shack with no toilet to a lovely villa in Dhesera.'

'Are the family of the boy still around?'

Bonaparte shrugged. 'I kept up with what they were doing through my gossiping mother. When my mother died, so did the information on the inhabitants of the villages around Suuj.'

'I see.'

'After the incident, it all went very quiet for Subrina and her family. Soon after, they moved to Delhi and, well, the rest you know from *Icon Bites*.' Bonaparte winked at Pankaj.

'And the sister?' Chupplejeep asked. 'Subrina Basi's sister? She's still in Goa?'

'Yes, she never went to Delhi. Although you won't see much of her.'

'Why is that?'

Bonaparte looked at his watch. 'Look at the time. I should be charging you for this.'

Chupplejeep leaned forward. It was Bonaparte who had told the story so slowly. 'We just need the name and address of the sister.'

'You can find her easily, I'm sure.'

'Why do you say that?'

'Subrina's sister, Suki, is exactly that these days. She's a Sister.'

Chupplejeep twisted the end of his moustache. 'I don't follow.'

'Suki has been convented. She is now a nun at the Sacred Heart Convent in Verna. She goes by the name Sister Valentine, now.'

'But they are Sikh!' Pankaj said.

'Suki never moved with the family to Delhi. She stayed in Goa to novitiate, after which she acknowledged God's calling and took her perpetual profession of vows, giving herself to God. Odd, huh?'

'Very,' Pankaj said.

Chupplejeep stood up. 'Come on, Pankaj. It's getting late and we don't want to keep Bonaparte from his dinner. Thank you,' Chupplejeep said to the journalist, once again extending his hand to him.

Bonaparte took it. 'No problem, Detective, as long as you remember our deal.'

Chupplejeep nodded and walked towards the front door. Pankaj followed. 'Oh, one other thing,' Chupplejeep said.

'What's that?'

'Did anyone see Subrina Basi driving the car when the boy was killed?'

Bonaparte nodded. 'Yes. Nitin's brother, he was about twelve at the time. He was right there when it happened.'

'And where is the brother now?'

Bonaparte shrugged. 'His family, with their newfound wealth, sent him off to study. I didn't follow what happened…by that time I had moved to the city. But rumour has it, he died as well.'

Chapter Twenty

Chupplejeep parked his faded blue Maruti outside the venue and made his way towards Christabel. 'What's this?' she asked, pointing to his uniform. 'You want to get married here or no?'

Chupplejeep opened his mouth to answer, but she didn't let him.

'Arthur, you better not throw your weight around. I like this place and I want to have our wedding reception here. You're a detective inspector. You don't even have to wear uniform. Why would you wear it today? No, don't answer that. Just don't act like a cop when you speak to the manager. It's enough that you wore that,' she said, looking him up and down.

Chupplejeep closed his mouth. He wasn't sure why he had decided to wear his khaki uniform today. But Christabel was probably right. On some subconscious level, he wanted to dissuade the manager of Sinquerim Jardin from letting them have a wedding there. The venue was much like the last one Christabel had dragged him around. A large concrete dance floor with a stage for the band was in one corner of what could only be described as a garden complex, with its mixed variety of trees, flowers and shrubs. In another corner there was a buffet area and some toilets, and in the third corner was, most importantly, the bar.

'So I told the manager that we would walk around first and then ask him any questions. Do you like the bunting?' she said, pointing above the stage.

Chupplejeep looked up at the white bunting tied between the trees.

'There is a wedding this evening. Look at how many staff they have.'

Chupplejeep looked around and began to sweat. There were people tying green bows on chairs and gardeners tending to the lawn. He wondered how much so many staff would cost.

'This wedding is for five hundred people. You know this place has capacity for eight hundred guests.'

Chupplejeep stopped walking.

'No, silly,' Christabel said, taking his hand. 'We'll only have a maximum of two hundred.' Christabel pulled him along. 'And it's in Bardez – so not too far from Larara, and Sinquerim beach is close by. Someone also told me there is a bird sanctuary near here.'

'What difference does that make?' Chupplejeep snapped. 'They'll be at our wedding, not enjoying themselves at a beach or an aviary.'

'There is no need to get all angry. I'm just saying it's a good location, no?'

They stopped walking and Chupplejeep looked around. Christabel looked so happy. He didn't want to dash her dreams so he kissed her forehead. 'Christu, it's a perfect venue,' he said, forcing the words from his lips.

Christabel smiled and squeezed his arm. 'Oh, here is the manager. Mr Agarwal,' she said, waving furiously at a man with a clipboard.

'Ah, madam. This must be your betrothed.'

'Yes, yes,' Christabel said, while stroking Chupplejeep's arm.

'Sir, do you like what you see here at Sinquerim Jardin? I think it will be perfect for a late January wedding. Most of the high season tourists have gone by then so traffic is less. And still the weather is nice.'

Chupplejeep let out a nervous laugh. 'It's a lovely venue, but I think January is a little too soon.'

'It is January that you mentioned on the phone, was it not, madam?'

Christabel nodded, still squeezing Chupplejeep's arm. Chupplejeep turned to look at her.

'Arthur, Mr Agarwal rightly pointed out that there are only fifty-two Saturdays in the year. And I think January is very auspicious.'

'Why is that? January is next month!' Chupplejeep asked.

'W-well it's the New Year for one, so it's a time for new beginnings. And, er, it's the month we celebrate Republic Day.'

'*Aacha*,' Chupplejeep said, still not convinced and wondering what Republic Day had to do with setting a wedding date. The three of them were silent for a moment. Chupplejeep looked at his fiancée and then

127

said, 'Mr Agarwal, how much would it cost to get married here say in January, maybe February-March time?'

'Firstly, let me tell you about the history of Sinquerim Jardin.'

Chupplejeep put his hand up. 'No, there is really no need for that.'

Mr Agarwal shook his head, signalling his acceptance. 'Fine, sir, okay. So exclusive of band, but inclusive of local spirits, soft drinks, buffet food and table linen, cutlery and glasses...'

'And table decoration?' Christabel interjected.

'Table decoration excluded, madam.'

Christabel pouted.

'For all this, for two-fifty guests on the last Saturday in January, you're looking at seventy-nine thousand, nine hundred and ninety-nine rupees.'

'Eighty thousand bucks? Are you serious?'

'Did I mention the local spirits and soft drinks are included?'

'Did I mention I'm a cop?'

Agarwal shook his head. 'I can see by your uniform.'

'I serve this great country. I keep you people safe...' Chupplejeep felt Christabel's elbow dig into his side. 'How about if we choose March? That's low season, no?'

'It would be good for business as we are very empty that time of year. But with all due respect, your guests will be fainting in the heat and the lawn doesn't look so fresh when the sun is so strong.'

'February?'

'I can give you a five thousand rupee discount.'

'On a Friday?' Chupplejeep felt another dig in his ribs.

Mr Agarwal opened his clipboard. 'Last Tuesday in February. Okay, I can give you another two thousand rupee discount.'

'And the table decorations. We want those also,' Christabel said.

Mr Agarwal pulled out a calculator from his jacket pocket and started tapping on the device.

'Tuesday?' Christabel whispered to Chupplejeep.

'What's wrong with that?'

Christabel pursed her lips. 'I've never been invited to a wedding on a Tuesday. All weddings are on a Saturday. What will people think?'

'That we have more sense than money. Think of what we could do with the savings. We could put that towards the band.'

Christabel was silent.

'Anyway,' Chupplejeep whispered, 'we don't have to decide today. We're not in any rush. We can call him later with our decision. It will give us both time to think.'

Christabel made a face.

'And I noticed Mr Agarwal mentioned two hundred and fifty guests, not the two hundred we agreed.'

'Tuesday is fine. Let's just book it,' Christabel said.

Chupplejeep felt uneasy at his fiancée's determination. He had never seen her like this before. Standing in this wedding venue amidst the crab grass, with the smell of citronella, was making him feel quite nauseous.

'Okay. Because you are such a lovely couple and because you, sir, work for our government as an officer of the law…'

'Detective,' Chupplejeep said.

'A detective, *wah*! Of course, then I will include the table decorations for a total price of seventy thousand rupees. So it's settled. Shall I put you down for the last Tuesday in February? All I need is a ten thousand rupee deposit from you.'

Chupplejeep felt another dig in the ribs. He put his hand in his pocket, but before he pulled out his wallet he said, 'Can we sample the food before we put our deposit down? You have a wedding going on here tonight. Are any of the foods ready?' Before he parted with any money, they had to sample the food. That was all that mattered at weddings. If the food was hopeless, the guests would remember it till their diamond wedding anniversary. Plus, he was sure a spicy curry would get rid of the queasy feeling he was experiencing.

Mr Agarwal smiled. 'Come this way.'

'Arthur, have you asked Joachim to be your best man?' Christabel asked as they followed Mr Agarwal, giving him that look of hers. The look that said she knew what he was thinking.

Chupplejeep shook his head. How did she always know what was going through his mind? He had wanted to ask Joachim, but at the same time he was nervous because by asking Joachim it meant he was one step closer to commitment and one step away from his carefree lifestyle, which wasn't so carefree anymore if he was honest about it.

'Ask him fast. Now that we have a date, we have to get moving on everything. I've spoken to my bridesmaids already.'

'That, my dear, is because you knew we were getting married soon, unlike me. I've only just found out.'

'I was just thinking his nephew is in that band, is he not?'

Chupplejeep nodded.

'You could ask his nephew's band to play. It could save some money.'

'So have a seat over here and I'll tell one of the waitresses to bring you a selection of foods,' Mr Agarwal said.

Minutes later Christabel and Chupplejeep were savouring wedding favourites of *soropatel*, prawn *balchao,* and beef tongue with healthy sides of carrot and lime pickle.

'How's the food?' Mr Agarwal asked with a confident smile.

Chupplejeep hesitated. He wanted to say that it was bad, anything to postpone setting the date. But he couldn't lie. The food was first class. He made a circle with his thumb and forefinger.

'Super, super,' Christabel said. Chupplejeep could see she had forgotten about her pre-wedding diet already.

Mr Agarwal stood expectantly while Chupplejeep eventually got the hint and handed over ten thousand rupee notes. 'Thank you, sir. You won't regret it. Sinquerim Jardin never disappoints. We'll catch up soon, madam, to iron out all the details. And sir, I hope I see you before the 29th of Feb.' With that said Mr Agarwal walked away, shouting as he did so at a gardener stringing up some lights.

Christabel's jaw dropped. 'Did he just say the 29th of February?'

Chupplejeep took another mouthful of *soropatel*. 'I think he did.'

Chapter Twenty-one

'No comment,' Chupplejeep said, slamming the green telephone back in its cradle. 'That's the second call I've taken this afternoon. If Bonaparte hadn't been so helpful, I would go around to his place and wring his neck! Pankaj, what have you got for me?'

'Sir, I've been trawling the internet for most of the day and the death of Subrina Basi has only gained a couple of column inches in *Icon Bites* and a couple in two e-zines. The papers are not giving her death much coverage at all, even the Delhi-based ones. The media circus Gosht predicted is nothing more than a one-man band.'

'Bonaparte.'

'Two calls is not so bad compared to what could have been expected. Maybe Gosht will take the pressure off.'

'I doubt that. Gosht hangs around with those big-shots in Delhi and he's gunning to be the next director general of police. Those Delhi people have solid influence. He'll still expect this case to be solved fast.

Anything that I should know about from the stuff you've read?'

Pankaj shook his head. 'One site claims that Subrina Basi famously said, "Death is certain for whatever is born." Apparently she said it after her first movie flop. They are saying that ironically this statement has come back to bite her.'

'Isn't that a quote from the *Bhagavad Gita*? The reporter must have misunderstood what Subrina was saying.'

'Still, it is an odd thing to say, sir.'

'Is it? We know about the child she killed. Perhaps she was trying to find some justification for the death of the innocent child.'

'She was high, sir. That's why the baby died. I see it all the time – drunkards riding home on their bikes or driving their flash cars home at three, four in the morning with not so much as a care in the world.'

Chupplejeep sighed. Goa, known for its hedonistic culture, always had a drink-drive problem. That was the beauty of third world, wasn't it? You could drink and drive and nobody gave a damn. Only recently had they started to police the issue in the tourist season with the introduction of *nakabhandhis*, checkpoints. But depending which traffic cop was on duty, it was something you could easily get away with, if you were willing to pay a little *baksheesh*. Twenty years ago when poor Nitin's life was taken from him, getting stopped because you were drunk and behind the wheel was unheard of, especially in a small village like Dhesera.

'She can't use a line from a sacred text to justify what she did,' Pankaj said.

'Her wealthy parents paid to have the whole incident go away. I looked into all reports filed at the time of the death.'

'And? Let me guess, it was never reported.'

'You're wrong.'

'I suppose the Nineties were not so long ago. It would had to have been reported.'

'If it wasn't, Subrina's family would have no reason to pay out.'

'What was it reported as?'

'Accidental death. They said that the boy ran out into the road and was killed by a driver who was going to pick up his employer from the airport.' Chupplejeep picked up the yellow folder in front of him and looked through it.

'We should go and speak to this driver.'

'Too late. After the incident, he retired. Now he lives in Gujarat with his daughter.'

'So he too got a payoff to take the blame.'

'It would appear so. A driver doesn't just relocate like that, without a large cash injection. The employer was named, but I couldn't track down anyone by that name. Sounds like the name was fictitious.'

'Which police officer filed the report?'

'Sub-Inspector Gustav. An old fellow who has long since died.' Chupplejeep put the yellow folder down and opened his drawer. He took out a packet of *grams*. He could hear his stomach rumbling and he knew he

135

wouldn't last till dinner. He popped a handful of the dried yellow beans into his mouth and chewed, swallowing them with a large gulp of water. They were fat-free at least, which was something. Although he couldn't help but stare at the potato chops sitting on a steel plate on Pankaj's desk. He tried to ignore the question forming in his head as to what filling was in the chops – traditional beef, or mutton. His mouth began to water. He took another sip of water. 'Anything else from your internet search?

'Subrina's death has been overshadowed by a new movie, which has just been released. It's set in Maharashtra but all the characters are fully Hindi-speaking. The Marathi-speaking people are up in arms.'

'These showbiz reporters have their priorities all wrong. You would think a dead movie star would make for better news.'

'She was D-list, sir.'

Chupplejeep shook his head. How awful to be categorized in such a way. The death of an A-list celebrity would have commanded so much more news coverage. In his opinion, the world of showbiz was pathetic.

'Oh sir, there was one thing I read that I found a little odd.'

'What's that?'

'Advani said that Subrina was his muse and that he loved her.'

'Yes.'

'Well, there was reason for that. Subrina was supporting Advani's work to be exhibited in an exclusive gallery in Malabar Hill. Recently she withdrew her support, or so this newspaper reported.'

'But Advani is a big artist. He earns thousands. Surely he could pay his own rent.'

'Yes, that is what I thought also, so I looked into the matter,' Pankaj said. 'The support isn't money. Subrina's grandfather owned the building and she has a vote on the board of directors. But for some reason she withdrew her support for Advani before she came to Goa for IFFI.'

'So Advani could be a suspect. Having your art suddenly withdrawn from an exclusive gallery would dampen anyone's spirits. But is that motive enough to murder someone?'

Pankaj gasped. 'He killed her to get revenge. Maybe she was blackmailing him too. If his work was vastly different from the artist he originally stole from, like Takshak suggested, maybe Subrina found out and sent him the letter. She was in Goa when he received it.'

'She withdrew her support but she had no reason to blackmail him. She didn't need the money.'

'He was with her the night before she died. Maybe he was trying to persuade her to change her mind about the gallery.'

Chupplejeep drummed his fingers on the table. 'Are you making any progress with the blackmail case?'

Pankaj shook his head. 'Sir, with the Basi death I haven't given his case my full attention. You could say that I'm putting the blackmail case on hold.'

'On hold? You can't just put one case on hold, Pankaj.' When would this boy learn?

Pankaj put his head in his hands. 'I'm not sure what to do, sir. That Advani is a character. It wouldn't surprise me if he sent the letter to himself to make himself seem important. I've read online that the reviews for his latest collection are not favourable. And I can't say I blame the critics, sir. Not after what I've seen.'

'And do you have any evidence that Advani forged a blackmail letter to himself? Because if you don't, it's a serious allegation you are making. We could charge him for wasting police time.'

Pankaj bit his lower lip. 'I don't actually have any evidence, but I am beginning to think that perhaps he has been wasting police time.'

'Why is that?'

'I tracked down Advani's art teacher. I made up a story about Advani's first pieces. He had one of the first ones he sold so he sent me a picture of it. Sir, even I can tell it is Advani's work and I know nothing about brush strokes. This teacher also had a piece of Vallabh's work. He sent me a picture of that also. It was very different to Advani's work. Takshak backed this up previously by implying that the artist Advani claims to have stolen from had terrible style. He said that the work was so bad no one would pass it off as their own.'

138

'Tell me more about Takshak. He looked a mess yet he said he was sleeping well. Something is troubling him and I'm worried it has something to do with Subrina's death.'

'Sir, I don't know about his link to Subrina, but he's very loyal to Advani despite how he treats him. I suppose Advani rescued Takshak from his brute father, so he has to be grateful.'

'You cannot be grateful for a lifetime. There is a point in any relationship like that when both people have to be realistic and let go of the feeling of gratitude or indebtedness. Get back on the case. Go speak to Advani. Tell him you suspect that he has lied to you about his secret and that you want to know the truth or you are dropping the case.'

'Can I do that, sir?'

'Yes,' Chupplejeep said. 'You can. If he has any brains, he will confess what it is he is actually hiding. Once you know his secret, you'll have a better idea of who is behind the blackmail. Advani and Subrina were close. This could have something to do with Malabar Hill and ultimately Subrina's death.'

Pankaj got up from behind his desk. 'I'll go there now.'

'And then go back to the Golden Orchid.'

'Why?'

'I want you to speak to the staff you haven't managed to speak to yet.'

'That slippery gardener fellow, Nishok?'

'That one and anyone else you haven't spoken to. I want to know if they had any means, motivation and opportunity to murder Subrina Basi.'

'Yes, sir.'

'That means you need to check their alibis.'

'Okay. But sir, shouldn't we wait to hear what the lab and toxicology reports come back with? I mean, what if Subrina did kill herself? She carried the guilt around with her for poor Nitin's death for so long it was probably too much to bear.'

The telephone on the detective's desk rang, interrupting their conversation. 'That will be Kulkarni now,' Chupplejeep said as he picked up the receiver. He put one hand over the mouthpiece and looked at Pankaj. 'Any news from Panaji on Dinesh?'

Pankaj shook his head. 'Nothing.'

Chupplejeep rolled his eyes. He removed his hand from the mouthpiece. 'Ah, Kulkarni, tell me.'

CHAPTER TWENTY-TWO

'She had enough drugs in her system to knock out a *ghoda*!'

'A horse! What?'

'Narcotic sedatives, analgesics and natural opiates. It's true what the papers had reported about her. She was high on drugs, that's for sure, eh.'

'Tell me in English.'

'A cocktail of codeine, pain relievers and sleeping tablets. There was evidence that she took cocaine before her death.'

'So the bartender was telling the truth.'

'Did he have reason to lie, eh?'

'If he murdered Subrina then yes, he would have had reason to lie,' Chupplejeep said irritably.

'Very quick today, Detective. Anyone would think you had set a wedding date already.'

Chupplejeep narrowed his eyes. 'Who told you?'

'My cousin-sister met your Christabel at the bakers this morning. Your fiancée was happy that the month for the marriage had been fixed but she mentioned something about changing the date slightly.'

'Why don't we get back to your results?'

'Ah, so you're still a reluctant groom. Poor Christu, does she know what *durgathi* she is marrying?'

'I'm not so miserable, thank you. Now back to the results.'

'Nothing suspicious found under the fingernails or on the vaginal swab. Like we thought, there was no evidence of sexual activity. The water in the bath had traces of Subrina's urine and faeces along with the contents of the maid's stomach. Not much trace evidence to go on, eh.'

'What else?'

'Her blood alcohol level was high at 0.12 per cent. She would have been feeling nauseous with this much alcohol in her system. The hair samples showed she was using cocaine and other illegal drugs over a continuous period of time.'

'Okay, so she was an addict. But how did she die?'

'Hypoglycaemic coma.'

Chupplejeep leaned forward. 'She was diabetic?'

'All her organs shut down one by one, until Subrina Basi was no more. The tests showed that there were elevated levels of insulin in the blood. Subrina Basi wasn't a diabetic.'

'How do you know that?'

'I did a full autopsy. There was no evidence. Plus, copies of her medical records came through, but they were not as comprehensive as I would have liked and some pages were missing. Typical of the system, but I'm sure you'll check with her doctor in Delhi.'

Chupplejeep said he would.

'From the puncture mark in her bottom, and the trace drug found in the tissue samples, I can tell you she was injected with insulin. It's pretty easy to get your hands on the drug. The insulin, once injected into her bloodstream, would have caused the cells in her body to absorb extra glucose from the blood. So her liver would have stopped producing as much glucose. Glucose is what we need to run. Running out of glucose is like that Maruti of yours running out of gas. She may have had a seizure but this was unlikely given the bruising on her body was not consistent with this. It's more likely she became unconscious and then died. The trouble is, insulin breaks down post-mortem so it is hard to detect in the body. We could have easily missed it had we not carried out the autopsy as soon as we did.'

'What are you saying?'

'I'm saying that the autopsy results in this instance have to consider the non-pathological evidence as well.'

'Which is the fact that there was no suicide note, the wrists were slit post-mortem or at least whilst the victim was dying, and the suspicious puncture wound in the left buttock?'

''Es, that is exactly what I am saying. Also, there were no fingerprints on the lipstick, none at all, not even the victim's. It was not a new lipstick so Subrina must have used it previously.'

'So the prints have been wiped.'

'Here is where the killer made a mistake. No prints anywhere to be found, apart from the maid, Indu's, and

Subrina's on her belongings in the bedroom, but four sets of fingerprints have been lifted from the knife used to slit Subrina's wrists. The knife if you ask me was a last-minute addition, the knife slipped to the bottom of the bath after the wrists were slit. Out of those four prints, one will match the victim's, because whoever did this would have pressed her fingers on to the knife first. In that respect, the killer was smart. But perhaps he was disturbed and because the knife was never part of his plan, he or she forgot about it.'

Chupplejeep smiled. 'Therefore failing to remove their own fingerprints. It makes sense, Kulkarni, it makes sense and now we have evidence to tie the killer to the crime.'

''Es, Detective. Now all you have to do is find out who did it. Simple.'

~

'You, girl, your painting looks like a cat's behind. And you? Did you paint that with your nose? You're supposed to be the next generation of artists in India. I worry for this great country if you all are going to represent our nation. I could paint better if I were blind!'

Advani continued walking around the room, taking his time to insult each student individually.

The students fell silent. Not a peep or a sniffle from a single one of them. Takshak walked behind Advani, solemnly agreeing with his boss's severe comments with a nod of the head. Occasionally he mopped Advani's brow with the end of his own *dupatta*.

Pankaj stood at the back of the room while Advani finished with his derogatory comments.

'*Hai*, so tell me,' Advani said to Pankaj, after he finished criticising his last student. 'Takshak, fetch this cop some water, na. It's so hot.' He turned back to his students. 'Class dismissed. Tonight I want you to meditate. Imagine you are back in your mother's womb. Our topic for tomorrow is birth.'

Pankaj looked at one of the student's paintings. He couldn't make out what it was, but he thought it best not to ask. If tomorrow's topic was birth then he could only imagine today's session was something just as obscure.

'Usually, when I run this class I offer one student an internship with me in my Malabar Hill Gallery. It's an honour and an experience of a lifetime for them. Being at Malabar Hill opens such possibilities. Rich Bombayites ready to spend their hard cash on art they know nothing about so they can impress their friends.'

'Isn't that soul destroying? If people buy your work and they don't understand or even like it?' Pankaj asked.

Advani shrugged. 'It pays the bills. My work is at other smaller galleries so it's accessible to everyone. It's in these small galleries that I touch people's souls.'

Pankaj wanted to speak to Advani about his big secret and ask him if it was all a lie, but this was too good an opportunity for him to pass up. 'So you would be more upset if you lost your place at one of the smaller galleries than if you lost your place at Malabar Hill?'

'Let's move from this small studio. I can't breathe in here.' Advani started walking towards the main gallery, once Bunty D'mello's living room. Pankaj followed. 'Yes. It's much cooler in here, don't you think?'

'I was asking about your exhibitions, sir.'

'So you were. Don't make idle chat with me. Are you not here to do your job? Have you found out who is blackmailing me?'

'I-I am here to do my job, sir.' Pankaj hesitated slightly, but he soon recovered himself. 'That's why I'm asking you about your gallery. I'm not just investigating your blackmail case, but also the suspicious death of Subrina Basi.'

Takshak entered the gallery with a carafe of water and two glasses. 'Takshak, I don't want water. Get me my wine and my special blue glass. I only want to drink from that.'

Takshak opened his mouth as if to protest, but then turned and started towards the kitchen.

'Fucking murdered? Is that what you are saying?'

'I said suspicious. We're still waiting for test results.' Pankaj noticed Takshak had stopped in the corridor from the gallery to the kitchen when he heard the word 'murdered'. Chupplejeep was right – there was something Takshak wasn't telling them. He turned back to Advani.

'Fucking slow, that's what its like here in Goa. Everything is slow. My Subby, who would fucking do that? She was such an inspiration.'

'That's what we're trying to find out. Hence my question about Malabar Hill.'

Advani folded his arms across his chest. 'I like exhibiting in all my galleries. Once, Leila came into the Malabar Hill Gallery and nearly had an orgasm looking at one of my pieces. I think it was *Fisherwoman at Night*.'

Pankaj's words caught in this throat. He had never before met someone who was so vulgar. He pulled at the collar of his shirt and took a deep breath. Advani was silent, lost in his memory. 'Who's Leila?' he asked eventually, not knowing what else to say.

'Leila Bhobe, stupid.'

'Oh,' Pankaj said. He used to want to marry the actress when he was in the seventh standard. Which young boy didn't? He wondered what it would be like to meet someone that famous in the flesh. He decided it was best not to ask Advani. It wasn't professional. Instead he asked a more pertinent question. 'How did you feel about losing your place at Malabar Hill?'

Advani uncrossed his arms and pulled a cigarette and lighter out of a pocket in his green harem pants. 'I haven't lost my place there.'

'It's not what I've heard.'

'You cops know nothing.'

The artist took a drag from his cigarette and for once didn't say anything. The silence was uncomfortable, but Pankaj knew he had hit a nerve. Advani stared at one of his paintings and didn't flinch even when Takshak returned with a bottle of red wine and his blue glass. Pankaj sensed that any minute now the artist was going to kick him out of his studio and that would be a disaster. He should have left the questions surrounding Subrina for Chupplejeep and only concentrated on the blackmail case, like he was supposed to.

Advani walked out onto the balcony. Pankaj followed. What advice had Chupplejeep only recently given him? 'Sometimes to make someone open up to you, you have to ask them something they are interested in. Then when they are comfortable with you, you can ask them trickier questions.' Yes, Chupplejeep had said those words, and now Pankaj had the opportunity to do exactly that. He smiled. He loved it when he got a chance to put theory into practice. Advani was leaning over the balcony blowing his cigarette smoke into the village. The sun was setting on Dhesera and the trees took on a magical glow.

'It's beautiful at this time of day, isn't it?' Pankaj asked.

'Ya,' Advani said tilting his head to one side, he straightened up and looked into the distance. Smoke was rising up from a fire. Someone in Dhesera was burning their rubbish or making a cooking fire. A low beat and a chanting voice like a mantra started.

'These villagers and their evening entertainment,' Advani said.

'What was she like?'

'Who? Subby?'

Pankaj was about to say no. It was Leila Bhobe that he really wanted to know about, but he supposed Subrina Basi was more relevant so he nodded.

'She was beautiful and troubled. We often spoke to each other about our own issues. But recently she was having problems with her boyfriend and some internal struggles. You know what it's like. Sometimes even when you are famous and you have people around you all the time, you can feel alone. It's not the lonely that you regular people feel. It's a soul-destroying loneliness. One that makes you think life is not worth living.'

'Was she depressed?'

Advani threw his cigarette on the tiled floor of the balcony and stood on the butt with his multi-coloured, embroidered *Phulkari jooti* slipper. 'All great artists are depressed. Subrina had many reasons to be depressed.'

'Like?'

'She was worried about her weight. She was a little plump but all the best Bollywood stars are. Or well, at least they used to be. Now they are getting ideas from the West. And then there was the whole Dollywood/Bollywood debate. She only stayed in Dollywood because of Dinesh. Dinesh was cheating on her also. That didn't do much for her self-esteem. Want me to go on?'

Pankaj wanted to say yes please, but he stopped himself. Instead he remembered something else Chupplejeep had taught him. 'Stay silent,' his boss had once said. 'People often speak to fill the void.' Pankaj started to silently count the bats flying around the breadfruit tree in the garden. When he got to eight, Advani spoke again.

149

'She said something had happened to her when she was younger. Something she was confused about. This thing happened here in Goa, in this very village. She wanted to come back and face the "demons of her past" or so she told me. She encouraged me to set up a gallery and art school here just until the New Year. She said she too would stay in the village and uncover some things.'

'Uncover?'

'Her words. I guess she did what she had to do and died in the process.'

'Do you think Subrina Basi could have killed herself?'

'I thought you said it was suspicious. Don't you cops know anything for sure? Subrina would never have killed herself.'

'But you just said she was depressed.'

Advani waved Pankaj's comments away with the flick of his wrist. 'I said all artists are depressed. I'm depressed. I wouldn't throw myself off a balcony.' Advani peered over the railings again. 'Although it does look tempting.'

'It sounds like you and Subrina were close.'

'Very,' Advani said, retrieving another cigarette from his pocket and lighting up.

'So why did Subrina stop supporting your contract at Malabar Hill?'

Advani took a drag of his cigarette and then looked at Pankaj. 'They made her,' he said eventually.

'Who?'

'The rest of the board at that pretentious gallery. They wanted fresh blood.'

'But didn't Subrina have a controlling vote through her inheritance? Her grandfather owned the Malabar Hill Gallery, didn't he?'

Advani studied his *jootis*. He looked wounded.

'Did you ask Subrina to change her mind?'

Advani looked up. 'You think I would have come to this back-end arse of a village otherwise?'

Pankaj took a step back.

'Yes, I came to commiserate with Subrina about her wasted life and the shit of her past but I also thought I could cajole her into changing her mind about Malabar.'

'You spoke to her about it whilst you were here?'

'I begged her to change her mind the night before…well, the night before her death.'

'And what did she say?'

'I think she was coming around. It was that bloody Dinesh who was getting in my way.' Pankaj noticed how Advani's hands formed into tightly clenched fists at the mention of Subrina's boyfriend.

'And where is Dinesh now?'

'That's your job. How the fuck should I know?'

CHAPTER TWENTY-THREE

'You look unwell,' Chupplejeep said. 'Did Advani explain to you another one of his paintings?'

Pankaj shook his head.

'What then? You didn't eat from that cart selling sausage bread near the circle, did you? That fellow is dodgy. If you don't cheer up, I may have to send you home. You may kill our only office plant with your sour face.' Chupplejeep looked over to the money plant on his officer's desk.

Pankaj had bought the plant last month in a bid to liven up their drab office. Now he wondered if a Christmas tree would have been more appropriate. There was no office budget for such luxuries, but the supercentre in Porvorim was selling them cheap. 'Sir, I've just come back from the Golden Orchid. I spent all morning interviewing the staff like you asked. It was very tiring so I needed to eat something. Sausage bread was the only thing appealing to me. But it's not that. Yesterday I went to see Advani like you said.'

'And you found out whether or not he lied about using someone else's art as his own?'

'Before I got to that we started talking about other things.' Pankaj explained Advani's confession that he had followed Subrina to Goa to persuade her to get him back into the Malabar Hill Gallery. 'Then when I asked him about his secret, he started to sob. He went into a room at the back and locked himself in. Takshak showed me out.'

'You were there to ask Advani about his lies, not question him about Subrina. I was planning to do that myself,' Chupplejeep said with a frown. 'I'll contact the chair of the board at Malabar Hill and get his version of what was happening with his contract.'

'Sorry, sir.'

'Oh never mind. Just cheer up.' He hated seeing Pankaj sad, the boy was like a son to him. 'Anyway, you still have some days before you need to solve the blackmail case. And the fingerprint analysis from the letter arrived from Kulkarni this morning. I put it on your desk.'

'That's not the reason.'

'What is it then?' Chupplejeep asked irritably. 'We haven't got all day. We also have a murder to solve, in case you forgot.'

'On my way home yesterday, after I met with Advani, I saw Shwetika at a *gado* buying some chocolate. She was on her own, sir. She's never on her own. She's usually with her sister, her mother or her friends.'

Chupplejeep smiled. 'Ah, I should have known, the girl you love from afar. You stopped to speak to her?'

'That's exactly what I did.'

'So, what's the problem?'

Pankaj's cheeks turned pink. 'I bought her the chocolate she wanted.'

'That's the way.'

'Yes, I'd seen Sailesh and Raja offer to buy girls things they want. Girls like that, sir.'

'Yes,' Chupplejeep said. He was about to say that he would be buying things for Shwetika forever more once they were friendly, but he stopped himself. He didn't want to ruin Pankaj's moment.

'Then I started talking to her as we walked towards her house.'

'You walked her home?'

'She didn't want her parents to see me, so I only walked her to the corner of the street.'

'That's it? That's why you are looking so pathetic?'

'That's not just it.'

'Then what happened? It can't be that bad.'

'It is.'

'How?'

'I asked her out.'

Chupplejeep suppressed a laugh. 'What did she say?'

'She agreed, sir,' Pankaj said, looking slightly pale.

Chupplejeep walked over to him and slapped him on the back. 'Well done, boy. I knew you had it in you.'

Pankaj shook his head. 'I was so nervous. But I did it. The problem is now…'

'What's the problem?'

'I don't know where to take her.'

154

'When's your date?' Chupplejeep asked, returning to his desk and rolling his eyes.

'Saturday.'

'No problem. Take her to Delhi Delights. The food is excellent. You can get good tandoori and *makhani* there.'

'You think she'll like it?'

'Of course she will. She's not veggie, is she?'

Pankaj's hand flew to his mouth. 'I didn't think of that.' He couldn't imagine his mother accepting a vegetarian into their family. Not when she loved her meat so much. But it was something he was prepared to fight his mother over, either that or lie, because he knew Shwetty was the one. He just knew it.

Over a cup of tea, Chupplejeep relayed to Pankaj what Kulkarni had said about the cause of death and Pankaj told him in detail what he had learned about Subrina from Advani.

'Demons?' Chupplejeep said. 'Sounds to me like she wanted to face her past. Perhaps get some closure for what she did to that little boy.'

'I was thinking the same.'

'Subrina finally wanted to take responsibility for what she had done. She thought that by speaking to Nitin's family it would make the depression go away. She came back here to ask the family for forgiveness.'

'And make amends with her sister, sir. Her sister would have witnessed the ordeal. No wonder she became a nun. Advani also said Subrina was confused.

Maybe she wanted to ask her sister what really happened,' Pankaj said.

'You would think she would remember something like that. But if she was out of it when she ran over the child, perhaps she thought her sister would remember it better.'

'Something like that would jolly soon sober you up, sir.'

'We need to speak to Suki. Find out what happened all those years ago and see if it has any relevance to the case. Kulkarni reckons she was killed not too long after that, given the state of decomposition of the body and her stomach contents, which was only partly digested. So we are looking for someone without an alibi and a motive to kill between one-thirty and, say, five-thirty on the morning of the 16th of December,' Chupplejeep summarised.

'Subrina was last seen by the hotel staff just after one, after their line of coke at the Firefly bar at the Golden Orchid. Dinesh dropped her to her room and then left the hotel at two-thirty. So Dinesh could have done it?'

'Dinesh had a good hour and a half to murder Subrina and put her makeup on.'

'He is suspicious by the very fact that he's not here. It's like something from the movies, sir, and Dinesh was familiar with movie making. Disgruntled lover kills girlfriend with a shot of insulin and then tries to cover it up by making it look like suicide. He must have heard about the death. If he were innocent, he would have come forward. It's been days.'

'And Ayesha Saxena is missing too. The police in Bombay can't locate her. Inspector General Gosht is fuming. Her parents want answers. Understandably, they are concerned. After I met with Kulkarni yesterday, I called some of the guests who had attended Ayesha's party and you were wrong, Pankaj.'

'Wrong, sir? How?'

'All this time we thought Dinesh was in Goa. We were wrong. Four guests confirmed he was at Ayesha's party. He turned up late, or should I say early morning, but he stayed till sunrise and then left with Ayesha.'

'What the hell?' Pankaj said, standing up. His chair scraped the stone floor, making Chupplejeep clench his teeth. 'I checked with the aviation authority. They said they had no record of him leaving the state. This is a joke!'

Chupplejeep nodded. 'Get on to them again. I want to know everything about what Dinesh did at the airport. If he had luggage, even if he ate a samosa, I want to know. Not only is he the key suspect in the Basi case, he is now a suspect in the case of the missing actress Ayesha Saxena. The fact we didn't even know he had left the country makes us look bad. Gosht won't forget this easily.'

'You think he killed Subrina and then flew to Bombay to do the same to Ayesha? He was dating both of them. He is the clear link, sir.'

'One of his girlfriends is dead, the other missing,' Chupplejeep said. 'It looks pretty bad to me. The Bombay police are searching for them following some tip-offs. I'm concerned that neither one of them has a phone with them. That tells me something is off. No one roams without a cell phone these days, especially these celebrity types. Nothing has been posted on social media and Ayesha Saxena was known for putting pictures up all the time.'

'Wait!' Pankaj said. He started to pace around the office, his hands on his hips.

'What?' Chupplejeep said, looking up.

'You said it was insulin that killed Subrina, sir?'

'Yes. Why?'

'Takshak is a diabetic.' Pankaj walked back to Chupplejeep's desk and sat on the chair opposite his boss.

'How do you know?'

'That day when I saw Takshak searching for Advani's tablets, I saw a drawer full of syringes. He openly told me he was a diabetic. I didn't know at the time it was insulin that killed the actress.'

'So, Advani and Takshak had ready access to the drug. Question Takshak, see if any of his supply is missing and ask him where he obtains his drug. Find out if anyone else with links to Subrina was diabetic, even the staff at the hotel.'

'Sir, that day when you were talking to Advani and I spoke to Takshak, he told me Subrina was an okay person, but his face betrayed his words. There is something that man is hiding.'

'What do you mean?'

'When he said her name, his top lip curled and he scrunched his nose like he had smelled a fart. And when I was with Advani, he stopped in his tracks when he heard the word 'murdered'.'

Chupplejeep twisted the end of his moustache. 'What else have you found out that you are keeping to yourself?' he asked.

'Nothing, sir. My mind has just been so busy.'

'Well. You're a cop. Get used to it. Did you have time to speak to the hotel staff this morning?'

'I went there first thing and took one of Kulkarni's men to get their prints like you asked. But most of them don't have any motive for killing Subrina Basi. The watchman is a drunk. He passed out shortly after Xavier went home. Furtado didn't hear anything and, sir, my gut tells me to believe him. The guy is a little slow. I can't see why he would want Subrina Basi dead. He relies on his job and the death of this star is going to ruin the Golden Orchid. That goes for Xavier, the barman, too. His family vouch that he arrived home at one-fifteen. His mother can't sleep until she hears him come home.'

'Sweet.'

'It is,' Pankaj said, thinking of his own mother. She was the same. 'Rosie was at home, her husband confirmed that. Then there is Indu. Indu's parents said she was at home, but she wasn't.'

'Tell me.'

159

'The neighbour saw her leave through her window that night. I questioned her and she was cagey. Her eyes were darting here and there when she answered my questions. But when I went back to ask her, it turns out she has an alibi.'

'Which is?'

'She was with her boyfriend that her parents don't know about. I tracked him down on my way to the office. He confirms her story, but he could be lying to protect her. She was the one who found the body. She was treated badly by Subrina, maybe she took it to heart and thought she would teach Subrina Basi a lesson.'

'That is hardly a motive. Half of all employees in India's tourism industry are treated badly. And not by foreigners, most foreigners know how to treat people. They treat them with respect. It's the domestic tourists that treat waiters and maids like dirt. I don't know why. They must think they are better than the people who serve them and clean up their mess.'

'That's true, sir.'

'Okay. Leave Indu to me. Who else?'

'The driver for the hotel was also at home. He was told he was not required. His wife says he came home and went straight to bed. There's no motive there. But he did have some information for me.'

'What?'

'You know how drivers talk to one another? Well, this chap got the cell number for Dinesh's driver.'

'And?'

'I called it, sir.'

'And?'

'No service. The cell is either out of range or the battery is dead.'

'Okay. Put a trace on that number too and keep trying both numbers we have for him. This could be our only hope of tracking him down. I've had that imbecile at the Delhi police station visit Dinesh's family but they haven't seen or heard from him since he took his flight to Goa. His family are now making a noise in case something terrible has also happened to him.'

'Unlikely,' Pankaj said, crossing his arms over his chest.

'Who else?'

'Nishok, the gardener. I tried speaking with him but all he did was look at the floor. He didn't say a word. And he ran that first time I tried speaking to him. That tells me he's got something to hide.'

'Maybe he's scared.'

'And he was trembling when Kulkarni's man was taking his prints.'

'Nervous?'

'Nervous because he's guilty.'

'Some people are just scared of cops, that's all.'

'Abhik said I would have to arrest him before I got anything out of him.'

'Abhik's the chef?'

'Now he looks suspicious, sir. No alibi – he was home alone. But there is something about him that tells me he is lying, and it's not just those cold black eyes of his or the anger he is holding inside.'

'Anger?'

'When he first saw me in his kitchen, I thought he was going to hit me with his frying pan. He was annoyed I was there, but it's a hotel kitchen. He should not be so alarmed if someone else is there, no? It's not his house. No motive that I have found yet. He earns well also. But he is smart enough to commit a crime and he had access to the knives. Also, when I first talked to him, he said he knew exactly where everything was. Yet he didn't know that the knife found in the bath with Subrina Basi was missing until I asked him to check.'

'Interesting. You've been busy this morning. What about Hari, the general manager?'

'He too was at home. This murder is not doing any favours for him though. Bookings are down and Furtado said that most of the guests for the New Year are now cancelling their stay.'

'And this isn't a case of fraud?'

'Sir, I don't know what you mean?'

'Did they want the hotel to make a loss so it will have to close? Some of these big-shots often pull such scams for insurance fraud. The Golden Orchid only got permission because Dinesh's father, the resident MLA, was bribed.'

'I can look into it, sir.'

'Do that. Anything else?'

Pankaj thumbed through his notes. 'Wait sir, the watchman said that he saw something suspicious when he woke up at around four in the morning.'

'Is he reliable? What did he see?'

'He saw the gardener leaving the hotel. Nishok doesn't stay at the hotel. He leaves after he waters the plants at around six in the evening.'

'Strange.'

'Very strange.'

'Nishok is the one not talking. The one who ran.'

'Motive?'

'He looks dirt poor, sir. He could have taken something of value from Subrina Basi to sell. Maybe she caught him in the act and so he killed her.'

'But is he smart enough to commit murder and stage it to look like a suicide? What you're describing is an opportunistic thief. So if he were caught, he would have stabbed her in the chest and ran. He wouldn't go to the trouble of carrying insulin with him. The fellow probably doesn't know what insulin is.'

Pankaj shook his head. 'But till now he hasn't said one word to me, why is that? It's normally the quiet ones, sir.'

'Okay, lets see what comes back from Kulkarni when he matches the prints on the knife to the prints from the staff. If we need to interview the staff again, we go back. We need to speak to the family of the boy who was killed.'

'You found them, sir?'

'Whilst you were interviewing the staff, I read through Nitin's records. I've got the address of the family right here.' Chupplejeep tapped his breast pocket. 'Bonaparte said that Nitin's elder brother, the fellow who witnessed the accident, was also dead.'

'He did, sir.'

'But when I checked with the Panchayat there was no record of the brother's death.'

'But you found a record of Nitin's death?'

'His was there. But it's strange that his brother's was not.'

'Unless he didn't die in Goa and his parents never registered the death here, or he is still alive.'

'Either way, we need answers.'

'Are you going to speak to them?'

Chupplejeep nodded. 'Yes, but there is someone else I need to speak to first, before Gosht calls me again.'

CHAPTER TWENTY-FOUR

Chupplejeep stepped into Sister Perpetua's office at the Sacred Heart Convent in Verna. He felt a chill run down his spine as he sat down in the wooden chair on one side of the desk. It reminded him of the Lemon Tree orphanage he had been thrust into as a boy of just two years old. Everything in that place had been hard and cold. Not soft and loving like an environment expected to nurture a child.

He rarely thought about his time at the orphanage. He found it best to avoid thinking of the overbearing mammas who would tower over him until he finished his tasteless porridge, not once but twice a day – for breakfast and dinner. Lunch had been the only time they received some kind of flavour in their meals. Mostly the food was vegetarian, but vegetables were better than water and rice. Even now, Chupplejeep struggled to eat any sort of *conjee*. It had been a sad existence living within the confines of the Lemon Tree, only made worse when the mammas made him go to church with them.

The wooden cross hanging on the wall in Sister Perpetua's office reminded him of those long, boring

Sundays sitting through sermons in Konkani, instead of playing outside with the other children. No wonder he had decided he would be an atheist when Nana took him in at twelve. At the time he didn't know the word 'atheist', but after spying a rosary on Nana's bedside table, he took precautionary measures and announced to Nana that he had no intention of visiting a church. After the words left his mouth he worried that Nana would return him to the Lemon Tree, but she didn't.

'How about the temple?' she had asked casually, as she finished reading to him under the large *badam*, almond, tree that had once stood tall in their garden.

Chupplejeep shook his head.

'A mosque?'

Chupplejeep carried on shaking his head.

'Okay, you're old enough to decide. If you don't want religion, so be it. But if you change your mind, you tell me,' she had said.

He hadn't believed her and, with a feeling of dread in the pit of his stomach, waited for her to persuade him to go to church with her. The last thing he wanted to do was disappoint the woman who had saved him from the terrible orphanage. Nana was someone he wanted to impress. His first Christmas came and went without any mention of church. Chupplejeep found himself beginning to relax and had even geared himself with the confidence to resist the promise of Easter eggs at church, that his best friend and neighbour Joachim had warned him about. But the offer never came and for that Chupplejeep loved Nana even more.

'You're so lucky *men*,' Joachim had said at the time. 'My mother forces me to go to church every Sunday. I wish I had a Nana.'

Chupplejeep had smiled at the time but he also remembered thinking that he would have gone to church willingly if he had a mother. At the time he didn't see how there could be a god who would let a child go motherless.

The only time he had entered God's house since his days at the Lemon Tree was when he had sat by Nana's coffin for her funeral. And if Christabel hadn't been dead set on having a church wedding, Chupplejeep doubted he would ever step inside one again.

'Detective, what can I do for you?' Sister Perpetua asked, as she entered the room and took her seat behind the desk. Her features were hard, a sharp nose and eyes that were a little too close together.

He knew that small talk would only anger the woman so Chupplejeep got straight to the point. 'Sister, I'm hoping to speak with Suki?'

She leaned forward, clasped her hands together and placed them on the desk. 'I'm not sure I know who you mean.'

'Oh,' Chupplejeep said, desperately trying to remember what Suki was now called. Bonaparte had told him, but he couldn't remember. 'Sister, this lady joined perhaps some twenty years ago. She was Sikh but she converted, you may remember this. She took two years to novitiate.'

'Converted to Catholicism?'

Chupplejeep nodded.

'That is a long time ago and my memory is not what it was.' She gave Chupplejeep a little satisfied smile. 'Perhaps you can come back another time, when you remember who it is that you want to see. We have many nuns at this convent and we are all quite busy. We have our chores and our needlework. Perhaps you would like to see some table linen we have in our shop at the chapel. It makes a lovely gift...'

'No...umm, let me think.' Chupplejeep closed his eyes, then opened them and smiled. 'Her name is Sister Valentine, I think. Yes, that's it. Sister Valentine,' he said, confident that was the name Bonaparte had told him.

Sister Perpetua wrinkled her nose as if she had just smelled something bad. 'I see. Let me go and see if she is available.' She rose to her feet and left the room.

Moments later, she returned with a woman. Suki, looked a little like Subrina Basi. She shared the same almond-shaped eyes as her sister. But her frame was petite and she had a heart-shaped face and a button nose. Her veil hid her hair, but nevertheless Chupplejeep could see that she was an attractive lady – delicate, unlike her brash sister with her Botoxed lips.

'Would I be able to speak to Sister Valentine in private?'

Sister Perpetua rubbed her brow as she thought about this. She stared at Suki for longer than was necessary. 'Okay,' she said eventually, and then left the room. Chupplejeep waited till he heard her walking away before he introduced himself.

'You're here about my sister,' Suki said.

'Correct.'

'So it's true. She's dead then?'

Chupplejeep pointed to the chair next to him and asked her to take a seat. Suki obliged, but not before tapping the chair three times with the palm of her hand. The detective noted her strange behaviour. 'I'm afraid that is the reason for my visit.'

'I see.'

He gauged her reaction. There was no outward show of sorrow. No emotion. People sometimes went into a state of shock at times like this – silent and thoughtful as they digested the information about their deceased loved one. 'When did you hear about her death?'

'My sister was something of a celebrity. People talk and I overheard some of the nuns say she was dead.'

'Overheard?' Chupplejeep shook his head. 'Did they not consider that you could hear them?'

'Nobody here knows Subrina Basi is my sister. Only Sister Carmina, and she has taken a vow of silence.'

'You kept it a secret?'

'They never asked.'

'Do you have friends here in the convent?'

'We don't like to talk about our lives before we joined Sacred Heart. It's difficult when your whole family has turned against you.' Suki looked away from Chupplejeep towards the window.

'But the convent is a place of worship and forgiveness, isn't it?'

'There is no need to mention my past. The sisters here know me as Sister Valentine. They don't know me as Suki.'

'Are Sister Valentine and Suki two different people?'

Suki looked back at the detective. 'I don't know what you're saying.'

'I'm asking if the Suki before joining the convent is different from the sister I see before me today.'

'Of course she's different.'

'How?'

'I was young, naive and stupid back then. Twenty years later I'm…I don't know. I made more than my fair share of mistakes.'

'Twenty years ago we were all a lot younger and more foolish,' Chupplejeep said, thinking of his recent birthday. Twenty years ago he would have been twenty – fresh out of Police Training College accepting his first job in Greater Larara. He remembered how he was socially awkward, not knowing when to address women as ma'am or mrs, and trying his best to impress his boss at the time, who was as crooked as a branch of a mandara tree.

It was a long time ago but Chupplejeep could still remember the mistake he made with his first case. How he had been so busy trying to do the right thing, he forgot to do the necessary task of labelling the evidence correctly. 'We all make mistakes when we are younger,' he said. 'But it's part of growing up.'

'I'm sure you're not here to talk about the milestones in my life. Surely you want to know something about my sister.'

'I do.' Chupplejeep hesitated. 'Do you have any questions about your sister's death? I imagine if you've only heard through the convent grapevine, you want some details.'

'I have questions.' Suki touched her head three times with her right palm. 'How? How did my sister die?'

'We believe your sister was murdered.'

Suki's hand flew to her mouth. 'Never!' she cried.

'Our forensic pathologist has reason to believe that her death was unnatural.'

Suki stood up and walked over to the window. She looked out. 'When I heard, I thought that perhaps it was an overdose.'

'You knew your sister used illegal substances, narcotics?'

Suki nodded. 'She was older than me and liked to smoke this and that when we were younger. When I heard she was a film star, I knew she would get into the harder things. My sister has...my sister had an addictive personality.'

'Always?'

'Even when we were kids, but then it was with chocolate and Thumbs Up. Who would want to do this to my sister?'

'Well, that's what we want to find out.'

'How was she killed?'

'Sorry, but I can't say too much at this point.'

Suki turned to Chupplejeep. 'But she's my sister. I have the right to know.'

The detective pressed his lips together before he spoke. 'Your sister was poisoned.'

Suki tilted her head to one side. 'Someone administered her a poison? She didn't give it to herself?'

Chupplejeep frowned. 'You have reason to believe your sister was suicidal?'

Suki turned towards the window again. She seemed lost in her thoughts. 'I can't tell you much about my sister. My life is at the convent. I rarely leave.'

Chupplejeep stood. He walked over to the window and waited for Suki to turn towards him. 'But you met her recently,' he chanced as she turned. He saw then a flicker of something in her eyes. Was it hesitation, or was it fear? Suki turned back to the window. She was concentrating on something in the distance.

'You hadn't seen her for some time, so it must have been quite emotional when she reached out for you after so long.'

'I met Subrina, yes.'

'Did she come here?'

Suki shook her head. 'She doesn't believe in all this.' She looked around her and touched her habit.

'She stayed true to the faith she was born with?'

'I don't think she believed in anything. After what happened, I will ask the Father to say a mass for her. He says masses for anyone. Even if they are not Catholics.'

'What did you talk about?'

'This and that?'

172

'This and that! You hadn't seen her in how long?'

'Almost twenty years.'

'You must have been desperate to catch up on her news.'

'She told me she had been married twice already. She said she was going to marry again. I can't recall his name. It sounded like she loved him, but something wasn't right. She didn't say what.'

Chupplejeep pulled out his notebook from his breast pocket and scribbled something down. 'When did you see your sister?'

Suki pressed her lips together. 'A couple of days ago.'

'Do you remember the date?'

'It was on the 14th of December. It was the day of the crochet sale at the church. I remember because I had to ask another sister to receive an order I was expecting for the sale, just so I could meet Subrina. Sister Carmina had to take my place. She wasn't happy because she is silent, so she doesn't like interacting with people from outside the convent.'

'I see. And where did you say you met your sister?'

'I didn't,' Suki said, eyeing the detective. 'I met her in the park outside the engineering college. Subrina called and begged me to meet. I didn't want her near the convent and she wouldn't have come here anyway. So we agreed to meet in the park. I have to walk or take the bus to get anywhere. Subrina could get a driver, so we met close by.'

'Your lives were very different.'

'We chose different paths.'

173

'And she begged you to meet her, you said. Did you not want to meet her?' Chupplejeep was reminded of the conversation the maid, Indu, had overheard. Indu must have heard Subrina begging her sister to meet her and not her boyfriend Dinesh, like she had thought.

Suki retuned to her chair, tapping it before she sat down. Chupplejeep sat down again too.

'She hadn't made contact in so long. I was apprehensive as to why she wanted to meet.'

Chupplejeep was silent.

'She had never bothered with me before, so why now, I asked.'

'Did she tell you?'

'She said she wanted to put the past behind her. She wanted us to be family again.'

'And did you accept?'

'The Lord teaches us to forgive and forget.'

'And how did your sister seem to you?'

'Sad, remorseful.'

'Because she had shut you out of her life? Or because of the child that she ran over when she was younger.'

Suki looked up with a start. She focused her dark brown eyes on the detective. 'I must get back to the others. Sister Perpetua will be here soon.' She stood up and wiped her hands on her tunic.

'Talking about the death of little Nitin worries you?'

'I remember that day as if it were yesterday. I don't wish to talk about it.'

'But it could help us solve the murder of your sister.'

174

'Why? That was so long ago. It's in the past.'

'It may help us understand your sister and her actions before her death. If we can understand this then we will find her killer sooner. We have reason to believe that your sister was trying to accept responsibility for what she did twenty years ago. The death of the little boy was troubling her.'

'I saw the child with my own eyes that night. He was at the side of the road looking the other way. He had long curly hair and a black string tied around his neck. I only saw him for a second, but I remember him so clearly. Then I heard the screams. They chilled me to the bone. Sometimes, in my sleep, I still hear those screams. If she too was thinking of that day then maybe she killed herself. I've thought about it myself…'

'For devout Catholics, suicide is a sin,' Chupplejeep said.

'I wouldn't do it. I said I thought about it and I go to confession after such thoughts, but Subrina didn't believe. So there a chance that she could have killed herself.'

'When you met, did she speak to you about the accident?'

Suki shook her head.

'Did she speak of any enemies?'

Suki pursed her lips. 'Enemies? No. Why would anyone want to kill her?'

'There are some evil people out there. Subrina would have made friends and enemies over the past twenty years.'

'I suppose you're right.' She looked around her. 'I have been protected from the outside world. Like I said, she only spoke of her boyfriend. Look, Detective, I really must get back to the others. They'll be waiting for me to say our afternoon prayers.'

'You've been most helpful. But before you go, can I ask you where you were on the morning of the 16th? The early hours of the morning. It's just a formality'

'I was here at the convent where I always am.'

'Did anyone see you here?'

'The day following the Christmas crochet sale, we hold a late-night prayer with candles. Sister Perpetua was there. You can ask her.'

'I will. How long did the prayers last for?'

'Perhaps an hour.'

'And then?'

'Then, like I do every year, I stayed on all night with another sister. At dawn I went to my room.'

'Is that so?'

'Of course. Is that all, Detective?'

'Yes.'

'You'll let me know as soon as you have more information on my sister.'

Chupplejeep nodded.

Suki stood up and smoothed her tunic. 'You know, Detective, earlier when I looked out of the window I saw a crow staring back at me.'

'I don't understand.'

'When we were children, Subrina always said she would die before me because she was older. She said that when she died she would come back as a crow and watch over me. Perhaps if what you are saying is correct, and my sister was killed, she won't be able to rest until you catch the person who did this.'

CHAPTER TWENTY-FIVE

Pankaj watched Takshak through the window as he dipped his paintbrush in water and then pulled it across the white canvas, making a single blue streak. Takshak leaned back and studied the stroke from different angles. Then he put his paintbrush down and looked through the window directly at Pankaj, catching him unawares. He stared at him like a lizard watching its prey. There was something venomous in his eyes.

Pankaj took a step back. How did Takshak know he was standing there? A shiver ran down his spine. He turned and walked towards the entrance of the gallery. As he approached the door, Advani's assistant was standing there his scarf loosely wrapped about his neck, his thick-rimmed glasses perched on his nose.

'Can I help you? If you are here to see Advani and talk to him about his case, then you are out of luck. You just missed him.'

'I wasn't here to see Advani.'

'Not working on his case then. Is it because of how he is? How we are?'

Pankaj frowned. 'What are you getting at?'

'Many people don't want to help us because, you know, we are gay.'

Pankaj wondered if this was the same Takshak he had previously spoken to. This fellow had an air of superiority, unlike before. The last time they spoke Takshak had confided in him about his past, about how his father had treated him. Now he was cold and aloof.

'I came to talk to you about your diabetes.'

Takshak frowned. He retreated into the gallery and Pankaj followed.

'Oh, that. What about it? It's not a crime to be a diabetic.'

'No. It isn't.'

'Then why are you questioning me about it?'

Pankaj looked at Takshak, his arms folded across his chest, his right foot at an angle in front of the left, as if he was getting ready to run. This man was hiding something, yet he seemed so cool and collected with his genuine look of innocence.

'Can I ask you how many vials of insulin you keep with you?'

He hesitated. 'Sev...no, six. Six vials.'

'Why so many?' Pankaj asked. He didn't have a clue about insulin and how many vials a diabetic would carry, but he asked his question all the same.

'When I'm travelling I like to have a supply, so I don't have to visit a doctor here.'

'Have you been to a doctor whilst you've been in Goa?'

Takshak shook his head.

'A pharmacy?'

Takshak hesitated. 'No. Look, what is this all about?'

'Just some questions we are asking people in the village.'

'Has this something to do with Subrina?'

'Can you tell me if you have all your vials with you now?'

'Follow me.' Takshak led Pankaj to the room he had been working in and opened the drawer.

The police officer glanced around the small studio. He looked at the paintings that stood along the floor, propped up against the wall. They were abstract designs in vibrant blues and yellows. He liked what he saw and he could see that Takshak had talent. He was glad Advani had encouraged him to continue with his work. The world needed more vibrant colour in it. Colour lifted your spirits and made you smile, which was more than he could say about Advani's violent images.

'Here are all the syringes that I need,' he said, pointing to the contents of the drawer. Then he walked over to a mini-fridge and showed him the vials neatly lined up on the top shelf.

'Only six?'

Takshak rolled his eyes. 'I said six, didn't I?'

'Not seven?'

'I said six,' Takshak said. He looked at Pankaj. 'Six, seven, what does one vial matter to you? It's me who has to go and get more if I run out.'

'Okay, thanks.'

'Okay, thanks. That's it. You're not going to tell me why you are asking me these questions,' Takshak said as he closed the fridge door.

'It is about Subrina's death. We have reason to believe she may have been poisoned with insulin.'

Takshak tapped his foot on the ground. He removed his glasses and pressed his temples. Pankaj watched him carefully. The man looked distressed but Pankaj wasn't sure why. Was it because they knew how Subrina was murdered and he was hoping that the insulin would have been untraceable in the body? Was it because he was supposed to have seven vials remaining but one was missing and he knew who had taken it? Or was he genuinely shocked?

Whatever the reason, there was something suspicious about Takshak and it made Pankaj think that he wasn't only an artist but an actor as well.

Chapter Twenty-six

Christabel bit into a prawn patty – to hell with her wedding diet. How could she diet at a time like this? She only told two people about the date for her wedding and it had already spread like wildfire around Greater Larara. Clearly, the rumour that Sandhu was sleeping with the cook from the Saldanhas' house was old news. The villagers wanted something else, something spicy, and Christabel's wedding date was just the thing.

She wiped the pastry flakes from around her mouth and bit into another patty, letting the sweet prawn and tomato mixture sooth her nerves. Patties tasted best when they were hot and straight from the bakers. Pastry always had a way of calming her. That's what they need in those big stressful offices, she thought, pastry. But although the patty was soothing, it didn't solve her problem. The 29th of February as a wedding date was a big problem. Not only was it renowned for bringing bad luck to couples getting married, but it also meant that most years she and Arthur would have to celebrate their wedding anniversary on the 28th, or only celebrate it once every four years, and that didn't sit well with her. In fact it gave her indigestion. She could have discussed it in detail with Arthur, but she knew he would just use it as another excuse to postpone the wedding.

'Don't worry,' her mother had said, which had at first been a surprise. But then she expanded. 'You can't marry this year. There will not be enough time for preparations. And you can't leave it another year. You're already too old to be walking down the aisle. Leave it another year and I might be in my grave. Better to have bad luck than a dead mother for your wedding, no? Forget about luck. The whole leap year is an unlucky time to marry. You'll just have to accept your fate.'

It wasn't just the date making Christabel reach for the delicious prawn puffs. She had told a lie this morning, and lying didn't sit well with her either. Well, sometimes it was okay, like when she told Lisa that her behind looked small in her new dress when in actual fact it looked like she had trapped a hot air balloon. And when she told Effermiana that her carrot pickle was tasty, when she had overdone the vinegar and the pickle was beyond repair. But these were small lies. The lie Christabel had just told was big and she had told it in a church, to a Father of all people! Now she made the sign of the cross and prayed for forgiveness. It was Arthur's fault, his fault entirely.

~

Christabel knew that after booking the reception venue for their wedding, the next thing she had to do was to book the church. It was highly unlikely that the church would be booked on the 29th February for any other auspicious occasion, but you never knew. These days foreigners were choosing to get married in Goa, even in the villages, and they didn't care about superstition – not like the Goans.

When Christabel gave Father Agnelo her date, he laughed. 'No need to check the diary,' he said. 'I guarantee it's empty.' But he soon registered Christabel's disappointment and, not wanting to make her feel bad about her chosen date, quickly added that the Lord would not have wanted people to avoid getting wed on that date.

'You think, Father?' she asked.

'Why else would our Holy Father add another date to the year? So that more people could join together in marriage.'

Christabel smiled. Father Agnelo had known her since she was a child and knew exactly what to say to make her feel better.

'Let's talk over the finer detail,' he said as they walked through the old church and into a back room where there was a kitchenette. Christabel always felt safe in the Larara church. It wasn't one of those pretty churches that looked perfectly proportioned and tempting from the outside. It was more of a rectangular block, with thick walls of unevenly plastered, whitewashed laterite stone, and roof tiles blackened by the elements. But inside it was like an oasis. Along with the great wooden altar and the hand-carved pews, the ceilings were high and the temperature in the church was always cool, even in the heat of the midday sun.

Christabel and Father Agnelo had a great deal to catch up on. After all, he had presided over her first holy communion and then her confirmation. And he shared the same birthday as her aunty. Two hours later, Christabel and Father Agnelo had decided on three readings and four hymns including her favourite, *Give me Joy in my Heart*. She knew all the words by heart. But just as she had finished her milky tea and her plate of *bolinhas*, coconut and semolina biscuits, they had wandered back into the church and Father Agnelo had asked after the groom. 'And Arthur is new to Larara, is he not?'

'Well, yes and no,' Christabel had answered. 'He grew up close by, in Porvorim, and was working in the villages after college.'

'But let me guess, he decided it was too quiet here and moved to the city, no?'

Christabel nodded.

'Oh, we are all like that when we are young.'

'Not you and me, Father.'

'No. People like us stay in the same village our entire lives.'

'Yes,' Christabel said with a little sadness. She had wanted to move to one of the cities, perhaps even go to Mumbai, but the chance never arose and now, well now it was too late. She wanted to settle down and have a family before her eggs dried up.

'He was the detective that solved the case of the serial killer, was he not?'

'He's the one.'

'So a Goan?'

Christabel nodded. She could see where this was going. She stood up. 'Father, I must be getting on.'

'You must. But I need some details of the groom, na.'

'Of course.' Christabel sat back down.

'So tell me. Who are his mother and father?'

Christabel hesitated. 'You see, his father and mother died when Arthur was young. He was put into an orphanage.'

'Oh no, how terrible. There were no relatives who could take him in?'

'No.' She refrained from telling the priest that the families of Arthur's parents had disowned them when they had married. In those days it had been a sin for a Catholic to marry a Hindu. In some places in Goa it still was. The Chupplejeeps had moved away to Porvorim and set up home there, away from the harsh words and unkind stares from people who they once called their friends, and a year later Arthur was born. Two years after that, Arthur's parents had been killed when a bus crashed into their scooter. A neighbour was looking after Arthur at the time. The relatives were eventually informed, but by that time Arthur had already been placed in the orphanage and the relatives thought it was the best place for him.

'He is the product of sin and bad luck,' one of the mammas at the orphanage relayed back to Chupplejeep only a few years ago when he bumped into her at the market. It was in the market, next to the sugar cane vendor, that Chupplejeep found out for the first time he had relatives, heartless relatives.

It had been a shock to Chupplejeep and when he told the story to Christabel, she had cried with him. She knew then that a man with so much emotion, like Arthur, was truly the man for her.

'Oh, what a terrible pity. So he lived at the orphanage until he was old enough to work?' Father Agnelo said, waking Christabel from her thoughts.

'He was taken in by Nana de Souza.'

'Oh, Nana. I remember her. She was a keen churchgoer and she loved to sing. She knew all the hymns. A truly good person. Ah yes, and she had a boy she adopted. It's coming back to me now.' Father Agnelo frowned. 'We never saw him here though. Or perhaps we did and my memory is failing me. Nana would have bought him up like a good Catholic. The church in Porvorim is probably where she took him.'

Christabel smiled apprehensively.

'So you'll be a de Souza?'

'No, Father. He is Arthur Chupplejeep. I will be a Chupplejeep.'

'Chupplejeep. I don't know this name. Nana didn't make him take her surname?'

'No.'

'I see. Very modern. So can you confirm to me that your husband-to-be has been baptised?'

Christabel's palms began to sweat.

'You know I can only marry two Catholics who have been baptised in church.'

'Of course, Father. I know how it works here.' Christabel swallowed. 'I know the rules of your church. I wouldn't have come here on the off chance that you would make an exception,' she said nervously.

'So you can confirm Arthur has been baptised?'

'Oh yes. They said at the orphanage that he had been baptised.' The lie slipped form her mouth so easily.

'You have the baptism certificates?'

Christabel looked at her empty cup of tea. 'Father, I only have mine.'

Father Agnelo was silent for a moment. He put his hands together and bent his head. 'We must take pity on orphans,' he said eventually. 'After all, they are all the children of God. You know we have an orphanage here in our village as well?'

'Really?' Christabel said diffidently.

'Arthur is a detective, perhaps he can give a donation to our orphanage. He would understand, more than anyone, what these orphans need. We always need donations, especially around the festive season. The children here won't see presents but at least they can get a good meal of *soropotel* and *sannas*.'

'I'm sure he'll do just that. I'll tell him to drop by tomorrow.'

'Good. I can see no reason not to marry you two here in God's house. We don't need a bit of paper to prove what you are saying, Christabel. You are a good Catholic woman. I know you would never lie.'

With that Christabel had bid Father Agnelo goodbye and hurried out of the church before she combusted with sin.

~

Christabel pushed the bag of patties away from her. After two of the rich, savoury treats she was feeling quite queasy. But she knew it wasn't the patties making her feel ill. It was the guilt of what she had told Father Agnelo. She briefly thought about confessing that Arthur had never been baptised, but she knew she could never do that. She wanted a church wedding and couldn't do anything to jeopardise that. She wondered if Arthur would consider getting baptised now. She shook her head – there was more chance of the Pope converting to Hinduism.

She would have to forget about her lie. It was no use dwelling on something she couldn't change. Now, all she had to think about was how she was going to get her fiancé to give the local orphanage a donation.

CHAPTER TWENTY-SEVEN

'So her sister believes she had reason to kill herself,' Pankaj said. The red mud along the track stained the hem of his trousers as he walked with Chupplejeep towards their destination.

'Or she is trying to throw us off the scent.'

'Sir, why? Do you think Suki had motive to murder her sister?'

'She had an alibi. I checked with Sister Perpetua and she backed up her story. They had a candlelight vigil that night. Sisters are not required to stay all night, but Suki always did. Another nun was with her.'

'So there was no way that she had time to drive over to Dhesera and kill her sister?'

Chupplejeep nodded. 'She doesn't have a car. She would have had to borrow one.'

'Perhaps Subrina did kill herself. Subrina was suddenly feeling remorseful for the death of little Nitin. Perhaps his death had been eating away at her for some time. After all, she told the Commissioner in Delhi that she murdered someone.'

'Okay, continue.'

'She went to see her sister to talk it through. From what you said, Suki was cagey about telling you what was actually said between them. Plus, Subrina was only a minor celebrity, which can be very depressing to such vain people.'

'Go on.'

'The best role she received to date was in Dollywood. And let's be honest, sir, Dollywood may be emerging, but it's not going anywhere fast. And Subrina was old.'

Chupplejeep bristled.

'Sir, I meant she was old to be an actress. Forty-three is grandmom age when you are in the *filmi* industry.'

'I suppose.'

'Plus, her boyfriend Dinesh didn't really want her. Despite the fact Suki said Subrina was talking about marriage.'

'Because they had separate rooms.'

'They hadn't slept together since his arrival,' Pankaj said, colour rising to his cheeks.

'And men like Dinesh – '

'Exactly, sir.'

'Have you managed to get hold of Dinesh's driver as yet?'

'I'm still trying.'

'Ayesha Saxena?'

Pankaj shook his head.

'We have to find them. Dinesh is my number one suspect at present.'

191

'I agree. But what I am saying was that perhaps Subrina was depressed.'

'So why did she slit her wrists and then inject herself with insulin? One of the methods would have been enough.'

'She wanted to use the drug, but it was taking too long and Subrina was impatient. So she got in the bath and slit her wrists to speed the process up, but died soon after from the insulin overdose so there was not much blood.'

'But I spoke to her doctor in Delhi before we came out.'

'And?'

'She wasn't a diabetic. And she only suffered from mild depression now and again. Her doctor didn't believe she would kill herself. All the evidence points to homicide. Just get over it, Pankaj. It isn't suicide.'

Pankaj bit his thumb. 'Okay,' he sighed. 'Fine. Where do we start?'

'The insulin. We know Takshak had access and so that means Advani also had access.'

'And Takshak, if he is involved, didn't give anything away,' Pankaj said as he repeated the conversation he had with Takshak to Chupplejeep. 'He was acting very strange though. When I asked him how much insulin he had with him, he started with saying seven vials but quickly changed to six. And there were six in the fridge and six syringes, but the slight slip made me wonder if he was trying to cover up the missing one. He was defensive when I arrived at the gallery, but when I told him that insulin was possibly used in Subrina's murder, he softened. He is a good actor but he is definitely hiding something.'

'Well, he had reason to be angry with Subrina Basi. She had taken away Malabar Hill from them.'

'And there was a ready supply of insulin at the gallery. Takshak owed Advani, maybe he killed for him.'

'Advani has a secret he is trying to protect and a gallery place he is trying to win back. That could be a motive. I am still waiting for the chair of the board at Malabar Hill to get back to me to see whether it was Subrina or the board against Advani's tenure.'

'I've checked the students enrolled on Advani's course because they would have had access to the insulin as well. But there are no motives there. Most of them are rich kids sent to Goa by their parents. They study art during the day and get stoned at night,' Pankaj said.

'Insulin is readily available in India. It could have been purchased by anyone. Although it is one of the more expensive drugs.'

'You're right. Why not use something cheaper and less sophisticated?'

'Maybe money isn't a problem for this person. That would rule out some of the staff at the hotel. But insulin is a class H drug,' Chupplejeep said.

'What does that mean, sir?'

'It means that you need a prescription to issue it. All pharmacists must therefore keep a record of purchase and sale of the drug. The Food and Drugs

Administration can ask for these records of a pharmacist at any time.'

'But with all due respect, sir, this is India. You don't always need to have a prescription to get the drugs you want. And if money is not an issue for this person then…'

'True.'

'Kulkarni may be wrong though. I've been reading why people slit their wrists in the bath, sir. The reason is because the warm water not only numbs and moistens the skin, but it allows for a smoother blood flow. Plus, there would be less to clean up.'

Chupplejeep stopped walking and looked at Pankaj. 'You are still following the suicide track? We just put that theory to bed. And for the record, from what we've learned about Subrina Basi, she didn't seem the sort to care about people cleaning up after her.' The detective started walking again.

Pankaj was silent for a moment before he spoke again. 'But, sir, the mind can do strange things when you are contemplating the taking of your own life.'

Chupplejeep opened the small metal gate at the front of the house and walked through. Pankaj followed, climbing the three red steps up to the front door of the mint-green bungalow.

A small woman with grey hair pulled tight into a bun answered the door.

'Are you Chaaya?'

'You're not welcome here,' the woman said. She met Chupplejeep's gaze with a steely look.

'We just want to ask you a couple of questions, that's all.'

'About that witch?'

'I'm not sure who you mean.'

'Oh, you know all right. A celebrity dies and everyone looks for the killer. A small child dies and just because his family have no money, he's treated like a nobody – his death swept under the *kambal*, blanket. When my poor Nitin died, you cops didn't want to know. You get a payoff from Subrina's family and you're only too happy to accept, na? It makes your life easier. You don't have to bother doing any hard work, like bringing justice, but you can go home with a nice fat pig to feed your family with.'

'I'm sorry if you feel that way…'

'Trust me, it is I who is sorry. I let you people into my house once. I'll never do that again.' Chaaya started to close the door.

'Ma'am,' said Pankaj, 'the case involving your grandson happened twenty years ago and I admit the policing system in Goa was not what it should have been. Mistakes were made and there was solid corruption.'

'Ha! You're going to tell me it's all changed. Please, boy, don't insult me. You young people today, have you not been taught to respect your elders?'

Pankaj looked as if he had been slapped. If there was one thing he knew, it was how to respect his elders. His mother and his aunty had always made that clear. It came above any other moral he was taught.

'You're right,' Chupplejeep agreed, 'corruption still exists and we are working to overcome this horrible disease we have in India – to accept money, to turn a blind eye.'

Pankaj found his voice again. 'T-there is still corruption in the state. I-I can't deny that,' he said with a slight stutter. 'But do you know about this detective? He is Detective Chupplejeep. Over a year ago, he was dealing with a case in Panjim involving one of our most influential politicians…'

Chaaya opened the door further and raised her hand to stop Pankaj continuing. She looked Chupplejeep up and down. 'I've heard of you. You were mocked and ridiculed for not taking a bribe. They demoted you.' Chaaya smiled with satisfaction.

Chupplejeep nodded.

'So, because we took a payoff from Subrina's family, that makes you better than us?' Chaaya asked.

Chupplejeep and Pankaj shared a look. What the hell, Pankaj thought. First the woman said the police were corrupt. Now she was accusing them of thinking they were superior.

'Sometimes our hands are forced to take something we do not really want to accept,' Chupplejeep said.

Chaaya was silent for a moment. 'Fine, fine, take a seat out here on the veranda,' she said, looking towards the cane chairs. 'I still don't want you people in my house. You want drinks?'

Chupplejeep and Pankaj sat on a small wooden bench. 'Water will be fine,' Chupplejeep said, speaking for the both of them.

Chaaya disappeared into the house and returned with two glasses. She took her place in her rocking chair. 'You should have not bothered coming all the way out here. I've nothing to say. I'm glad the witch died.'

'Why is that?' Chupplejeep asked.

'You're here, so that means you know about my grandson and how he was taken from us. The woman got what she deserved.'

'Can I ask how you found out about Subrina Basi's death?'

'You think because I'm poor I can't read? I read it in the papers.'

Pankaj looked around the spacious veranda. It had a granite grindstone in one corner. He imagined the maid grinding masala for the week's curries as she looked over the well-kept gardens – the coconut and caju trees, the white bougainvillea, and dark green and red rubber plants.

Chaaya stared at him. 'Don't look at my house like that!'

Pankaj snapped his head back to look at Chupplejeep then took a sip of his water.

'Yes, we built this house with blood money. That is what you were thinking, was it not?'

'I don't think my officer was thinking that. Pankaj is interested in architecture and planting,' Chupplejeep said. Pankaj shot his boss a look of thanks.

'I told my son not to take the money. The money brought bad luck to this family. But he was stubborn and he was strong. No one could oppose him. After all, I named him Balbir and his name means strong.'

'What bad luck came with the money?'

'My daughter-in-law was on my side. She didn't want to take the money. She wanted that woman to go to jail, but my Balbir, he said that Subrina was just a child.'

'Subrina was young at the time of the incident.'

'At first he said no to the money, but the family came back with a better offer. Balbir was a carpenter at the time. He made money but not so much. Everyone was a carpenter twenty years ago. The money they offered meant we could move out from the hut we were living in and build a big house. He could send his remaining son away to school – a good English-speaking school. And he would never have to worry about money again. But the money was bad. Blood money never brings anything good.'

'What happened?'

'My daughter-in-law loved Nitin like any mother loves her son. She saw Balbir and her other son moving on, and for their sakes she tried to get over the death of poor Nitin, but she couldn't. Every night I would hear her cry. In her dreams she would scream out exactly in the same manner she did when she saw his bloodied little body on the roadside. Every night she was reliving the death of her youngest son. It was only a matter of time.'

'Only a matter of time?'

'Before she killed herself. Do you know how she died, Detective?'

Chupplejeep shook his head.

'She set herself alight after dousing herself in kerosene. She did this in the back yard, whilst my Balbir was at work. I was at home, but you know she didn't make a sound. There was no screaming, no running about trying to put out the flames. She had no regrets of what she was doing even as the flames burned her skin. She accepted the most painful death she could think of, so that she could be with her son.'

Pankaj saw Chupplejeep staring at him. He quickly closed his mouth and turned his attention to the glass of water in front of him. He took a sip of water and steadied his breathing.

'Eventually, the smell of burning flesh got my attention. That fetid smell still fills my nostrils to this day,' Chaaya said, scrunching her nose. 'But by the time I got to her, it was too late. I found her charred body in the yard close to the broken-up pieces of furniture we were using as firewood. She was careful not to go too close to the *lakud*, firewood. She was considerate like that. I put out the remaining flames. Then I called my son. He has never been the same since.'

'You stayed in this house?'

'You cannot avoid your fate, Detective. These rich people move far to get away from their past, but it always catches up with you. That witch's death is proof of that.'

Chaaya looked up as an old bald man with a hunched back approached the veranda, carrying a bag. 'This is my Balbir,' she said with a warm smile.

'Ma, who are these people?' Balbir asked.

'The police, son.'

'They've found him?'

Chaaya pressed her lips together and shook her head. 'No, son, they're not here about that. They are here just to see me. Why don't you go inside and start cleaning the vegetables, *haan*? Then I can make soup later.'

Balbir stared at Pankaj. Then he bent down and put his hand under his chin. He lifted his face up and looked into Pankaj's eyes. 'Son, you came back. Good. Very good.'

Chaaya stood up. She put her hand on Balbir's back and rubbed it. 'No dear. This is not your son. They are no longer with us. Come now. Go inside and clean the carrots and the kohlrabi for dinner.' Balbir looked at his mother and then back at Pankaj. He smiled and then went into the house. 'Excuse my son. He's been like this since the day his wife took her life.'

'It must be difficult.'

'You wouldn't know,' Chaaya snapped. 'So don't give me your fake sympathy. Now what is it that you want?'

'I'm sorry that I have to ask this of you, but as part of our investigations we have to rule out all eventualities.'

Chaaya sat back down. 'What is it that you want to know?'

'I have to ask the whereabouts of you and your family members the night of the 15th December, early morning of the 16th December.'

Chaaya let out a cackle. 'Ha! So the witch was murdered! Detective, if I knew that she was staying in the Golden Orchid, just a stone's throw away from my house, so close to where she murdered my grandchild, I would have killed her myself!'

'Were you and Balbir here on the night of the 15th December?'

Chaaya stood up and clenched her fists. 'How dare you?' she asked. Her face began to turn the colour of a *brinjal,* aubergine. She pointed to the front gate. 'Get out, get out of my house and don't you ever come back here again.'

Chapter Twenty-eight

Pankaj picked up the folder containing the fingerprint analysis in the blackmail case and then put it down again. He couldn't concentrate, not when he wanted to remember every detail from his date last night. He looked up at the old clock on the wall. It was ten minutes to eight. Chupplejeep would be in any minute now and he would want to know how it went. Pankaj wasn't sure what his response would be.

He had picked up Shwetika from Café Coffee Day to avoid her parents finding out about their date. His friend Raju had warned him, 'Once the parents find out, you're screwed. Means they will soon expect marriage and formal introductions. You don't want that shit. Keep it casual. There are plenty of women out there.' Pankaj could see himself marrying Shwetty, but Raju did have a point. The parents would interfere and pressure them to marry as soon as they found out. He was stressed enough as it was with dating, let alone having her parents watching his every move.

From the coffee shop, Pankaj had taken her on his scooter to Delhi Delights. It was a new place which opened after its predecessor, a Chinese restaurant called the Rising Sun, closed down. The food at the Rising Sun had been terrible and after rats interrupted one couple's main course, they closed down before the Food Hygiene Authority of Goa forced them to. People said that rats were still a problem in the building, but what could you do? Rats were everywhere and Delhi Delights served the best tandoori this side of the Mandovi River.

Pankaj breathed a sigh of relief when they arrived at the restaurant and didn't see any familiar faces. He chose a booth in a dark corner of the restaurant, initially thinking the obscure corner was a design feature, but soon realising that it was dark because a bulb had blown and was 'too difficult to replace' or so the short, rotund waiter had said, as he shook his head from side to side with visible disappointment. It was a perfect spot because other guests didn't overlook the table and it had a good view of the front door, so he and Shwetty could watch out for anyone they knew entering the restaurant. There had only been one uncomfortable moment – just after they had sat down at their table, a second cousin of Shwetty's stopped by to pick up a takeaway. Shwetty had conveniently slipped away to the bathroom as her cousin was paying and didn't return until he had disappeared.

When it came to ordering, Raju had suggested that he 'be a man and take control'. But Pankaj didn't know where to start in making a decision for someone else, especially on the matter of food. His friend had pointed out that it was what real men did in the movies and that he and Sailesh did it all the time. Raju wasn't lying,

Pankaj had seen them in action, but he didn't think he had it in him. After all, food was a very important thing, and if he chose something Shwetty didn't like, she may never want to see him again.

He had decided on onion *bhajis* to start – a safe option given that he still hadn't asked her if she was a vegetarian yet. But when the portly waiter in his starched white jacket came to their booth and stood, pen poised over his notepad, Shwetty cleared her throat and summoned the waiter over to her side of the table.

She ordered the chicken lollipops and fish *tikka* for starters and then a *daal makhani, aloo palak* and butter chicken for mains to be accompanied by two *chapatti* and boiled rice. No tandoori, thought Pankaj, but never mind. Shwetty was a confident woman, not the meek girl in the *shalwaar* he had assumed she was, and she had an appetite that her figure betrayed. In that moment Pankaj knew it was love.

With their order sorted and two fresh lime sodas on their table, their date was in full swing. It wasn't until Shwetty squealed that it was eleven o'clock and that her curfew was midnight that he realised just how quickly the evening had passed.

He had paid the bill, she let him do that, and then drove her back to her village, stopping his scooter a few metres away from her house so her parents wouldn't see. 'My parents think I'm with my friend, Madhul. They think we're helping to get the venue ready for her brother's engagement ceremony tomorrow.'

'Smart,' Pankaj had responded. He had wanted to kiss her then. Not a French kiss, but perhaps a peck on the cheek. But it was difficult to turn around while he was on a scooter, even though they had stopped. He made a mental note to practice. She had stepped off the scooter and coyly fluttered her eyelashes at him, but she was too far away for Pankaj to kiss her and he was nervous of doing anything like that in her village. Someone, somewhere would be standing on their balcony with their phone in hand ready to tell their closest friend what Shwetty was doing with a boy, in the middle of the village, for all to see.

'So can I see you again?' Pankaj had asked.

Shwetty looked at the ground. 'Sure.'

Pankaj liked that she was shy, even though she was the opposite when it came to food. A smile formed on his lips thinking about how she and his mother, both lovers of food, would get on.

Now he smiled, remembering the date. It had gone well. As well as he could have hoped. He opened the folder on his desk and looked at the fingerprint analysis in front of him. Thinking about his date last night wasn't going to help him solve his case. He looked at the results. They didn't tell Pankaj anything he didn't already know. Advani and Takshak had both handled the letter, no other prints had been found.

Instead of moving forward on this simple case, he felt as if he were taking a step back. Chupplejeep had made him the lead on this case. It was his opportunity to shine and instead he was failing. He blamed Subrina Basi.

205

If she hadn't died then he would have had all the time in the world to solve Advani's problem. But, Pankaj knew it was wrong to take out his frustrations on the poor dead woman.

He put the folder down and studied the blackmail letter. What other clues could he find in the letter to help him? The culprit had addressed Advani as Advani, but there was no clue in that. The whole of India knew the artist as Advani. It would have been more of a clue if he had been called something else. *You have secret.* The writer of the letter was confident. He knew that Advani had a secret. So Advani had either confided in this blackmailer or the culprit had been witness to it, whatever 'it' was. The forged paintings? Pankaj shook his head. Every lead he had followed about the forgery just gave him more evidence that Vallabh's paintings were completely different to Advani's. Pankaj had seen pictures of Vallabh's work from his former teacher, and even with his untrained eye he could tell that the gaudy paintings of lotus flowers and temples were starkly different to the passionate art Advani created. Pankaj had to admit though, despite Vallabh's paintings being described as saccharine, he still preferred them to Advani's. At least they did not depict mutilated lady parts.

If it wasn't the forgery that was Advani's big secret, what was he hiding? Had Advani murdered someone? Or held someone to ransom? Or was he the blackmailer, himself? After all, everyone knew Advani rose from rags to riches. He had written a full article about his upbringing in the *Times of India* and he had talked about it on a popular chat show on Star TV.

I will expose you if you dant live 40 lakhs in yellow garbage can outside your galleri on the eve of Christmas. Dant live – those two words jarred, they didn't fit. And then the letter ended with a simple: *Do not disregard this.* Disregard was certainly not a word used by someone who didn't know how to spell 'don't' and 'leave'. There was no signature or sign-off mark, and the criminal was smart enough to use gloves while constructing the letter because no other fingerprints had been found. The blackmailer was not a simple soul as he wanted the police to believe, with his engineered misspellings and fountain pen. He was smart.

Pankaj rubbed the paper of the letter between his thumb and forefinger. It was a good quality paper of medium density. The ink could be analysed further but it looked like standard royal blue Bril or Camel ink, which you could buy all over India and in shops in Panaji like JD Fernandes. Pankaj slapped his forehead – it was useless, he was going around in circles.

He had to know Advani's real secret to move the case along. Time was running out. Every time his mother bought another pack of festive *nureos,* he felt a knot tighten in the pit of his stomach. He put the letter along with the fingerprint analysis in his top drawer and pulled out his mobile phone from his pocket. He punched in a series of numbers and hit the call button.

~

Chupplejeep let himself into the office and rubbed his tired eyes. Christabel had phoned him last night in a fit of tears – although he was sure they were crocodile tears. Apparently the unlucky wedding date was already affecting them as she had been forced to lie to Father Agnelo about his baptism. Now she had promised Father Agnelo some money, which was no better than a bribe, to get married in the church. What cheek. Chupplejeep had never paid a bribe before, and now he had to pay one to a man of the cloth for a marriage he wasn't really sure about.

But he had Christabel to consider in all of this. She would easily forget the bad luck a wedding on the 29th February could bring, but she would not forgive him if he put any barriers in her way to getting married in the church she had been baptised in. And her mother would soon be paying Chupplejeep a visit if he didn't sort out this problem soon. It was a visit, Chupplejeep thought, best avoided and so, against his better judgement, he decided to pay Father Agnelo a visit. This whole wedding situation was getting out of control. Last night he had woken in a cold sweat after he dreamt he had been standing in front of the altar. 'It's too late to back out now, though,' he said to himself, thinking of how Christabel would react if he told her how he was really feeling.

He had to forget about his nerves. Instead he had to concentrate on the issue at hand. Could he forget his morals and give the church money so that they would overlook that he had not been baptised? Would that not undermine him as Goa's most moral detective? And Father Agnelo, using the orphanage as an excuse, annoyed him afresh. He was certainly stuck between a rock and a hard place. There was only one thing he could do in a situation like this: visit Father Agnelo after work and sort out the problem once and for all. After all, he had caught Goa's only serial killer, he could sort out a wedding in a church.

'Ah, Pankaj, there you are,' he said as the police officer walked into the office with a red hibiscus flower in his hand.

'I was in the garden watering the plants. I had so much going around in my mind I couldn't think straight. Being around nature always calms me down.'

'So the date didn't go well?'

'On the contrary, sir, it went very well, very well indeed. I invited her to Sailesh's wedding.'

'Sailesh Krinz is getting married?'

'Yes, sir,' Pankaj said, putting down the flower he was holding on his boss's desk.

'To the maid?'

'The same one, Utsa.'

'I remember her from our last case, when we found the body of that driver under the coconut tree.'

'Yes sir, the same one. Sailesh's mother, Meenakshi, is doing her nut. First, she threatened to set fire to herself then she threatened to send her beloved son to his uncle's house. Poor Sailesh was beside himself, sir.

He didn't want to lose his family, but he's in love with the girl.'

'Then what happened?'

'Eventually, his father saw sense after getting to know her. Now, the wedding is all set for just after Christmas.'

'That was quick,' Chupplejeep said, thinking of his own impending wedding. He picked up the flower and put it in an empty glass on his table.

'Sir, in the villages, once you are friendly things move fast, very fast. That's why Shwetty and I have to keep our relationship under wraps. As soon as the gossips start, her parents will find out and we'll have to get married.'

'It's a relationship now?'

Pankaj blushed.

'I'm lucky I didn't have that kind of pressure.'

'You are, sir. Although some pressure is okay. I wouldn't want to get to forty without a wife.'

'Okay, enough of that. Tell me, what thoughts are going around your mind that you have to waste valuable police time watering plants?'

'Two things – I checked with the staff at the hotel if anyone had diabetes.'

'And?'

'Not the staff nor any of the guests that were staying at the hotel the same time as Subrina had diabetes.'

'And you know this because?'

'I checked the records of the staff at the hotel. They have to declare things like that. Also, I called the guests. They could be lying, sir. I have already thought of that.

But there was no need. All of them had alibis. They had left the country long before Subrina was murdered. So it's just Takshak that's diabetic, with a ready supply of insulin.'

Chupplejeep looked at the red hibiscus. 'You said you had two things to tell me. What else?'

'Oh yes, this news is good, sir. Are you ready for this, sir?'

'I'm always ready.'

'Good, because I know where Dinesh is.'

CHAPTER TWENTY-NINE

Suki slipped the small envelope into the fire and retrieved the pink rosary from her pocket. She rubbed a plastic bead between her fingers and said another Hail Mary as she walked back into the courtyard. But her mind wasn't on her prayers, it was on what she had said to the detective.

She replayed the conversation over and over in her mind. She had been careful as to what she said, giving him information she thought was relevant. The detective had been cunning, calling Sister Perpetua to confirm her story. She had stopped in the little alcove outside Sister Perpetua's office to listen as she answered the detective's questions in that guarded way of hers. For the first time in twenty years, Suki was grateful that the woman was naturally untrusting of people.

'She was at the candlelight prayers,' Sister Perpetua had said into the telephone. 'No, I didn't stay all night...Because she was with another sister who has categorically stated she was with her...No, Detective, we are not a prison here at the Sacred Heart Convent. We don't even lock any of our doors. My office, for instance, is always open. I don't check on the other sisters at night. There is no guard on the door…No, no watchman either. We trust in the Lord to keep us safe.'

Sister Perpetua paused then as she listened to what the detective was saying. Suki couldn't help wonder what it was that had Sister Perpetua so unusually quiet.

'I suppose you're only doing what's right, Detective, but I don't want you bringing scandal into my convent. We cannot help it if some of the families of our nuns are so, so promiscuous…No, I'm not saying that Ms Subrina Basi brought this on herself. Of course not. But one should look at the company in which they keep… No, she would not be in God's favour if she did. It is a sin for us. Sister Valentine never tried to kill herself. I really cannot be talking of such things with you. One more question, Detective, and then I really must go.'

Suki leaned in closer.

'Did she occasionally leave the convent at night?' Perpetua repeated into the phone. 'You mean did she go out after dinner-time?'

There was a silence. Suki's palms began to sweat. With the base of her hand, she gently tapped the wall of the little alcove where she stood.

'You are very inquisitive but I suppose, Detective, you are only trying to do your job.' She cleared her throat. 'Sister Valentine does occasionally leave the convent at night, yes. And,' she said as she lowered her voice, making Suki lean closer towards the door, 'I think she has been meeting someone.'

Suki let out a small gasp. Sister Perpetua turned and closed her office door. Suki had no choice. She ran across the courtyard, to the kitchen where she knew a fire would be burning.

How did Sister Perpetua know? Her room was at the rear of the convent, away from the entrance. When she first arrived, to avoid her night terrors she used to often leave the convent late in the evening under the cloak of darkness. She didn't want anyone to see her because they would ask questions and she didn't want that. It was a transitional period between her old life and new. Walking down to the engineering college, watching the students eat *Bhel* and drink Kingfisher straight from the bottle, made her comfortable with the decisions she had made.

After a couple of years, the need to leave at night subsided. She still had nightmares, her thoughts still clouded by memories from her past. But she had made friends and was comfortable spending all her hours in her room, the chapel or within the confines of the courtyard.

But it all changed one Sunday, a year ago, when after mass a tall man with deep-set eyes, glasses, thick dark hair and a kind smile approached her as she was collecting hymn books. She didn't often talk to parishioners and would have made her excuses, but this man was different. There was a deep sorrow in his eyes and his hunched shoulders told her exactly how he was feeling. As she stood close to him, she experienced something she had not experienced before. A warm feeling spread through her and for the first time in years, she felt alive.

'Are you okay?' she had asked, surprising herself with the question as it left her lips. And he answered her. She knew then that she had found a kindred spirit and she wanted to help.

The other nuns and priests had guided lost souls before, but she had never been given the opportunity. Finally, she had the chance and she wouldn't let him down. It was at a time when she had started to question her faith, and she knew that by helping him, her own faith would be restored.

The man started visiting the chapel every Sunday and after the church had emptied, they would sit on the front pew and discuss all sorts of things. Once he told her he liked greens because it reminded him of nature. She confessed her love for pink and even told him how she disliked the brownness of the convent, a comment she later said three Hail Marys for. Another time, he told her about his love for birds and how cruel it was when people imprisoned them in cages. She told him she had recently seen a woodpecker. When she described its red and golden back, he pronounced it a flameback and reached out to touch her cheek, but she had swiftly turned away and he had quickly moved the conversation along. Later, he told her that almost three-quarters of wild birds in India died before they were six months old and that had sobered up her mood. Her sister was like a wild bird, but she didn't know then that she would die young, like one of India's wild birds.

Suki wondered if her behaviour with this man was appropriate, after all they were only talking, but she didn't dare ask. He was smart and funny and after a few months, when the warm feeling crept up on her every time she thought of him, she realised she was falling in love. It was then that she had agreed to meet him late at night, when darkness fell and the other nuns were asleep. Her late-night wanderings commenced again, but this time he accompanied her.

She didn't think anyone knew what she had done, was still doing, but Sister Perpetua did. It was all Subrina's fault. Why had she wanted to get in touch after all this time? Why couldn't she just leave things as they were? There was no need to dredge up the past. It was better left buried. She had made the ultimate sacrifice. If it hadn't been for what happened all those years ago, she would never have been in a convent.

But things were different now. Her life was no longer just an existence. She had someone to live for and he had given her a way out. Soon she would leave the Sacred Heart and live a full life. She had every right to do that. Too much of her life had already been taken from her. It was her time to live.

Suki said a Hail Mary and looked up before moving on to the next rosary bead. Birds were chirping in the pomegranate tree and some of the nuns were gossiping by the fountain. She recalled the conversation she had with her sister and her nostrils flared at the thought of what Subrina said, but she had been strong. In broad daylight, on her favourite bench outside the engineering college, she had grabbed her sister by the arms to make her stop talking and it worked. Subrina had momentarily lifted her black sunglasses, looked in her eyes and then stopped speaking. It was better that way because no one wanted to hear what she had to say.

CHAPTER THIRTY

'Let me get this straight,' Chupplejeep began. 'You got hold of Dinesh's driver and he told you that at around two-thirty on the morning of the 16th December, he drove a very inebriated Dinesh to his private plane stationed at Dabolim airport, but he doesn't know where he is now.'

'There he boarded the plane and took off to Mumbai.'

'We know that from what the guests at Ayesha's party said. Did you check with the aviation authority like I asked?'

'Of course.' Pankaj opened his notebook. 'He boarded the plane at three-thirty and landed at Mumbai's Chaatrapati Shivaji airport, domestic terminal 1.'

Chupplejeep shook his head. 'Why the hell didn't they tell us this the first time we asked?'

'They only looked at their records from ten that morning when we first asked them. You see, it's unusual for a private plane to take off from Dabolim so early in the morning.'

'All the more reason for them to know about it, no?'

Pankaj shrugged. Chupplejeep supposed there was no accounting for what some people thought.

'You'd think that with all the terrorism around they would be extra vigilant.' Chupplejeep sat at his desk and pressed the space bar on the keypad of his computer. A window popped up reminding him of his impending church visit. He turned back to Pankaj. 'From the party, where did Dinesh go? And why the hell has he not bothered to contact the Goa police, given that his girlfriend has been found dead? He better not be dead also.'

'Perhaps he has been knocked out these past few days.'

'Knocked out?'

'On a cocktail of drugs and alcohol, similar to what was found in Subrina Basi's system. *Icon Bites* recently reported that Ayesha Saxena's parties are legendary, and we all know what that means, sir.'

Chupplejeep nodded. Pankaj was right. These celebrity types were drugged up to the eyeballs and passed out on day-beds overlooking infinity pools, after parties such as Saxena's. But in the age of smartphones, he couldn't believe that Dinesh was ignorant of Subrina's death.

'Sir, there were no smartphones allowed at the party,' Pankaj said as if reading the detective's mind. 'Saxena is paranoid that something will get leaked to the press. She guarantees the safety of all her guests to her parties this way.'

Chupplejeep thought of the stick-thin Bollywood actress in a bright pink *gagra choli,* a picture Christabel had recently showed him in one of her magazines. He couldn't deny the actress was extremely good-looking, even though he liked women who carried a little more weight and didn't look like they were in need of a large portion of mutton *biryani.* 'Don't these big-shot actors and actresses mind?'

'Sir, it's the party of the year and it was only for one night. Also, these days there is a trend not to post everything on social media. It is known as MOMO.'

'MOMO?'

'The mystery of missing out. When someone is not posting anything or checking in, it makes their followers and friends feel anxious because knowing what they are missing out on is much better than not knowing.'

'I can't keep up with this generation. But never mind that. It's been nearly a week since the party.'

'Rumour has it that Dinesh and Ayesha are now officially an item after they were seen at the party.'

'But where the hell are they?'

Pankaj opened his mouth to say something but Chupplejeep interrupted him by banging his fist on his desk. 'Dinesh wanted to be with Ayesha and Subrina wouldn't let him go. There is motive in that. He could have planned her murder before he arrived in Goa. That night he killed Basi, put her sunglasses on her face, painted her lips and then left. Or,' he added, twisting one end of his moustache, 'maybe he left the Golden Orchid and got someone else to do his dirty work. That's just typical of someone like Dinesh. Here, look at this.'

Chupplejeep picked up a blue file and passed it to Pankaj. 'What's this, sir?'

'It's the fingerprint analysis from the knife used to cut Subrina's wrists. Kulkarni said four sets of fingerprints were found on it.'

Pankaj started to read and as he did so, his eyes widened. 'One set of prints belonged to Subrina Basi, that's understandable, the killer must have pressed her fingers to the handle.'

'Carry on reading.'

'One set is unknown.'

'The other two, Pankaj.'

'Nishok and Abhik!'

'You said that Nishok wouldn't talk, well make him talk. Make them both talk! Arrest them on suspicion of murder if you have to. I want answers. I need answers.'

Chupplejeep took out his mobile from his top pocket and looked at the display, then he replaced it. 'Gosht will be calling again. I'm going to Mumbai. I'll bloody find that Dinesh myself.' Just then his top pocket started vibrating. He retrieved his mobile again and answered the call. He listened intently.

Pankaj could see the detective's grip tighten around the phone. He was angry. When he disconnected the call, Pankaj asked him if he should arrange a ticket from Goa to Mumbai for him.

'No need.'

'Sir, why?'

'Dinesh's on his way here. He found out about the death last night and is flying over. His plane lands at lunchtime. He phoned the Commissioner in Delhi, who in turn phoned Inspector General Gosht. Apparently, Dinesh wants to help any way that he can. I'm sure he does. That bloody Delhi Commissioner, why didn't he call me straight? Now Gosht will think he came to us instead of us finding him.'

'But that, sir, is partly correct.'

'I know you know that, but the bloody Inspector General doesn't need to know that, does he?' Chupplejeep looked at his watch. 'I'm going to meet Dinesh. Go and find out why exactly Nishok and Abhik's prints were on that knife. If they have motive and opportunity, I want to know. If you have any reason to suspect that Dinesh hired them, call me immediately.'

Chupplejeep closed his eyes. Gosht was gunning for closure to the case but if his suspicions were correct, when an arrest was made Gosht was not going to be happy.

CHAPTER THIRTY-ONE

Pedro's Bar and Grill, an eating place near Dabolim airport, had made a half-hearted attempt to get into the festive spirit. A few garlands of fake ivy and balls of cotton wool were stuck to the walls with tape, and a cardboard cut-out of Santa Claus in red shorts and a white singlet was taped to the bar. Chupplejeep's best friend's five-year-old daughter could have done a better job.

He looked at the menu. When the waiter appeared he ordered a simple plate of fried kingfish, chips, salad and a Limca. He may as well eat something while he waited for Dinesh to arrive.

Speaking to Father Agnelo before he left Larara one hour ago had worked up an appetite in the detective. Chupplejeep had listened to Agnelo explain how the orphanage was always the last to receive any donations, and that they were in desperate need of food and clothing supplies. At the outset Chupplejeep was convinced that he wouldn't concede to giving a bribe, determined to appeal to Agnelo's Christian nature and use the power of persuasion to secure a church wedding for Christabel. But after looking at the sorry state of the orphanage, he had parted with a larger sum of money than Christabel first suggested. The money was handed over under the guise of a donation, which soothed Chupplejeep's conscience, and he relaxed even further when Father Agnelo suggested he visit in a couple of months to see just how his money had been spent.

As he left the orphanage to make his way towards the airport, he felt elated. He had never thought of himself as being a patron to an orphanage as Father Agnelo suggested, but now the thought quite appealed. After all, no matter how bad it was, without the Lemon Tree he would not be here today. He found himself already looking forward to his impending visit in two months' time, and perhaps he would even pay them a visit at Christmas.

The detective pushed the white plastic chair out and stretched his legs as he waited for his food and for Dinesh to arrive. Pedro's was on a stretch of road from Dabolim towards Panjim. It was a badly designed restaurant with the seating area facing the road and the kitchen facing the garden. But Chupplejeep liked it. Not only was it a good spot for people watching, you couldn't beat the fried fish which always came with a few *rawa* fried *shinaneos*, as well. He watched as the cars passed outside, stirring up the red mud into clouds of dust. Finally, as his plate of food was placed before him, he saw Dinesh pull up in a white Mercedes. His driver, whom he had earlier asked to bring his employer to

Pedro's, quickly got out of the driving seat and opened the passenger door for him.

Chupplejeep put a juicy, fried mussel into his mouth. He swallowed it down with a large gulp of Limca and twisted the end of his moustache, happy that Pedro's food was better than his decorating skills. He watched his suspect enter the restaurant. He was just as he had imagined. Tall and fair with short black hair and a bit of stubble, which seemed to be what all the *filmi* set did these days. He was dressed in a white linen *kurta-shalwaar* and he wore dark glasses, which Chupplejeep assumed he wouldn't take off.

As Dinesh walked over, Chupplejeep felt something stir inside him. The man walking towards him thought a lot of himself. He was violent too. Bonaparte had told him about his abusive nature towards women, and Subrina's friends had backed it up. Plus, Ayesha Saxena was still missing. The Mumbai police had confirmed this to him when he called on his way over to the restaurant. Ayesha hadn't been seen since her party when she left with Dinesh. If he had killed once, had he got a taste for it and killed again? Would some other housekeeper find Ayesha wearing red lipstick and sunglasses in a bath in a boutique hotel somewhere in Mumbai? It was a possibility and Dinesh was his number one suspect. He would have to treat him accordingly, despite Gosht's warnings. 'Let them think you are looking for him because you are concerned for his safety. Do not, under any circumstances, let on that he is a suspect. That family have a lot of influence here,' Gosht had said.

He stood and greeted the rich kid.

'Any food?' Chupplejeep asked as they both sat down.

Dinesh put a packet of cigarettes and two mobile phones on the table. He touched his hand to his stomach. 'No, nothing for me, it's much too early.'

'It's past one o'clock,' Chupplejeep said. The man was clearly hungover.

'Breakfast time then.' Dinesh raised his hand and called a waiter over. 'Get me a juice. What fresh juice you have? You have watermelon?' Dinesh turned to Chupplejeep. 'No chance of them making a Bloody Mary here, right?'

Chupplejeep faked a smile.

'Get me a whiskey also. You have Johnnie Walker?'

The waiter nodded and disappeared into the kitchen.

'Not too early for alcohol then?' Chupplejeep asked. He couldn't help himself.

'It's never too early for a slug of whiskey, right? No doubt it will be counterfeit stuff. These people in these small states, *yaar,* they don't know whiskey from rum.'

'Not all of us have been brought up with the privilege of drinking different brands of whiskey.'

Dinesh clasped his hands on the Formica table and studied his watch. 'So Detective, I know what I've read in the papers, but I can't believe that someone would do what they did to Subrina.'

'What have you read?' Chupplejeep asked. Since Bonaparte's article, there was very little in the papers and the journalist had kept to his word. He hadn't written anything since. But Subrina lived in Delhi and he had since seen a couple of articles online speculating about her death.

'The papers said it was suspicious. Online they say it was suicide, some sites say murder. Tell me, *yaar,* did she suffer?'

Chupplejeep raised an eyebrow. 'I can't say too much at this point, but I do have some questions for you.'

'Like what, Detective? I wasn't even here at the time.'

'You were one of the last people to see her alive. Tell me, how did she seem to you when you left her?'

'She was her usual self. But she was preoccupied with her baggage.'

'Her baggage?'

'One of the reasons she wanted to come to Goa was to clear up some family matter.'

'Do you know what this family matter was about?'

Dinesh stretched his arms above his head. 'Nah, I was only half-listening when she told me. Lately she was always going on about her past. Some accident that happened years back when she forced her sister to go with her to some party, bribing her by letting her wear her makeup. She was talking about how her sister was going to be some big-shot doctor, but now she's a nun.' He laughed. 'Subrina's sister is a nun, can you believe that? It was some stupid story and she sounded very confused. I told her, "Fucking forget your past. The past is where it should be, in the past." She hadn't spoken to her sister in years and Subrina was high more than she was sober recently, so I wasn't sure if she just talking nonsense. Why the hell did she want to talk to her sister now?'

Dinesh suddenly looked solemn. He looked at the detective. 'I suppose I should have listened better. Perhaps it would have provided some clue.'

Chupplejeep nodded. He was often guilty of switching off when Christabel was talking about her relatives. Talk of relatives could be really tiring on the ears. But he often wished he had a brother or sister in his life so he understood why Subrina wanted to get back in touch with her sister after all this time. Some bonds were difficult to break, no matter how hard you tried, no matter how long you left it. He guessed that Dinesh didn't have any siblings. Either that, or he was one of those heartless fellows. 'Did Subrina often make things up?'

Dinesh rubbed his forehead. 'I suppose not. But I never really checked up on all that she said.'

'Did Subrina know you were heading back to Mumbai to Ayesha Saxena's party?'

'Waiter,' Dinesh said. He looked around him. 'Where is my fucking whiskey, *yaar*?' he asked, the watermelon juice forgotten. 'She didn't know I was going to the party.'

'But you had a fight before you left?'

'Do you have a woman, Detective?'

He nodded.

'Well then, you know how it is, *yaar*. You know what these females can be like. They can be so clingy. She wanted me to stay back in Goa with her and she ate my brains about it from the day I landed. I mean, come on, what was she thinking, booking some hotel in the middle of nowhere. She should have booked something in Baga or Calangute, Anjuna even. This village stuff is not my scene.'

'So you told her you were leaving.'

The waiter arrived with a tall glass of watermelon juice, a glass full of ice, a measure of whiskey, and a small carafe of soda. He placed the items on the table. Dinesh picked up the glass of whiskey and took a large sip.

'That's exactly what I said. There was no way that I was going to hang around in Goa, when the party of the year was happening in Bombay. I said I would join her back in Goa for New Year's after she cleared up all her shit.'

'Her shit?'

'Are you fucking joking me? I didn't literally mean her actual…never mind. You villagers are all the same. No, I said I would come back to Goa when she had finished sorting out her past or whatever *natak*, nonsense, she wanted to do.'

'Did she know it was Ayesha Saxena's party you were attending? Did you know that Subrina and Ayesha were enemies?' Chupplejeep asked, remembering what Pankaj had said about the warring actresses. He took a bite of fried fish. The flavours of the meaty fish mingling with the slightly spiced breadcrumbs danced on his tongue.

'You read too much, Detective.'

229

'But surely, your girlfriend would be annoyed if you were leaving her to spend time with another woman, especially a woman she didn't like. And you're dating this Ayesha now. Subrina Basi was your girlfriend, wasn't she?'

'Come on Detective, we're not in fifth standard at school where we have girlfriends and boyfriends, are we? Subrina and I were occasional lovers. Ayesha is also my lover. Don't tell me you are one of those grandfathers who doesn't believe things like this happen. It's the twenty-first century, *yaar*. It happens. Subrina was older than me, it was never going to last.'

Chupplejeep looked at Dinesh. He must have been in his late thirties and although Chupplejeep wasn't the violent sort, he felt a sudden urge to punch him right between his eyes. The boy not only had no manners, his head was so far up his own backside he couldn't see anything else. And what was his claim to fame? He had a rich grandmother and had done two Palmolive commercials. Is that all it took these days to become a *gadhaa*, donkey? Chupplejeep took a deep breath and pushed away his half-eaten plate of fried fish. This man had ruined his appetite. He took a deep breath. 'But you hadn't slept with Subrina recently?' he asked.

Dinesh squinted. 'Our schedules didn't allow us to meet up so often.'

'Oh, are you filming something at the moment?' He couldn't resist the question.

Dinesh finished his whiskey. 'Waiter,' he shouted, raising his empty glass, 'get me another. I'm not filming.

I have a lot of business enterprises. Something you cops know nothing about.'

'But you had separate rooms at the Golden Orchid.'

'That was another reason she was angry with me. She didn't like the fact I wanted my space. Come on, what did she expect, to share a bed every night? I like my time alone. She knew that right from the off. But like I said, Detective, these females are all the same.' The waiter returned with another large measure of whiskey.

Chupplejeep looked at his plate of barely eaten food. 'You didn't sleep with her at all when you were in Goa?'

'Don't ask me when clearly you already know. We didn't. Is that such a surprise?'

'Well, actually.'

'That was one of the reasons it wasn't working out between Subrina and me. She didn't have the same appetite I did. Mostly, she just wanted to cuddle.'

'Perhaps, being in separate rooms wasn't conducive to…'

'Whatever, Detective. Other girls don't seem to mind. I like sleeping in my own space.'

'Ayesha Saxena?'

Dinesh nodded.

'You don't seem very upset that Subrina is dead.'

'I'm fucking heartbroken.' Dinesh removed his sunglasses and lit a cigarette. Chupplejeep smiled, his initial assumption that Dinesh wouldn't take off his sunglasses was wrong. He looked at the man's puffy, red eyes – likely to be the effect of drugs rather than mourning the loss of his late girlfriend.

'I'm surprised it took you so long to make contact with the police. You were impossible to trace. Were you not surprised that Subrina didn't contact you this past week?'

Dinesh put his sunglasses back on and drained his glass again. He took a long drag on his cigarette. 'After Ayesha's party we went to her place in Amboli Hill Station. The mobile reception is fuck-all there.'

'Didn't you check the news? Did nobody tell you that your lover was dead?'

'No. Ayesha has the same appetite as me, if you know what I mean.' Dinesh winked at the detective.

'We spoke to Ayesha's friends. They say it was rare for her to go completely off the radar like that.'

'Rare is not never, Detective. What can I say? She wanted some alone time with me. No disturbances. Her words, not mine.'

'It is known that you have raised your hand to women in the past. The friends of Subrina's that we spoke to said you left her with a bruised arm just a few months back.'

'Her friends? What friends? I wouldn't call those hangers-on friends or believe anything they have to say. This is a joke, Detective.'

'So you're not denying that you struck her?'

'Is there a police report for this incident? No? I didn't think so. Then this is all conjecture.'

'Subrina didn't make a complaint because of her career, because she didn't want some trashy website like *Icon Bites* to write a story about it.'

Dinesh stared at Chupplejeep. 'What are you fucking accusing me off, huh, cop?'

'You don't seem to have been interested in Subrina in the least, either that or you're a very good actor. Your history of violence against women doesn't stand you in good stead.'

'I defy you to get a woman to make a statement that I raised a hand to them. I wouldn't hit anyone. It's not in my nature.'

'You hit the waiter at the Firefly restaurant at the Golden Orchid. Or does he not count? Is he not a person?'

Dinesh sneered.

'I'm trying to make sense of what your relationship was with the deceased. She told her sister that she was going to marry you.'

The suspect laughed. 'Marry Subrina? That's original. The woman was deluded. I would never have married her.'

Chupplejeep couldn't help but feel sorry for the dead woman. He didn't know her but he was sure she could have done better than a spineless snake like Dinesh. 'Will Ayesha Saxena corroborate your story?'

'Of course.'

'And where is Ayesha Saxena? We can't get hold of her and as you can imagine we are getting quite concerned. It would be odd, no, if two of your lovers ended up dead.'

'Now you're really taking the piss. Ayesha is still in Amboli. She is staying there for some time.'

'Without a landline?'

Dinesh nodded.

'Her parents are worried too. You're telling me her parents don't know about this place of hers?'

'How the fuck should I know?'

'You can see how this looks.'

'What do you want me to do?' Dinesh said, leaning back in his chair.

'Give me the address so we can check she is where you say she is.' Chupplejeep handed Dinesh his notebook and pen. He noticed tiny beads of sweat had formed on his brow. So this cool character was beginning to sweat. Was it the heat of the day, or something more sinister?

'You'll find her there,' Dinesh said. He scribbled something in the notebook and handed it back.

'You better hope we do.'

'Have you questioned that fag, Advani? That artist was chasing after Subrina. He wanted Subrina to reinstate his tenure at Malabar Hill, what the hell. I had to listen to his shit for one hour whilst he told her how pretty she was just so that she would put in a good word for him with the board. But she never would because I told her he had to go. He was holding that gallery back. My grandmom is one of their best customers.'

'Did you think he was really doing the gallery harm? Or did you want him out because he knew some things about your family that you didn't want to get out?'

Dinesh stared at Chupplejeep. 'You're a joke, Detective. Have you asked Advani where he was when Subrina was killed?'

'We've spoken to Advani, yes. But surely Advani wanted Subrina Basi alive so that she could take his case to the board at Malabar Hill?'

'He must have been angry that Subrina wouldn't listen to him.'

Chupplejeep made a mental note to check in with Pankaj about how the blackmail case was going. Dinesh was clearly still angry with Advani for sleeping with his father. He didn't need the forty lakhs, but perhaps he wanted him to suffer.

Dinesh rose to his feet and stubbed out his cigarette.

'Where are you going?'

'Am I under arrest, Detective? Because, otherwise, I'm not going to sit here and take abuse from you.'

Chupplejeep was silent. Let him talk, he thought. He doesn't know what's coming.

'Instead of asking me questions speak to Advani, and while you're at it why don't you speak to the maid at the hotel?'

'The maid?'

'The girl fawning all over Subrina, the one stealing from her. You didn't know, did you? Go and do your job. Find out who murdered Subrina and stop sticking your nose in my business.'

'I see.'

'I'm going back to Bombay. If you try and harass me again I'll call the Inspector General. He and my father go back.'

'I'm sure they do,' Chupplejeep said.

'Meaning?'

'Your father was one of the key politicians who allowed permission for the Golden Orchid Hotel to be built.'

'So?'

'So, I can imagine he knows everyone. A man who has such power has contacts everywhere. I am sure he could get his son out of trouble if he needed to. But if you haven't heard, I am a cop who cannot be easily bribed.'

'Watch yourself, Detective, or you may not have a job soon.' Dinesh turned and walked to his car. The driver, who had been snoozing in the front seat, woke with a start when Dinesh called to him. He leapt out of the vehicle, running around the car to open the passenger door.

'*Ek minat,*' Chupplejeep said, walking up to Dinesh. He could smell the whiskey on his breath.

'What now?'

Chupplejeep unclasped the handcuffs from his trousers and swiftly placed one around Dinesh's wrist.

'Fucking…what the hell do you think you're doing?' Dinesh asked incredulously.

'I think that night, after Subrina's party at the hotel, she pressed you to commit to her. She begged you to stay in Goa with her. After all, she loved you.'

'So, she loved me. Big deal.'

'You couldn't handle it. You wanted your freedom. You wanted to party with Ayesha Saxena and you wanted Subrina Basi out of the way. You wanted to shut her up once and for all so you did what all you rich fellows do.'

'What's that, Detective?'

'You throw your weight around.'

'Geez. Just because you don't have two paise to rub together, don't take it out on me.'

'You are a violent man.'

'A slap that you can't even prove is very different from murder. Anyway, I told you I was in Bombay. I couldn't have killed her.'

'You flew out of Goa very quickly, that's for sure. And you've been uncontactable – turned off your phone because you were scared. Usually you young *filmi* types can't go two minutes without looking at your smartphones.'

'You're really pathetic, Detective. My driver took me to the airport. He can tell you.'

Chupplejeep looked at Dinesh's driver with his *paan*-stained teeth. The man nodded. 'I drove him, sir. Correct.'

'I left Subrina, then I left for the airport.'

'I think you did leave Subrina, yes. You were seen together just after one, but you didn't leave till two-thirty and you were heard arguing. Before your driver took you to the airport, you had time to kill Subrina Basi. There was no sign of any forced entry into her room. She knew

237

her attacker. You entered her room, you murdered her and then, only then, did you seek out your driver to take you to the airport.'

Chupplejeep pulled Dinesh's other hand behind his back and cuffed him. 'I'm arresting you for the murder of Subrina Basi…' Chupplejeep started. He couldn't afford to lose his main suspect again. Inspector General Gosht wanted an arrest today, what luck! He was going to get one.

CHAPTER THIRTY-TWO

Pankaj was pleased that he had quickly managed to confirm to Chupplejeep that Dinesh's father took a bribe to provide permission for the Golden Orchid. All it had taken was a telephone call to the local government office and a request for the name of the official who pushed the permission through for the hotel. He had been lucky the secretary who answered his call worked in the office at the time of the decision. She knew everything about the case, official and unofficial, and gladly passed it all on to Pankaj. He could only imagine that she must have been having a quiet day.

With that information passed on to his boss and buoyed by his initiative, he decided that a background check on Abhik and Nishok would stand him in good stead for his impending interviews with them. 'You don't make a curry without chopping the onion first,' Chupplejeep had once said, and Pankaj knew that knowledge was power. But the five-minute task he envisioned took a lot longer. First, he had to call the Golden Orchid and speak to Hari, the general manager of the hotel. Then he had to wait for a fax. A fax! He was

239

sure they never used a fax machine on *CSI*. One hour later, and after two failed attempts, a fax containing the references for the two suspects came through.

Pankaj called the local police station where the silent gardener, Nishok, used to live. 'So that's where the scoundrel has gone!' Officer Jerry said.

Pankaj's ears pricked up. 'So, you're on the lookout for him?'

'No, not really. It was a petty theft we were after him for. But too much time has passed now to bother coming after him.'

'What did he steal?' Pankaj asked eagerly. He had always known that Nishok was a dodgy fellow.

There was a silence on the end of the telephone. 'You know, *baba,* I can't remember. If you can hold, I could check our records if you'd like.'

Pankaj looked at his watch. He needed to leave soon if he was to interview both Nishok and Abhik before Chupplejeep returned from his meeting with Dinesh. He drummed his fingers on his desk. 'Okay,' he heard himself say.

Several minutes later, Officer Jerry came back on the line. 'Oh, *tho,* perhaps he was not such a terrible person after all. I must have been confusing this Nishok person with some other man. It seems he was only stealing some foodstuffs. Oh yes, I remember the fellow now. Miserable, he was. He had a face like the backside of a *bakri,* goat.' Officer Jerry laughed at his own joke. 'Not cooperative at all, if I remember correctly.'

Pankaj thanked Officer Jerry for his time and disconnected. It sounded like they were talking about the same man. Nishok certainly had a desolate look about him. But the man wasn't as suspicious as he thought, simply a small-time crook. Had he just stolen something from Subrina? Is that why he looked so afraid all the time? Is that why he had refused to talk to Pankaj and took flight instead?

But if he was so innocent then why was he spotted at the hotel at four in the morning? Nishok had only been stealing petty items in his old village and here, in Dhesera, perhaps he had moved on to…to what? Murder? A simple villager like Nishok didn't go from stealing *mankurads*, mangoes, to plotting a heinous and cunning crime just like that. He needed answers from the gardener. Keeping his mouth shut was not going to help him, not now that his fingerprints had been found on the knife. The same knife used to slit Subrina's wrists.

Pankaj scratched his head. There had to be a reason why Nishok's fingerprints were on the knife. What exactly was his motivation? Perhaps Dinesh had paid Nishok to kill Subrina Basi. He was a simple villager who, like most villagers, needed money to survive. He had already shown himself to be a crook, running away from the police in the last village he lived in. He would have to get the man to speak.

Then there was Abhik. His prints were found on the knife as well. He picked up the Nepalese cook's reference.

It was as Pankaj had suspected, the chef had come all the way over from Nepal. It would be tricky trying to get answers from the local police officers in Abhik's village. He picked up the green telephone on Chupplejeep's desk once again.

After talking to the phone operator to find the correct number and trying to get an international line, Pankaj finally got through to a sub-inspector at the Nepalese police office close to where Abhik last worked.

'I-I see, I see,' the sub-inspector said nervously. 'But, you know, I can't just give out information on our citizens.'

'I completely understand that,' Pankaj said, trying to empathise with the sub-inspector. 'But this is a life or death situation. A crime has been committed. Not just any crime, but a murder and I need as much information about this person as possible.'

'Is h-he a suspect?'

'I suppose,' he said, pulling his chair out from behind Chupplejeep's desk and sitting on it.

'Oh, I see. You know, I think I would have to check with my superiors first.'

'Hmm, but I am in a hurry for this information. This fellow could be getting away with murder as we speak, literally. Can you tell me, at least, if you have a file on him?'

The sub-inspector was silent while he contemplated this. Pankaj heard tapping away on a computer. Eventually, he cleared his throat. 'Y-yes, we have a file on him,' the sub-inspector stuttered.

Pankaj closed his eyes. He knew that there was some sort of information-sharing agreement between Nepal and India, but he couldn't remember what exactly it was. 'In 1950 Nepal and India signed a friendship treaty,' he said. It was all Pankaj could remember from his schooling days. He hoped that it would encourage the sub-inspector to part with his information on Abhik.'

'Y-you know, I'm still not sure. I'll speak with my boss and call you back.'

'I don't have time. Can you at least tell me if Abhik has committed similar crimes?'

'Like murder?'

'Yes, murder.'

'Similar?'

'Yes, like another murder!' Pankaj said, losing patience.

'You could say that, I suppose.'

Pankaj straightened in his chair. So Abhik had killed before. This was interesting. Abhik could be placed at the crime scene with his fingerprints all over the knife. He may have worked in conjunction with Nishok or Dinesh. 'Okay, speak to your superintendent fast and call me back straight away or else I'll have to get Detective Chupplejeep to call your boss. You don't want that, do you?'

'O-okay, okay. I-I'll call you back.'

Pankaj gave the sub-inspector his mobile number. He placed the old green handset back in its cradle. He didn't expect a phone call any time soon because he knew what it was like in these small rural police stations. Nothing was a priority.

He thought about what the sub-inspector had said. Abhik with his dead eyes and quiet confidence, and now possible record for murder, was the perfect suspect. Plus, Abhik was calculating and smart. He remembered how the chef had excused his missing knife only minutes after declaring that everything in his kitchen had a place. Yes, thought Pankaj, the man was certainly smart enough to plan a murder. Now all he had to do was find his motive.

Pankaj heard the door to the station open. He looked up. 'Sir, back already? I was just on my way to the Golden Orchid. I still haven't questioned Nishok and Abhik.'

'I've made an arrest,' Chupplejeep said.

Pankaj leaned forward in his seat. 'You have? I may have a suspect...' Pankaj trailed off, putting his theory about Abhik to the back of his mind. His boss didn't go around arresting people without good cause. His notion about Abhik could wait. 'Excellent, sir,' he said. 'I want to hear everything.'

CHAPTER THIRTY-THREE

Chupplejeep sat at his desk and wiped his brow with a handkerchief from his trouser pocket. He was pleased with his work today. He had made an arrest and he was confident that he had got it right. It made sense. The motive was there – Dinesh had wanted Subrina out of the way. The opportunity was definitely there – Dinesh was the last known person to see Subrina Basi alive. Her arms had been bruised where he had grabbed her earlier in the day, he was sure of it. The man was a thug and he had taken one step too far.

Rinnnnng, rinnnnng. The green phone on his desk broke his train of thought. 'Ah, Inspector General,' he said into the receiver. He braced himself to tell Gosht the news. Gosht would be angry of course. But justice had been served and it came with a price. Plus, he couldn't afford to lose his main suspect again. He had no choice but to arrest him.

'You imbecile!' Chupplejeep heard through the receiver. He held the phone away from his ear. Gosht was loud, loud and angry. 'You utter idiot. What have you done?'

'I've made an arrest. Dinesh…'

'I know what you have gone and done, you fool. Let the man go.'

Chupplejeep heard the Inspector General's voice boom around him. At first he thought he was going mad. He could hear Gosht's voice through the phone but it also sounded like the man was standing in the room with him. He looked up from his desk and saw Pankaj's wide eyes and open mouth. He turned and saw a small, dark, bald man in a white shirt and perfectly pressed grey trousers. He disconnected the call. 'Inspector General,' he said. 'You've come all this way.'

'Because you made me!' Gosht barked. He put his mobile phone in his pocket and walked over to Chupplejeep's desk. He had small beady eyes and when he spoke they bulged out. He was angry, extremely angry.

'I've taken him to the main station in Greater Larara. He's in a cell,' Chupplejeep said, standing up. Although he instantly regretted it as he towered over Gosht.

Gosht ordered him to sit down. 'You call them this instant and get him out or I will. And believe me, if I have to make one more call in relation to getting an MLA's son out of the Greater Larara holding cell then I will fire you.'

'But with all due respect, we have every reason to make the arrest. If I didn't arrest Dinesh, he would have taken off again. We wouldn't have jurisdiction to arrest him in another state.'

'You have every reason? I have had his father and his mother on the phone. His mother wept, wept I tell you.

246

She said that I've personally brought shame on their family. Irreparable damage, she said. They are not going to let this go lightly. They will make a fuss and they want to blame us and then screw us for all we've got. They will bring a witness to give Dinesh an alibi if that's what it takes. They have the means to do that. You know what these people are like. I should never have accepted you at this branch, Chupplejeep. You with your morals, you're causing me nothing but grief.'

'He had motive and opportunity.'

'And the insulin. Can you tie Dinesh to the insulin?'

'Give me twenty-four hours. I'll be able to tell you…'

'And the knife used to slit her wrists. Were his prints found on the knife?'

'They are running his prints now, against the set of prints we found on the knife.' Chupplejeep looked at his watch. 'They'll have the results any minute now.' He had noticed when he arrested Dinesh that he had thin, wiry fingers which Kulkarni had profiled for the unidentified set of prints.

Gosht was quiet.

Chupplejeep took a breath.

'Let them run the prints, but if they don't match, you release that man, you hear me. I want to know today.' And with that Gosht left the police station as quickly as he had arrived.

Chupplejeep and Pankaj looked at each other for a moment, in silence.

'You go, Pankaj. Go and do what you were going to do. Find out what you can on Nishok and Abhik. I'll find you when I know the results.'

'But the arrest?'

'Their prints are on the knife. They could have been paid to do it.'

'Oh yes, I see.'

Chupplejeep was silent. Despite what he had said to Gosht, an uneasy feeling about the arrest began to creep up on him, and it wasn't just because of Gosht's threats. He knew he needed concrete evidence in order to charge Dinesh. How did Dinesh get hold of the insulin? Had he taken it from Takshak's supplies? As far as he was aware, Dinesh had never been to the gallery. He and Advani were not friends. Unless Takshak and Dinesh were connected. Unlikely, but a possibility.

Chupplejeep rubbed his forehead. He had acted rashly when he arrested Dinesh. There were still too many loose ends and he hated loose ends. Takshak was one of them but so were Abhik and Nishok. Both their prints were found on the knife. 'We need to know if the fingerprints match, but in the meantime let's not drop the ball with our other suspects. Let's carry on.'

'Okay sir,' Pankaj said, rising to his feet and making his way to the door.

Chupplejeep heard the station door close behind Pankaj. He looked at the green phone on his desk, willing it to ring. Kulkarni was sure to have fingerprint analysis by now. Just as he reached out to the phone to call Kulkarni, it rang.

CHAPTER THIRTY-FOUR

Pankaj parked his scooter and made his way past the gulmohar tree, with its long brown seed cases swaying in the warm breeze, towards the stone-tiled entrance of the hotel.

He was surprised that his boss had made the arrest so quickly. Normally Chupplejeep liked to get everything in order before he pounced. But he also understood. Dinesh was a slippery fellow. He had left Goa immediately after the murder and was almost untraceable. If Chupplejeep had let him go, who knows if they would have found him again. But if the fingerprints didn't match then there would be hell to pay. Pankaj heard the anger in Gosht's voice. He saw it on his face. If Dinesh was wrongfully arrested, he and his family would want blood – Chupplejeep's blood.

Pankaj's mobile rang. He answered it and listened intently as Chupplejeep spoke. 'I see,' he said eventually, before disconnecting. The unidentified prints on the knife didn't match Dinesh's, which meant that they had to let him go.

Had Dinesh got some other fellow to slit Subrina's wrists for him? He could have easily paid someone to do it and obtain the insulin for him. It was easy when you had his kind of money. It wouldn't be the first time a rich man paid for a kill. His driver's prints didn't match, so it wasn't him. But it wasn't too far a stretch of the imagination to believe that Dinesh was part of the Bombay mafia. They had contacts everywhere and could make people do things they didn't necessarily want to. Dinesh may have used Abhik or Nishok and it was Pankaj's job to find out.

~

Xavier, the barman and waiter at the hotel restaurant Firefly, offered Pankaj a plate of *rawa* fried prawns and a cold mango *lassi* while he waited. The prawns were just how Pankaj liked them – dipped in masala and coated in semolina before they were fried a golden brown. And because they were on the house, they tasted even better. He hadn't eaten prawns in a while. They were always double the price at the peak of the tourist season. Tourists loved prawns, almost as much as Goans.

Pankaj savoured his last mouthful and looked around the restaurant. It was well decorated for Christmas with silver and red tinsel hanging from the rafters and snow painted on the windows. There was even a tree in the corner, with brass cooking pots placed around its base, like presents. There were only a handful of diners in the restaurant. The news about Subrina Basi had ensured that only the perversely inquisitive dared to enter. No wonder they were giving him free prawns.

Pankaj stood up to greet his first suspect as Nishok inched through the double doors of the kitchen. 'I have some questions to ask you. Do you want to go somewhere more private?'

Xavier looked at Nishok and back at Pankaj. 'Nishok can't sit in here with you. Not when there are other guests. It's hotel policy.' He took away Pankaj's plate, briefly hesitating as he did so.

Nishok fiddled with the hem of his shirt and looked longingly through the window at the landscaped gardens. In his old shorts and faded blue t-shirt, he looked out of place in the modern confines of the Firefly. His hair was unkempt and he looked like he was in need of a good wash, but it was understandable. He was the gardener.

'Perhaps we step outside,' Pankaj offered. 'It's not too hot out there. We can sit on one of the outside tables. I'm sure that won't be a problem. There are no guests out there.' Without waiting for an answer, he led the gardener to the outside eating area. But instead of taking a seat at a table, Nishok sat on one of the stone steps that led to the garden.

Pankaj followed suit. 'You like it out here?'

Nishok nodded, his eyes fixed on the yellow and pink flowers of the imposing frangipani tree in the distance.

'They say that if a snake bites you and you eat the seeds from that tree then you'll be cured,' Pankaj said.

251

Nishok looked away from the tree but not before Pankaj saw recognition in the man's eyes. Pankaj knew a passionate gardener like Nishok would have heard this old Indian tale. He imagined Nishok was dying to tell him a story or two involving seeds and whatnots. Every keen gardener in Goa had a head full of plant stories they were desperate to tell, but the man didn't say a word. Pankaj decided to try a different tack.

'Earlier today I spoke to someone you know.'

Silence.

'Officer Jerry. Does the name ring a bell? He's the local officer where you used to live, am I correct?'

Nishok looked up, his eyes wide and moist. He started picking at something on the stone step.

'Officer Jerry told me what you did before. He told me why you ran away from the last village you used to live in. Don't look so worried. They are not coming after you. But you can't keep running like that.' Pankaj could hear Nishok's shallow breathing. And even though he wanted to stay objective, he couldn't help but feel sorry for the man. 'Do you know Dinesh?' he asked, watching Nishok's eyes carefully.

Nishok shook his head.

'He was Ms Basi's boyfriend.'

Nothing.

'Did he ever speak to you?'

Nishok shook his head again.

Pankaj sighed. Nishok certainly wasn't talkative. What was he hiding? 'Your prints were found on the knife at the crime scene and you were seen leaving the hotel at an unusual time the morning Subrina Basi was killed. Can you explain that?'

The shallow breathing quickened but still Nishok didn't speak.

'I can't help you if you don't help me. If you don't talk, I'll have no choice. I'll have to arrest you,' Pankaj said, even though his palms had begun to perspire at the thought of having to make an arrest on his own.

Nishok opened his mouth. Pankaj looked intently at his suspect.

This was it. The man was going to speak.

There was a noise behind them. Pankaj clenched his teeth and turned towards the restaurant where the noise had come from. Xavier was walking towards them. When Pankaj looked back at Nishok, his lips were pressed together.

'What do you want?' Pankaj asked curtly.

'I've come to help.'

'Help?'

'It looked like you wanted some answers from Nishok.'

'This isn't your business. You're interrupting a police interview.' This was why it was better to take people back to the station. It was more conducive to interviewing suspects. Although, Pankaj knew that kind of environment would have been wrong for Nishok and his mouth would have been closed tight like a clam, a little like it was now.

'Oh.'

Pankaj shook his head. 'Never mind, just leave us now.'

Xavier sheepishly turned back towards the restaurant.

'Sorry, Nishok,' Pankaj said. 'You were about to say something.'

Xavier stopped walking. He turned. 'But do you know?' he asked Pankaj.

'Xavier, I'll talk to you later. First, I need some answers from Nishok.'

'What I am trying to say is that you won't get any. Didn't Abhik tell you?'

'Tell me what?'

'Nishok can't speak. He's a mute. An insomniac and a mute. He's always been like that. Born like that.'

Pankaj looked at Nishok. The man was smiling now, exposing his crooked teeth and pink gums, nodding at what Xavier was saying.

'Why didn't anyone tell me this before?'

Xavier shrugged. 'I can help you converse with him if you like.'

Pankaj thought about whether this was allowed or not. He couldn't remember seeing anything in the *Good Practice Policing Handbook* that told him that you couldn't use a layperson to help translate, and as far as he and Chupplejeep were concerned, Xavier was not a suspect. He had an alibi. 'Okay,' he said reluctantly. 'How does he communicate?'

'He has his own special sign language. It took us some time to get used to him around here. But he's a good worker, ask anyone. Hari will tell you just how much everyone likes him.'

'And Abhik?' Pankaj asked, wondering why the cook had failed to tell him Nishok couldn't talk. 'Will he say Nishok is a good person?'

Xavier walked over to where Pankaj and Nishok were sitting. 'Who cares what Abhik says?'

Pankaj nodded. 'Don't you like him?'

'He's okay. He likes to be the big gorilla here.'

'Big gorilla?'

'Makes a noise when things don't go his way. Thinks he can solve all his problems with his fists. When I first started working here, he gave me a black eye because I got two of his orders wrong.'

'Did you notice what he was like around Subrina Basi?'

'Same. A bit quieter, I suppose. I think he had a crush on her,' Xavier said with a grin. 'But when he spoke to her, she was rude to him. Ha! That put the gorilla in his place.'

'What did she say?' Pankaj asked. Abhik had no alibi, so he had plenty of opportunity. Could this have been his motive to kill the star?

Xavier shrugged.

Pankaj knew how debilitating crushes could be. 'Okay. So first ask Nishok if he minds you doing this?'

Xavier didn't need to translate. The gardener was nodding. He made a few signals with his hands.

'He says he's glad I am here. Your questions were getting very tiring.' Nishok smiled. 'He said he never met or spoke to Subrina's boyfriend. But he once saw him advertising Palmolive soap on a billboard near Betalbatim some years back.'

Pankaj shifted and let Xavier take his place. He watched as Nishok started signalling rapidly with his hands, suddenly animated in his expressions.

'Okay, okay slow down,' Xavier told him. And without taking his eyes off the gardener, he started relaying to Pankaj what Nishok was desperately signalling. 'So he claims he had taken the knife on the evening of the 15th December to cut the fish heads of the *gobbro,* rockfish?'

'Does he often do work like that?'

Xavier shook his head. 'No.' He looked at the floor. 'Nishok was stealing the heads to take home.' Xavier whispered the word stealing, as if he was committing a crime by the very mention of the word.

'So he took the fish heads home with him that evening to make curry?' Pankaj couldn't help it, but his mouth had begun to water. *Gobbro* head curry was the tastiest.

'It's not such a big sin,' Xavier said. 'We don't use the heads here much, unless Abhik wants to make a stock and then he tells Nishok.'

Nishok was nodding.

'So you all know that he steals from the kitchens. Abhik knows?'

'We all know, except Hari. Hari would not accept stealing. He would rather the fish heads went in the bin than to feed Nishok and his family. You won't tell him, will you?'

'I won't if I don't have to.' Pankaj made a note in his diary. It explained why a fish scale was found on the knife as well. 'Okay, but answer me this, you say that Nishok cut the fish heads at around six in the evening after he watered the plants for the day and before he went home.'

'Yes.'

'Why then was Nishok seen at the hotel at four in the morning on the day Subrina Basi's body was found?'

Chapter Thirty-five

Chupplejeep disconnected his mobile phone and slid it back into his top pocket. He had made it to the Golden Orchid in record time, especially as he had to make two stops on his way over.

After Kulkarni gave him the terrible news about Dinesh's fingerprints not being a match to those found on the knife, he had decided to hold off telling Gosht. There was nothing to say that Dinesh hadn't paid someone to kill off his girlfriend, and Ayesha Saxena was still missing. The officer in Bombay, despatched to check on her whereabouts, had got lost and ended up at a hill station miles away. He was now making the long journey back to her house in Amboli to verify what Dinesh had said. Chupplejeep would have sent another officer out, but what they did in Mumbai wasn't in his control.

The detective's first stop had been to Dinesh's cell to interrogate him further, but when he got to the station, his cell was empty. 'What the hell!' he screamed at the officer in charge, calling him all sorts of names. The officer, too scared to make a sound, had showed him the release forms. Gosht had signed them around the same

258

time that Kulkarni phoned him with the results from the fingerprint analysis. Chupplejeep threw the papers back on the desk. He knew he had been the first person Kulkarni told which meant Gosht had undermined him, releasing his primary suspect without even having the decency to tell him. He punched the wall of the holding cell, smarting at the pain. Then he made a face at the officer and left, calling Gosht on his way out.

'His parents have assured me he will be fully contactable at all times,' Gosht said. 'And I just got off the phone with Kulkarni. The prints don't match. It is you who should be apologising to me.'

Chupplejeep had to use all his willpower not to disconnect his superior. He always thought Gosht had good morals, but he was mistaken. His boss was clearly more interested in pleasing the rich and influential than serving justice.

The second stop he had made was at a little village. He needed to speak to an old acquaintance. If his suspicions were correct, there was a good chance that this fellow would have some information on Indu, the maid who found Subrina's body and whom Dinesh said had been stealing from the late Subrina Basi.

Now, after asking Kulkarni to start checking with pharmacies on the recent sale of insulin, he sat on the bed in room 13, the room Subrina Basi had been murdered in, and waited for his officer who he had just called. Two minutes later Pankaj arrived, out of breath.

'I was interviewing Nishok and Abhik, sir, like you asked.'

'Did either Abhik or Nishok have anything to do with that rat?'

'Dinesh?' Pankaj shook his head.

'Fine,' Chupplejeep said, twisting one end of his moustache. He didn't think it was fine at all. If it wasn't Abhik or Nishok who had killed for Dinesh then who had? There was one set of unidentified prints on the knife. But whose, the bloody hell, were they? 'I wanted you here when I question Indu. Two cops may be better than one with this girl. The last time I spoke to her she came across as very naive, but now I know better.'

He briefed Pankaj on what he knew before he heard a knock at the door.

'Come,' said Chupplejeep as he moved from the bed to one of the armchairs. Indu walked in to the room, her head bowed and her hands buried deep in her apron pockets.

'Are you okay?' Chupplejeep asked.

'I've not been in this room since...since that day. It's odd seeing all her things in the room like this without her. Her makeup, perfume and jewellery on the dresser.'

'Do you want to go elsewhere to talk?'

'It's okay. In time another guest will be staying here and the horrors of what I saw that day will go.'

'Why don't you take a seat?'

'I already told you everything I know.' Indu made no attempt to sit.

'Actually, I don't think you told us everything.'

'I did,' she said, her eyes darting around the room.

'I don't think so. We've reason to believe that you stole some valuables from Subrina Basi.'

The maid looked though the glass balcony doors. 'Lies. It's all lies. Who told you these lies? The woman was a drunk. She went around saying all sorts of things.'

'What did she say?'

'That she used to live in the next village. That she had family here. All lies. We would have known if she had been a local.'

'She was telling the truth, Indu. She did live here in Suuj, one village away from Dhesera, and her sister still lives in Goa.'

Indu turned her face away from Chupplejeep.

'Now, the poor woman is dead,' Pankaj said.

She sat on the bed and looked at her feet. 'Yes,' she whispered. 'I'm sorry.'

Chupplejeep shrugged. 'No need to be sorry if you didn't like the woman.'

'She treated you badly?' Pankaj asked.

Indu's shoulder's dropped. She tried a smile.

Chupplejeep smiled. Pankaj always had a way of getting the younger ones to open up. His caring manner invited people to trust him. The beauty of it was that Pankaj didn't know he had this gift. The boy was going to make an excellent detective one day.

'She treated me like dirt.'

'And she didn't care for her things,' Pankaj said. 'Last time, you told my boss that she didn't even know what jewels she had. She chucked them around her room like junk, no?'

261

'You didn't think she would miss a few pieces?' Chupplejeep asked.

'I didn't take anything.'

The detective opened his notebook and glanced at it. 'Subrina Basi was untidy, but she knew what pieces she had with her. You took a pearl necklace and a gold and diamond brooch.'

Her face hardened. 'I didn't take anything.'

'Are you sure?'

Indu frowned.

'Less than an hour ago, your manager confirmed these items had been reported as stolen by Subrina Basi. He also confirmed that Ms Basi had suspected you.'

'Hari?'

'He was the one who gave me the details.'

'M-madam gave me these items.'

'You just said Madam treated you badly. Why would she give you jewellery? And jewellery she was only recently photographed wearing in *Icon Bites*. She received many compliments on those pieces in the press. One paper reported the necklace alone as being worth seventeen lakhs.'

Indu shifted her eyes from Chupplejeep to Pankaj. 'She felt bad for the way she was treating me. Asking me to iron her five rupee notes and telling me to do my work fast, fast. How could I clean fast when it took me half an hour to put all her things away first? Hari never mentioned anything to me. He would have fired me if he believed Madam.'

'Hari didn't have time. He was only told of the theft the night before Subrina's body was discovered. With all the commotion of her death the next day, it slipped his mind.'

'There's no proof. If Madam was missing something, she should have taken me to the police. These rich people are the same. Always looking for someone smaller to blame. She must have misplaced the items herself.' Indu stood up and started looking on the dresser and in the drawers. Then she walked over to the cupboard and opened the wooden doors. She squatted as she looked inside for several minutes.

She stood up with a small black pouch in her trembling hand. 'Here they are.'

'Can you take them out so we can see?'

Indu emptied the contents of the pouch on to the palm of her hand. 'Here,' she said, lifting up a gold necklace with a single pearl and a gold brooch. It was in the shape of a flower with a large diamond in the middle.

'Come on, Indu,' Chupplejeep said. 'Don't take us for fools. Those are not the items.'

'They are.'

'No they're not. You're lying and it makes me wonder what else you are lying about.'

'How do you know these are not the items?'

'Because I have the real items here,' Chupplejeep said, tapping his top pocket. 'It's easy to see what exactly a celebrity owns just by putting their name into a search engine on the world wide web.' Chupplejeep retrieved a similar pouch from his pocket and pulled out a string of pearls and a gold brooch with a cluster of diamonds.

Indu's face fell.

'When I was told some jewellery was missing, I made a few calls. Larara is a small place and there are only a few people who deal with such items. I found out who had bought these items from you. It was a loan shark in the village of Utol who you met with, wasn't it? His name is Sanjog.'

Indu was silent.

'He handed over the jewels to me. You see he's a mild fellow, keen to stay on the right side of the law. You told him that these were your great aunt's, didn't you? He bought them from you, but they were not as valuable as you had believed, they were not the seventeen lakhs the papers reported, were they? He only gave you a few hundred rupees for the items.'

'You may as well tell us now,' Pankaj encouraged.

'The pearls were freshwater pearls and the diamonds were just glass. It was cheap costume jewellery, made well. It was why Subrina didn't bother going to the police, that and I assume the fact she didn't want people to find out that her jewellery was all fake, if the items were found.'

Silence. Indu's shoulders were hunched.

'If you lied about this, perhaps you lied about what really happened when you found the body. Maybe Subrina Basi confronted you about her jewels that day when you went to clean her room and you didn't like it. You got angry and attacked her.'

'No, no. Rosie was just with me minutes before I found the body. I screamed. You know that's true. You've spoken to Rosie. She told me.'

'We're going to get to the truth of the matter, no matter what the cost.'

'Why don't you just tell us the truth,' Pankaj said softly. 'It'll be easier this way.'

'Okay,' Indu said eventually. 'I took the jewels. But when I found her I had a suspicion that she was dead in that bathroom behind the curtain.'

'You knew?'

'I expected.'

'How? If you didn't have anything to do with it.'

Indu looked at the floor. 'It was the smell – the faeces and urine. That and I glimpsed the bloody bathwater. That is why I knew what to expect.'

'Really?'

'I swear, Detective. I didn't kill her. I wouldn't know how to kill anyone. You have to believe me.'

Pankaj and Chupplejeep shared a look.

'When I spoke to you last,' Chupplejeep said, 'you said that you often overheard Madam on the phone. The day before she died, you said she was talking to someone and she was angry. She said something about the truth being told. You thought it was about her boyfriend. Do you remember anything else about the conversation?'

Indu sat on the bed. She started to bite her fingernails. 'She was angry. That much is true, and her boyfriend was a cheater. He looks like a cheater. But I can't remember…Oh wait. Yes. She mentioned another man, I think.'

'Who?'

'Let me think. Hmm, I can't recall the name. She said it was terrible what was happening and that he was to blame. She said it was because of him that she could never be free.'

'Could she have been talking about Dinesh?'

Indu shook her head. 'It was a familiar name. I just can't remember it.'

'Think.'

'I am. Could be one of her friends here.'

'Advani?' Chupplejeep asked.

'Takshak?' Pankaj tried.

Indu looked up. 'The man with the artist. I remember that name, yes. Subrina had certainly mentioned him. She said he had met her one evening. They must have been friends.'

'Without Advani there?'

Indu nodded.

Pankaj wrote down what she had said in his notepad. It was strange that Takshak would meet Subrina without Advani. He had never shown any affection for the actress.

Indu shrugged. 'But that wasn't who she was talking about. Oh, now it's coming back to me.'

'Yes?'

'The man she was talking about was Runit, no Rohan. No. Rohit. Yes, that was it. Same like my cousin-brother.'

'Are you sure?'

'Positive.' Indu shook her head from side to side, happy with having recalled the information.

'You didn't mention this before.'

'I must have forgotten about it, with everything that happened.'

'Did she say anything else?'

'I don't remember anything else. But she did say that it was this man's fault this was happening.'

'Do you know what *this* was?'

Indu shook her head. 'No. Can I go now?'

Chupplejeep nodded.

'Am I still in trouble? I took the jewels because my father is sick. We need to pay for his medical bills.'

'If we ever catch you stealing again…'

Indu thanked the detective before scurrying out of the room, closing the door behind her.

'Sir, you look worried. You don't think that Indu had anything to do with Subrina Basi's death, do you?'

'No, no, of course not. She just took a chance, that's all. She won't do it again, not now that she knows Hari knows about her behaviour. This man she mentioned bothers me though. Rohit was the name of the brother of the boy Subrina killed. Do you think that name is just a coincidence?'

'Rohit is a popular name, but Chaaya told us that both her grandchildren were dead.'

'Dinesh said Subrina was fixated on her past. Rohit was part of that past. I don't think it's a coincidence.'

'Like the ducks, sir?'

'The ducks?'

'The two ducks that went missing the night Subrina Basi was killed.'

Chupplejeep stood up and shook his head. 'I don't know what goes through your head sometimes. Is there even a brain inside there?' he asked, pointing to Pankaj's skull.

Pankaj looked at his watch. 'It's late. I hadn't finished my interview with Abhik and he will have gone home now.'

'Did you say on the phone earlier that you are waiting for the sub-inspector to call you with information from Abhik's criminal record?'

Pankaj nodded.

'You could go to his house. Interview him there. Or wait for the sub-inspector in Nepal to call and you can carry out your interview better informed. It'll save you having to interview him again. In the meantime I think we need to speak to Chaaya, find out about Rohit. How did you get here?' Chupplejeep asked as they left the hotel room and made their way to the hotel lobby.

'I came here with my scooter.'

'Okay, let's leave it for tonight. Have you looked into the insurance of the hotel I asked you to look into?'

'The report's on my desk. I need to review it.'

Chupplejeep's phone rang. He answered it. 'Keep looking,' he said into the receiver. 'And make enquiries with her friends and family.' He disconnected the call and slipped the phone back into his pocket.

'Ayesha Saxena?'

'They have been to Amboli. They can't find the actress. Her family is worried. Her phone was found in the house. Her sister said it was unlike Ayesha to be parted with her cell. Damn that Gosht for letting Dinesh go.'

Pankaj stopped walked. 'He did what, sir? But what if Dinesh has killed Ayesha Saxena? I'm worried.'

Chupplejeep twisted the end of his moustache. He couldn't help but think of one of Poirot's famous quotes: 'Fear is incomplete knowledge.' He thought about sharing this gem with Pankaj but then thought better of it. Pankaj never understood Poirot at the best of times. 'We don't know for sure that he has killed her. Officers are searching the premises at Amboli with sniffer dogs. We must question Dinesh again.'

'But what about his family? They will have you fired. If they managed to twist Gosht's arm to release their son, how will we be able to investigate this properly?'

'One thing at a time. Let's meet outside Chaaya's house tomorrow at nine.'

'And Dinesh?'

'If he is the killer, we will catch him. It doesn't matter what his family threaten us with.'

'Yes sir!' Pankaj said, with slight apprehension. He started walking in a different direction to Chupplejeep as they left the hotel.

'Now where are you going?'

'There is something I want to check.'

Chupplejeep shook his head and walked towards his car.

~

Pankaj walked up to the pond that at one time housed the two ducks. Long grasses and shrubs surrounded the pond and a large tamarind tree towered over it, the long brown furry casing of the tamarind hanging temptingly above. He saw that the string that held the netting and wire mesh together had been cut.

He looked up towards the rear entrance of the hotel and the shrubs around it. Then he folded his arms across his chest, took a deep breath and made his way back towards his scooter.

CHAPTER THIRTY-SIX

Abhik only managed to greet Officer Pankaj and answer a couple of questions about Dinesh before he was called away on urgent business. For that, Abhik was glad. The chef had hoped Nishok would be arrested after he was questioned earlier, but he wasn't. The gardener had walked back into the kitchen with a wide grin as if someone had just given him a big bowl of pistachio kulfi.

Typical, that Xavier should go to the rescue of the gardener. Everyone loved Nishok despite his ignorant ways. Whereas they had no time for Abhik, even though he made them *momos* and *thukpa* whenever they wanted. Racists, the lot of them. They didn't mind eating Nepalese food, yet he was sure no one would come to his rescue, the way they had done for Nishok.

Abhik opened the fridge and pulled the rubbish bin close behind him. His mind drifted to Subrina Basi. He had always fancied the star, since he watched her first movie. He loved it even though everyone else had said it was hopeless. He knew from *Icon Bites* that Subrina was just like him. Always trying to fit in – never quite succeeding. When he saw her at the Golden Orchid, he couldn't believe his luck. It wasn't often that a chef in a back-end Goan village got a chance to be so close to a celebrity. He had even plucked up the courage to speak to her.

He had approached the actress telling her that he knew of her troubles, that he too faced the same struggles as she, that he understood her. But as he spoke, she had laughed. Laughed at him! He couldn't believe it at first, but as her signature red lips parted and a cackling sound came from her mouth, her black glasses firmly in place, he realised that the actress was nothing but a bitch! He had clenched his fists so tight that his fingernails almost pierced his skin.

He chucked two rotten *brinjals,* aubergines, and bags of coriander into the garbage can.

'I don't like those policemen,' a voice said behind him.

Abhik turned around. It was Indu. She sat on a stool playing with the hem of her dress.

'Especially the one with the moustache. He looks funny with that thing on his face. If I were his wife I would tell him to shave it off.'

Abhik closed the door of the fridge and pulled up another wooden stool to sit opposite her. 'You're not old enough to be that man's wife. What are you, eighteen?'

'Nineteen in May.'

'Anyway, the detective doesn't have a wife, not yet anyway.'

Indu frowned. 'What are you doing? Stalking him?'

'If they're keeping an eye on me, there's no reason why I shouldn't keep an eye on them. Anyway, it looks like what you were worrying about the other day just caught up with you. Your eyes look red. They questioned you? They didn't make you cry, did they?'

'I did something I shouldn't have. They found out. I don't know why I did it in the first place and I don't know why I didn't think the police would find out.'

Abhik stroked his chin. 'Well, you're still here so whatever you did can't be that bad. They didn't arrest you.'

Indu's eyes widened. 'I didn't think of that. Imagine the shame if that had happened. My mother would have disowned me. The whole village would be talking. Do you think they'll tell everyone what I did?'

'Depends what it is?' He waited for a response. When he didn't get one he continued, 'I'm sure it's nothing. The police are many things, but I've checked up on these two fellows. They don't gossip like other police. They are what people call professional.' He gave her a weak smile. The girl was a kid. She wasn't a threat to him. No point in making her feel even worse. Out of all the staff at the Golden Orchid, Abhik thought she was the most genuine. He would even go so far as to say he liked her.

'They are good at detective work from what I've seen. They are thorough, not like these regular village cops. I heard from Xavier they were questioning Nishok about things he did back in the village he used to live in. It seems he too has done some things he is ashamed of.'

'We've all done things that we shouldn't have,' Abhik said. It was true. Everyone had a past. Indu had confessed to doing something she shouldn't have, Nishok used to pilfer food, and Abhik had even caught the watchman stealing liquor from the kitchens before his shift started. But all these were minor offences. And if he thought about it, they didn't really affect anyone. Okay, the Golden Orchid was losing out financially, but the financial loss was negligible and nobody had been physically harmed. No one had even been verbally offended! His own offences were something different though. He had a problem, an inherent problem that he wanted to desperately get rid of, but no matter how much he tried, it was there with him, always.

He first realised he had this problem at school. His teacher was always scolding him for being rowdy and fighting with others at break time. She asked to speak to his mother several times. After his fifth offence, his father found out. He remembered having to endure ten lashings across the backs of his legs with a cane for what he had done. The marks were visible for days afterwards and all his friends had laughed. But still he couldn't control the anger that would swoop down on him even when someone looked at him the wrong way. And as the years went by, he would often come home with a swollen face or grazed knees after fighting with the other boys in school. Eventually his parents got fed up and pulled him out of school altogether. At just twelve, they sent him out to work. It solved their problem. But it didn't solve *his* problem.

When he started working, he found it wasn't just other school children which angered him. Daily, he was irritated and angered by people and even animals. Bouts of rage would catch him, sometimes unexpectedly. He ended up having to move from one village to the next after some fight or other. Then, in the last Nepalese village he stayed in, something dreadful happened and he knew he had no choice but to leave the country altogether.

He should never have done what he did. If only he had thought about it before he picked up the knife, he wouldn't be in this mess. But he couldn't think, not when the red mist was clouding his mind. The two policemen were smart. They knew about Nishok's past. They would soon come for him. They would be making a case against him now in that little police station of theirs.

He didn't have to sit and wait though, he could leave. He could leave right this moment. Nothing was keeping him in Goa. But then he would be running again and he had spent his whole life running. He didn't think he had the energy to run anymore and for the first time in his life, he liked where he was. Perhaps he would just wait and accept his fate, accept responsibility for what he had done. It was about time that he did.

'Abhik, Abhik!' Indu was shouting now, shaking his shoulder.

'Sorry,' Abhik said, freeing himself from his thoughts.

275

'Your mind was far away. What were you thinking? I'm worried about you. You are not yourself these days. Usually you are always telling us off, banging your fists on the table. Now you're so quiet. Even the receptionist, Furtado, noticed and he never notices anything.'

'I'm fine.'

'Good. Because apart from Rosie you are the only friend I have here.'

Abhik smiled. He wasn't going anywhere.

CHAPTER THIRTY-SEVEN

Chupplejeep checked his phone while he waited for Pankaj outside Chaaya's house. There were two messages from Christabel. The first had asked for his opinion on wedding colours. Did he prefer peach or green to go with pink, the colour she had already chosen?

He didn't like pink and he certainly didn't like peach. But pink had been decided. And he knew it was Christabel's favourite colour. Hadn't his friend Joachim said last night, when he popped round to his place to ask him to be his best man, that it was best to let the bride choose all the colours for the wedding? 'Let her pick everything,' Joachim had said. 'Then if something goes wrong she can't blame you.' Chupplejeep liked his friend's way of thinking, but every time he thought about his impending wedding he felt a little nauseated.

Chupplejeep pressed reply and typed the word 'green' into the message box. He hit send. Then he read Christabel's second message, asking if he had spoken to Joachim about the band. Organising the band was the one thing Christabel had tasked him with. He would normally have left arranging the band till the last minute, but given that the front man of the band was Joachim's nephew, the first duty he had given his best man was to sort out the music. 'The 29th?' Joachim had asked when Chupplejeep told him the date, as he slapped him on his back. 'Of February? Oh, how unlucky! You must have got it cheap. Did a moth fly out of your wallet when you opened it to pay the deposit?'

'Yes,' Chupplejeep had said. 'Get all your jokes out of your system now. Because believe me I've heard them all.'

'Okay, okay. Chill *rae baba*. I'm just saying, no. I'll tell my nephew to keep the date free. First dance?'

Chupplejeep hesitated, his hands beginning to sweat. 'Err, of course, we'll have a first dance.'

'What's your song?' Joachim asked.

Chupplejeep was desperate for the conversation about the wedding to end. Why couldn't they talk about cricket? The number of runs Dhawan achieved at the last match? He felt a little light-headed thinking of wedding songs. He hadn't expected these difficult questions so he wasn't prepared with any answers and didn't have a clue as to what Christabel was thinking. He imagined he felt like how his suspects did when he questioned them. He had no idea what *their* song was. Was it something they had first danced together to? Would Christabel expect him to remember the song? He tried to remember some slow numbers. The first that came to mind was Phil Collins's 'Sacrifice'. But that was hardly a first dance song, was it? Although Chupplejeep thought the song was quite apt. Marriage was a sacrifice, wasn't it? One long sacrifice.

'You sly dog!' Joachim said. 'You're keeping it to yourself. Okay, be like that. But you'll have to tell me soon, no? I'll have to see if my nephew's band can play it. But don't worry, for you, if it's something they don't know then I'll make them learn it.'

Chupplejeep was relieved when Joachim's wife called out to him because their daughter was refusing to go to sleep. He saw his opportunity to leave and took it.

Now he looked at his phone. He had an idea. He started typing a message to his fiancée. *Spoke 2 Joachim. Band sorted. First dance?*

Perfect, he thought as he hit send. Now he wouldn't have to worry about Christabel asking him and she couldn't call him…what was the usual word she reserved for him…reactive. Yes, she couldn't call him reactive. Chupplejeep slipped the mobile phone back into his pocket, satisfied with himself. He looked up at the mint-green bungalow. The house was silent and he wondered if anyone was home. Or if they were, perhaps they were still asleep. He looked at his watch. It was almost nine. It was rare for people to get up late in the villages. They were used to working hard without the luxury of waking up past ten like some of the rich folk.

The village was quiet too, just an egret making a *kraa-kraa* sound in the distance. Chupplejeep watched the house until he saw some movement. Chaaya's son, Balbir, appeared on the veranda. The bald man with his hunched back squatted near the wooden railings and started rubbing a piece of paper along the grain of a single balustrade. Chupplejeep opened the metal gate and started walking towards the man. As he approached, he was struck by just how sad Balbir looked. But of course the man was sad. He had lost two sons and a wife.

'It takes time to sand down a balcony,' Chupplejeep said.

Balbir kept his eyes on his task. He simply nodded.

'Is your mother here?'

He carried on sanding down the wood. Chupplejeep noticed just how chapped the old man's hands were. 'You enjoy your work?'

Balbir nodded and then looked up. His smile froze and then suddenly he beamed. He dropped his sandpaper and the reached his hand past the detective. 'Son,' he said. 'You've come back.'

Chupplejeep instinctively looked behind him, hoping to see Rohit, but instead Pankaj stood there.

'Balbir, you are mistaken,' Pankaj said. 'I am Police Officer...'

Chupplejeep raised his hand to stop Pankaj from saying anything further.

Balbir walked up to the officer and put his hand on his cheek. 'Boy, I've missed you, but I'm glad you're back.'

'Err...well, sir...I've miss...err...How have you been?'

'Son, my back, it hurts me. Do you have something for my back? You never let me suffer. I remember that.'

Pankaj looked at Chupplejeep and raised his shoulders as if to ask, *'Now what?'*

'You miss your son?' Chupplejeep asked.

'Every day, I miss Nitin. But this one, I see him occasionally. I wish he lived here with me and ma,' Balbir took a step closer to the detective and whispered, 'but she won't have him here.'

'I see,' Chupplejeep said. 'Why is that?'

'Because of what he did. But you cannot blame him, no?'

'What did he do?'

'My son is very clever. We paid for him to go to English-speaking school. He was good boy. He didn't waste his education. You know some boys are not good. They are being educated and do nothing with their lives. They are sitting at home all day getting fat, waiting for bride to come with dowry. Not my son. He used his education. Now he solves everyone's problems. He is a magician.'

'You must be very proud. Does he live nearby?'

'Ma won't let him live here because of her.'

'Who?'

'The child.'

'Which one?'

'The other one.'

Chupplejeep glanced at Pankaj, but he looked as confused as the detective.

'Tell me where do you see your son. Does he come to the house?'

'My son is here,' Balbir said. He put his arm around Pankaj's waist.

'This is not your son, Rohit,' Chupplejeep said. 'This is a police officer.'

Balbir shook his head. 'This is my Rohit. They took my other son. They cannot take this one. He is rich and clever.'

'Who is rich and clever?' a woman said.

Chupplejeep and Pankaj looked up. Balbir immediately let his arm drop from Pankaj's waist.

It was Chaaya. She emerged from the house with her fists clenched, her thin top lip curled up like a snarling dog. 'I thought I told you never to come here again. Get out of my house. Look at you, trying to get information from my Balbir. He's not in his right mind. You know that and still you question him. Is this a game to you, Detective? Are you hoping for some kind of promotion for catching the murderer of Subrina Basi? Well, I for one hope the murderer is never found. That woman got what she deserved. The person who killed her is a saint in my eyes. What goes around comes around, na?'

'We are still investigating her death. We have some questions to ask.'

'So ask me! Don't you ask my son. He cannot think straight. What do you want to know?'

'We want to find out more about your grandson.'

'Nitin? What more is there to say? He died at the age of two when that witch took his life.'

'Not Nitin.'

Chaaya narrowed her eyes. 'Rohit? What do you want with my other grandson? He is no business of yours.'

'You said last time that Rohit was dead. But we can't find any records of his death. Can I ask you how he died?'

'I-it was…you cops don't know anything. Why should I tell you how he died?'

'We're not going to drop this matter until we get to the bottom of this.'

Chaaya crossed her arms across her chest. 'He took an overdose.'

Balbir started to cry.

'Happy?' Chaaya pointed up to the sky. 'Since Nitin died a black cloud has stayed over this house. I have lost everyone close to me. Even my own son doesn't know my name most days and still you have the courage to question him in my absence. You police will stop at nothing to get your medals. You come here looking for answers, but you'll find none. I'll say this one final time, Detective – both my grandsons are dead.'

And with that Chaaya took Balbir by the hand and marched him into the house, slamming the front door, leaving Chupplejeep and Pankaj on the veranda in a cloud of dust.

CHAPTER THIRTY-EIGHT

The taverna in Dhesera was attached to somebody's house. Half the building was painted bright yellow, the other was painted with the Bacardi bat and a bottle of the rum on an off-white background. Chupplejeep considered how many villagers in Dhesera could afford to drink Bacardi. Surely, all of them drank the cheaper and local alternative, Old Monk. He wondered if these marketing people working for multi-national companies had any brains at all.

'Two Limcas,' he said to the barman and then joined Pankaj at a wooden table in the corner of the bar. The taverna was surprisingly busy at ten in the morning. Most people in the bar were labourers drinking hot tea and eating chapattis, no doubt taking a break from the mid-morning sun.

When their drinks arrived, the detective took a large swig of the sugary lemon drink. 'I came here last night,' Chupplejeep said.

'With Christabel?'

Chupplejeep shook his head. 'We need to know more about this accident that happened twenty years ago. So I thought I would ask around.'

'And?' Pankaj looked expectantly at his boss.

'There was talk amongst the villagers of a farmer who goes by the name of Mario. He was friends with Subrina twenty-odd years ago. He knew her at the time of the accident.'

'Subrina friends with a farmer? Never!'

'Not a single fellow in here last night could deny it. A retired school teacher said that he would arrange a meeting between Mario and me today.' Chupplejeep looked at his watch. 'He is due to meet me here in a couple of hours.'

'This could be the breakthrough we need,' Pankaj said.

'It could be. So, tell me, what have you found out about the Golden Orchid?' Chupplejeep looked around the bar. No one seemed bothered by their presence. A man in a red and blue checked shirt and white *lengha* on the table closest to them looked more concerned with the consistency of his *conjee* than with them.

Pankaj pulled a folder out of his bag. 'They're clean, sir. I looked into the ownership of the building. There is no insurance policy for anything like this.'

'So even if the hotel makes a loss because of this death, no claim can be made?'

'Correct, sir.'

'What else have you got?'

285

'There was no insurance policy on Subrina Basi either.'

'Really?'

Pankaj shook his head. 'She was young, sir. She didn't have any children so there was no need for a life insurance policy.'

'Dollywood didn't make her take out a policy to protect themselves?'

'No one benefits financially from her death.'

'Will?'

'No will, sir. Her divorces were legal, so her family will get any money she has. Her parents were in Delhi and they're too old to do something like this for money. And her parents have more money then their daughter, so there is no motive there.'

'Does her sister Suki stand to gain anything?'

'Not a penny.'

'Ex-husbands?'

'Both happily married and not in Goa at the time of Subrina's death.'

'So we can rule out money as a motive.'

'Well, there is the question of Advani and his place at Malabar Hill.'

'Dinesh suggested that Advani killed Subrina because she refused him a place at the gallery.'

'Sir, I can't imagine the artist killing Subrina because of that. He wouldn't want to get his *jootis* dirty.'

'No. And I spoke to the chair of the board at Malabar Hill. They were against the artist staying on, not Subrina. Subrina could have put in a good word for him so he needed her alive. Plus, he doesn't strike me as a cold-blooded killer.'

'Maybe Takshak did it of his own accord.'

'He had access to the insulin, but what is his motive?'

'He cares for Advani a great deal. He didn't want to see his boss suffer by losing his place at Malabar Hill, so he went to speak to her, we know that already from Indu, and he killed her because she didn't listen.'

'But this murder was well thought-out. It was planned, not a spur of the moment thing and someone had to know that she had a beauty spot on her behind.'

'Takshak could have known that. He may have seen her when she was posing for Advani when he painted her.'

'Then there is the note in Subrina's phone,' Chupplejeep said.

'Oh yes, I had forgotten that, sir. Be careful of the Cobra. Cobra with a capital C. Who is the Cobra?'

'A friend, a lover. Clearly someone dangerous,' Chupplejeep said, taking a handful of nuts from the little metal bowl on the table.

'Kulkarni said he got the impression that she was laughing at this reminder she made herself.'

'I've seen the note. I don't know how he got that impression just from one exclamation mark. Wait a minute…' Chupplejeep said.

'What?'

'Oh bloody hell, why didn't I realise before!'

'What?' Pankaj asked.

'Takshak – his name is the clue. Think about it.'

'I'm not following, sir.'

'In Bengali, Punjabi, even in Tamil, Takshak means cobra. The capital C makes sense because she is referring to a name. How could Kulkarni have missed that? The man is from Tamil!'

'I see, sir. You're right.'

'Of course I'm right. Remember how we found Subrina's body. She had her bright red lipstick on and her dark glasses. She didn't do that herself.'

Pankaj bit his lower lip. 'Someone made her up. Like an artist would.'

'Indu said Subrina had met him a few days before her death. Why? What reason did she have to meet him? Advani doesn't remember much when he drinks – he admitted as much. Takshak could have snuck out of the gallery that night when he was sleeping. We know Advani was drunk, but Takshak doesn't drink much because he is diabetic.'

'It's possible,' Pankaj said. 'But it is possible that Advani knew? He has a secret, one he has taken great care to conceal. Perhaps the secret is that he murdered Subrina.'

'You've changed your mind very quickly. Just now you said Advani didn't want to get his slippers soiled. Now you say he did it.'

'You told me that sometimes a gut instinct is not always right if there is no other evidence to suggest it is. I thought this was a suicide at first remember, sir.'

Detective Chupplejeep smiled. 'Advani came to you with the case of blackmail before Subrina was murdered.'

He playfully hit the police officer on his forehead. 'You must get him to tell you just what exactly his secret is.'

Pankaj nodded. 'I'll try again.'

'Are Takshak or Advani's prints on the knife used to slit Subrina's wrists?'

Pankaj shook his head.

'They could have been wearing gloves. But there is still one set of unidentified prints.'

'If only we knew who the last set belonged to, sir. It would make life easier.'

'What about the staff on our suspect list? We've discovered Indu is nothing but a petty thief.'

'So is Nishok. His prints are all over the knife used to slit Subrina's wrists because he had used the knife to cut the fish heads to take home.'

'A fish scale was found in the bath with Subrina's body, so that fits. He was seen leaving the hotel at four in the morning though. Maybe he cut the fish heads and then later went to kill Subrina Basi. That is a possibility. Otherwise why was he at the hotel that morning?'

'I know why.'

'Why?'

'The ducks.'

'Again with the ducks?'

'Remember when we first attended the crime scene, Hari told you that nothing was out of the ordinary except that two ducks went missing the same night that Subrina Basi was killed.'

Chupplejeep scratched his head. 'I remember.'

'Nishok is an animal lover. Even Abhik told me when I first asked him about his missing knife. He said that Nishok loves animals more than humans and that he often took a knife to free a trapped animal that may have got caught in the grounds. He didn't like seeing the ducks kept in such a small pond, with netting all around it. So he returned that morning to free the ducks.'

'And he did this at night when no one would see him?'

'He was just unfortunate that the same night he chose to free the birds, was the same night Subrina Basi was killed. Xavier told me that Nishok suffers from insomnia. The idea came to him and he decided to act on it. He used a different knife but he did say that he put the knife used to slit Subrina's wrists back in the drawer after he took the fish heads. So someone must have taken it from the kitchen. Abhik had access.'

'Anyone could gain access to that kitchen. Security that night, or any other night for that matter, is weak and the watchman is a drunk.'

The man in the checked shirt and *lengha* turned around, looked at Chupplejeep and Pankaj, and smiled before turning back. Chupplejeep took a sip of his drink. Was this fellow listening to their conversation? Everyone's ears seemed to prick up with the mention of the deceased actress. Of course Bonaparte was patiently waiting for his scoop. Murder always shifted newspapers. The journalist called Chupplejeep at least once a day to check on progress. Sometimes, Chupplejeep didn't answer his phone when he saw Bonaparte's number flash on his mobile screen, but recently he had been calling from different numbers.

'I think that farmer is laughing about Nishok freeing the ducks.'

'How do you know he's a farmer?' Chupplejeep asked.

'Look at the blisters on his hands.'

'I see.'

'That's from hand harvesting the rice plants. It's an odd thing for Nishok to do, isn't it?'

Chupplejeep looked at the man in the *lengha*. Was this Mario? Or was he just a nosy villager? Chupplejeep looked at his watch. It was still early. He was told last night that Mario knew his face and would approach him. It couldn't be his man. He looked towards a quiet table at the back of the taverna. Then he stood up and took his drink with him. Pankaj followed. 'That's better. He won't be able to eavesdrop here. Now back to Nishok. The man felt sorry for the ducks. If you felt sorry for something in a cage, you too would want to set it free.'

'I suppose. It's just that the man is stealing food and he has to kill the chickens they eat at the hotel.'

'Sometimes you have to do something for a job, and killing a chicken is not the same as watching something suffer daily.'

'He could have stolen the ducks to eat?'

'You think Nishok is lying?'

'No, I don't. I think the man is simple, that's all.'

'Sometimes it is better to be simple. And you've told me about Furtado, Xavier, Hari and Rosie?'

'Yes. They have alibis and none have motive for the murder.'

'The watchman?'

'Same. And I'm still waiting to hear back from the Nepalese police about Abhik's previous crime.'

'Do you think it could be him?'

'The other staff at the hotel don't like him much. Xavier wasn't keen to give him a character reference. I wouldn't trust him. He looks angry and suspicious.'

'And his fingerprints were on the knife.'

'When I asked him why he laughed. Said he was the chef after all, what did I expect?'

'From what you told me, he's a very organised fellow. Everything has a place and yet he said that he didn't notice that a knife had gone missing. He's a liar, so what else is he hiding from us? And what's his motive?'

Pankaj and Chupplejeep were silent for a moment.

'Love,' Pankaj finally said. 'He has no wife that we know of. He could have been in love with Subrina Basi. Xavier said that Abhik had a crush on the actress. Perhaps he worshiped her from afar and he could have told her of his love when he saw her. Xavier said Subrina was particularly rude to Abhik when he tried speaking to her. He may have seen that as rejection. Some men can't take rejection. Perhaps he thought if he couldn't have her than no one else could. So he killed her.'

'Let's see what the Nepalese police have to say about Abhik. And we already established no other guests staying at the hotel had any motive.'

Pankaj nodded. 'Dinesh is the most likely candidate, sir. He had used his fists on Subrina before so he has form. His temper could have got the better of him. It's likely he was fed up of her and so planned her death. Now Ayesha Saxena is missing. He could have killed her too, but this time buried the body.'

It wasn't only Bonaparte's questions which had been making the detective weary. Inspector General Gosht was calling daily as well, still angry that Dinesh had been arrested despite the fact that they were unable to locate Ayesha Saxena.

Chupplejeep pointed out to Gosht that Dinesh was the last to see both Subrina and Ayesha alive. The same fate Subrina suffered could have happened to Ayesha. But Gosht wouldn't hear any of it. Instead, the Inspector General threatened him. 'This reflects badly on me!' he had snapped at Chupplejeep only yesterday. 'First you wrongfully arrest the son of an MLA and then you fail to arrest anyone else. If this case is not solved quickly there will be a price to pay. Chupplejeep, I'm warning you. It'll be a hefty price to pay indeed.'

'We're getting close,' Chupplejeep had responded but Gosht ignored him, instead reminding him of Dinesh's threats. He would be fired and would never be able to work as a detective in Goa again. Not even a sub-inspector, Gosht had confirmed.

'Subrina was injected with insulin and then her wrists were slit. It was pre-meditated,' Chupplejeep said. 'Dinesh has opportunity and motive. There was no forced entry into the room. Subrina knew her attacker.

And Dinesh had time from when he was last seen with her, just after one, to kill Subrina and then put her makeup on before he left at two-thirty. Dinesh is used to getting his way,' he added. 'He wants to have his cake and eat it. And if murder was the only option to enable him to go have a relationship with Ayesha Saxena, then maybe he took it. Have you heard from Kulkarni's man about the insulin records from the pharmacies he has been checking?'

'I've received a list. Nothing suspicious as yet, sir.'

They had to find the evidence that would tie Dinesh to Subrina's death. They had to link him to the insulin. They hadn't found any empty vials in Dinesh's possessions or at the crime scene, so he had either taken the syringe and vial back to Bombay with him, or buried it well. But it was unlikely to be the latter. The hotel grounds had been searched and no freshly dug areas had been spotted. The Delhi and Bombay police had returned nothing on pharmacies issuing or selling the product to Dinesh or any of his known contacts. At the moment, only Takshak seemed to be the likely source.

The detective rubbed his forehead. Takshak was another unknown quantity. There were too many unanswered questions. They needed to find Ayesha Saxena. He was certain that when they did, they would find the answer they were looking for.

CHAPTER THIRTY-NINE

The taverna was filling up now. Labourers at the bar were ordering Kingfisher beer and *choris pao,* sausage bread. Outside, the sun was beating down on the green paddy fields and coconut trees. Bullock carts were kicking up clouds of red dust as they passed.

'Chaaya's hiding something,' Pankaj said. 'Both times we visited her house she made sure we didn't talk to her son, Balbir. Do you think she could have something to do with Subrina's death?'

'She's old.'

'That's not an alibi. We both know these grannies can be a lot younger than they look. They marry young in the villages. They have a hard life. It ages them, but often they are full of strength.'

Chupplejeep smiled at his protégé. He was learning quickly. 'Perhaps Chaaya and Balbir were in it together. And his forgetfulness is just an act.'

Pankaj leaned back in his chair. 'I never thought of that, sir. He looked so sad. But you're right. He lost his son and his wife because of Subrina Basi. And perhaps Rohit too took an overdose because he had lost his mother and brother. He was the one who saw his brother die. He saw Subrina Basi run his brother over. How do you recover from something like that? Living with that image must have been unbearable. Chaaya and Balbir certainly have the motive. They have the opportunity also. They have not come forward with an alibi.'

The man in the checked shirt had moved closer to where they were sitting. Now he shifted in his chair. Chupplejeep eyed him with suspicion. 'This could be my guy,' he whispered to Pankaj.

Just as Chupplejeep was about to stand up and approach him, the man in the checked shirt stood up, took his newspaper from the table and left the bar. Chupplejeep and Pankaj exchanged glances then Chupplejeep ordered another two Limcas, a plate of beef croquettes and some prawn rissoles. That would keep his hunger at bay.

He noticed the makeshift tinsel behind the bar and realised he hadn't yet decided what he was going to get Christabel or her mother for Christmas. He would get something for Pankaj too. With a murder to solve and all the talk of the wedding, he hadn't had the time. But he had to give Christabel something on Christmas Day. She would never forgive him. He wondered if she would call the wedding off.

'Chaaya never said why Rohit killed himself. But witnessing the death of his brother, coming home to find his mother dead and then seeing his father lose his mind could have all been too much for him. If he was twelve at the time of Nitin's death he would be thirty-two now. Balbir said he was educated. Said he's a magician, solving other's problems.'

'You think he really is a magician?' Pankaj asked.

Chupplejeep shook his head. 'A therapist or a lawyer perhaps. Maybe a doctor.'

'But Balbir thought I was Rohit. Can we really believe what he says?'

'And why can't we find out anything about Rohit's death? Nothing reported. Nothing registered.'

'Maybe he's missing in another country.'

Chupplejeep scratched his head. 'Indu overheard Subrina on her phone saying she blamed Rohit. She said, because of Rohit she would never be free.'

'But who was she talking to?'

'I think I have an idea. Did you cross-check her phone records?'

Pankaj looked up. 'I'll check them today.'

Chupplejeep rolled his eyes. It should have been done as soon as knew they were investigating a homicide. 'We need to know more about Rohit.'

'Sir, this is Goa,' Pankaj said.

'Your point?'

'Village life! People don't just disappear in villages like they do in big cities. Everybody knows everybody's business whether they live here or not. If I had failed my Police Training College exams, my neighbours would have found out before I knew. When my uncle's cousin's brother was caught stealing from the local cart, my mother knew before his mother knew. In the villages good news travels fast, bad news travels even faster. If Rohit killed himself, someone in this village will know about it.'

Chupplejeep thought about this. Even Poirot had once said, 'Everybody always knows something.' The detective twisted the ends of his moustache. Perhaps he didn't look like Poirot, but he certainly was beginning to think like him. 'Bonaparte said Rohit was dead also. There must have been talk at the time of his death.'

Both Pankaj and Chupplejeep were silent for a moment as they thought about this. 'Then there is Suki.'

'Suki? Sir, she had an alibi and no motive.'

'Sister Perpetua was quite clear in telling me that Suki was meeting someone regularly at night.'

'Who?'

'She didn't know. But she said that Suki's behaviour, especially in the run-up to Subrina's death, was peculiar. Her gut feeling was that Suki no longer believed in her faith. She thought Suki was going to leave the convent.'

'Thought?'

'Well, later when she came to know about Suki meeting her sister after all that time, she thought that Suki was just unsettled by her sister's return.'

'Suki confided in her about her sister's visit?'

'No. She overhead Suki telling Sister Carmina.'

'The one who's taken a vow of silence?'

'The very one. Suki wanted to tell someone but she didn't want any rumours to spread, so she told the one person who could keep her secret.'

'She didn't realise Sister Perpetua was eavesdropping?'

Chupplejeep nodded.

'So how was Suki behaving?'

'She started tapping things.'

'I don't understand.'

'Counting and tapping. Before and after she did things, she would tap the back of a chair or a table three times, sometimes her head.'

'That's odd.'

'It can be a compulsion brought on due to stress or anxiety,' Chupplejeep said.

'So, she was stressed about the meeting with her sister.'

'Yes, but why? Either she was worried about something to do with her sister or maybe it was brought on by her anxiety of wanting to leave the church, like Sister Perpetua thought. Either way Sister Perpetua said she had the same peculiar behaviour when she joined the church, soon after Nitin's death, which is curious. Sister Perpetua also said that Suki started looking behind her regularly when she walked, when she prayed, even when she ate, like she thought someone was following her.'

'Sir, you might be onto something.'

'I think it's odd that the sisters met only days before Subrina was found dead.'

'You don't believe in coincidences.'

'I think the conversation Indu heard was Subrina talking to Suki about Rohit,' Chupplejeep said.

'Why's that?'

'Well, Indu said she heard Subrina begging someone to meet with her. We now know that was Suki and not Dinesh because Suki confirmed this. Tell me, if you are a nun, why would you not want to forgive and forget your own flesh and blood? Why then did Subrina have to beg her sister to meet with her?'

'Because she saw Subrina kill baby Nitin and get away with it. Suki had joined a convent to get away from her sister. Subrina had been the one to force her to go out that night. She was only seventeen.'

'After Subrina and Suki met, Suki was distressed and started her tapping. Subrina was upset as well, upset about Rohit. When I spoke to Suki she said they didn't talk about anything of interest, but something tells me she's lying. They talked about the day Nitin died, the day Rohit watched Subrina Basi kill his brother. Suki may have an alibi, she may not be the murderer, but there is a link here somewhere. There has to be.'

CHAPTER FORTY

The drinks and snacks arrived and while they ate, Pankaj and Chupplejeep put the case to the back of their minds. Pankaj bit into a crumbed beef croquette. 'I haven't eaten one of these in years.'

'Your mother doesn't make them anymore?'

Pankaj shook his head. The taste of the cumin and the chilli with the beef made his mouth water as he ate.

'Why not?'

Pankaj took a swig of Limca before replying. 'I don't know, but I'll certainly ask her to start making these again.'

'She should start making Goan snacks. Soon she will have to impress Shwetika's parents, no?' Chupplejeep said with a grin.

Pankaj fidgeted in his chair.

'How many times have you messaged or called Shwetty since your big date?'

'She prefers messages. She can message me without her parents finding out.'

'So you're a long way off from telling her parents,' Chupplejeep said, watching as people walked into the taverna.

Pankaj nodded.

'But you've invited her for your friend's wedding, haven't you?'

'I have. But we are not *that* friendly yet. I think she wants to play it cool.'

'Ah, so she is playing that game, is she?'

'Sir, there is no game with Shwetty. She just wants to date for a while first before we make any serious commitment.'

'A modern girl.'

'I suppose,' Pankaj said, picking up a prawn rissole.

'But you're not a modern man?'

'I know she's the one. We've only just met. But I just know it.'

'We're different, you and me. Look how long it took me to get engaged and even now I'm...Never mind. I think Shwetty has the right idea. What's the rush? You have the rest of your lives together.'

'I know,' Pankaj said, looking at his plate. 'That much is true. I certainly don't want any pressure from her parents yet.'

Chupplejeep held the bottle of Limca to his lips. 'I think Shwetika will do you the world of good.'

'So what do we do now, sir?'

Chupplejeep wiped his fingers on a paper napkin. 'You're going to check Subrina's phone records. Look for any calls made to the Verna area. And call the police in Amboli again, and Saxena's family and friends – see if there is any news on Ayesha Saxena's whereabouts. Since they couldn't find her at the house Dinesh claimed she was staying at, her family are a little spooked. Let's not take our eye off the ball on this one. If Dinesh had something to do with her disappearance, I want to be the first to know.'

Pankaj nodded. 'Are you worried that Dinesh's family is going to come after you?' Dinesh's family would not let his arrest go unpunished. Pankaj knew that the son of an MLA had enough power to get Chupplejeep fired and he couldn't imagine working with anyone else. He silently prayed that they would soon be able to link Dinesh to the crime with enough evidence for a conviction or that the family would forget about the arrest. The latter, he knew, was unlikely.

'I want you to check the pharmacies in Larara and any local villages around here that have a pharmacy,' Chupplejeep said.

'There is one between Dhesera and Suuj.'

'You mean Kulkarni's guy didn't start his search there?'

'Apparently not.'

'That should have been first on his list. Yes, check that one. See if anyone bought insulin without a prescription recently. See if anyone matching Dinesh's description was seen at the store.'

'But sir, it's so simple to get prescription drugs here without the right papers. And if you were cunning you would go to Panaji, Mapusa or Margao to get your drugs.

You wouldn't just go to the closest one. Dinesh could have got the drug from any pharmacy in Bombay or he could have paid someone to get it on his behalf. Linking him to the insulin is going to be difficult.'

Chupplejeep made a face. 'Just check them.'

~

Chupplejeep scanned the bar again. 'I'm going to ask around about Rohit,' he said. He looked up and saw the farmer from earlier propped up against the bar. The one wearing the *lengha* and the blue and red checked shirt who had been eavesdropping on their conversation. When he caught the man's eye, the farmer quickly looked away.

Pankaj's phone began to vibrate in his top pocket. He pulled out the telephone and answered the call. Suddenly his eyes lit up.

'What is it?' Chupplejeep asked.

Pankaj put his fingers over the mouthpiece of his mobile. 'It's the sub-inspector from Nepal,' he whispered. 'Yes, yes I'm listening,' he said, removing his fingers from the phone and speaking into it. 'So can you tell me what crime Abhik committed in Nepal before he left?'

Chupplejeep leaned in closer.

'Tell me,' Pankaj said.

Chupplejeep watched as the colour drained from Pankaj's face. 'What?' he mouthed.

This time Pankaj didn't bother to cover the mouthpiece. 'Murder,' he said. Pankaj stood up, his ear glued to the phone as he walked out of the bar.

If Abhik had killed before, he could do it again. If he had worshiped Subrina from afar and she had snubbed him, perhaps it was enough to drive him over the edge. Chupplejeep looked at his watch. It was now well past the time that the farmer was supposed to meet him. He sighed. Perhaps last night had been a waste of his time. He reached into his back pocket and pulled out his wallet. He put two one-hundred rupee notes on the table and was about to stand up when the man with the checked shirt sat down at his table.

'Can I help you?' Chupplejeep asked.

'I think I can be helping you,' the man replied.

CHAPTER FORTY-ONE

'So you are Mario. You knew Subrina when you were young?' Chupplejeep asked.

'You're checking because I'm a farmer and she was actress?'

Chupplejeep shook his head. 'They told me last night that you two were friends.'

'My talking was better. Means, I knew to speak properly, but now no practice.'

Chupplejeep nodded. 'So what can you tell me?'

'I heard you talking,' Mario said.

'I gathered that earlier.'

'I was checking. Means, I wanted to know if I could trust you. I think I can. So I'm telling you what I know.'

'How old were you then?'

'I'm knowing Subrina since sixteen. She was same age. A sweet and kind girl.'

'Different from the woman everyone has described.'

The farmer shook his head.

'When was the last time you spoke to her?'

'Long time back. I've met many people in my life. Some good, some bad. She was good inside. Good at sixteen, means, good today.'

'Okay, what information do you have for me?'

'Firstly, Subrina was good woman. She was my friend even though I'm a farmer. She made sweets for my family. She even ate at our table. No hang-ups like her sister. Her sister was, how you call it, with her nose in the air. Always looking down on us.'

'A snob?'

'If you say so.'

'Her sister was shy too,' Chupplejeep said.

'Her sister was quiet, yes. I never knew Suki. Subrina was the one I knew. Means, she could talk to me. And she did. She told me about boys she liked, her friends at school, she even told me about her family. They were a close family. But her father was strict. Means, he wasn't taking any nonsense. Bullied the young one, Suki. He would get so angry with them if they were doing anything wrong. But he loved them also. Otherwise he would never have done what he did.'

'What did he do?'

'He paid off that boy's family when Nitin was killed. Poor Subrina. She was broken after that day.'

'She had been drinking that night?'

'She was drinking too much back then. My mother would never have allowed me to drink like that. But Subrina only drank because she wanted to have a good time. And she always wanted to be an actress. Her daddy was against all that. But I'm glad she got to be what she wanted before she died. Subrina was full of life and she was smart. She never studied but always got first-class results. But her father was strict. Sometimes I would find her at the back of her house crying and crying, because her father wouldn't let her go out. But as she got older she started standing up to him. They realised,' the farmer said with a smile, 'they had no choice. Means, they had to either kick her out of the house or let her go out. Subrina wasn't one to listen to rules and her mummy and daddy didn't want to lose her.'

'She got her way.'

'She was happier then. But her sister was smaller than Subrina and quiet. Means, she didn't stand up for herself. Subrina would protect her like a mother.'

Chupplejeep leaned in closer to hear what Mario was saying. 'A mother?'

'Yes. Their mother was only there in body. She didn't care for her children. Subrina would often stand up for Suki when their mother didn't.'

'He hit the girls?'

'Not like that. His, how you say? His bark was worse than his bite. He had this look of thunder, used to shout at them all the time. The younger one was so scared of his shouts. Once Subrina told me Suki failed in maths and she was so scared to show her father her report card she wanted to run away from home. Subrina took the report card and changed all the marks so it looked like Suki had passed. Their father accepted the marks, no questions. How she laughed when she told me. I never went to school after my fourth standard. I'm an uneducated fellow, but still Subrina was my friend for years,' the farmer said fondly.

Chupplejeep leaned back. If what Mario was saying was true then why did Subrina and Suki fall out? And why did Subrina have to beg to see her sister? He wasn't going to get an answer from the dead actress and Suki certainly didn't want to talk about her relationship with her sister. But before he could pose his question, the farmer started talking again. Chupplejeep caught the bartender's eye and ordered Mario a drink.

'So that is my first point. Subrina was a good person. My second point is this.'

'What?'

'What do you know about Chaaya?'

Chupplejeep raised his eyebrows.

'You think both Chaaya's grandchildren are dead.'

'Yes.'

'You know how Nitin died?'

'Yes, the car accident.'

'Let me guess,' Mario said. 'Chaaya is saying that Rohit is also dead.'

'Yes.'

'She's correct and she's not correct also.'

'I'm not following you.'

'Rohit is dead in Chaaya's eyes. Means, in actual fact he is very much alive.'

'Alive?'

'I saw him just the other day, walking back from his workplace.'

'He works here in Dhesera?'

Mario nodded.

Chupplejeep thought of poor old Balbir confusing Pankaj with his son. He had felt sorry for the man and his delusions, but perhaps the old man wasn't so deluded after all when he said he saw his son occasionally. 'Why would Chaaya say Rohit was dead? He's her only remaining grandchild.'

'Because like I said, he's dead in her eyes.'

'He must have done something fairly horrific for her to disown a grown man.'

'Oh yes.'

'What did he do?'

The farmer smiled. 'I'll tell you.'

CHAPTER FORTY-TWO

Pankaj's mind was reeling after what the Nepalese sub-inspector told him about Abhik. He wanted to tell Chupplejeep straight away but his boss was deep in conversation with a farmer. Instead he decided to return to the office.

He felt sick to the stomach just thinking about what he had heard. So Abhik had committed a felony and was a wanted man. What was it like to be a man on the run?

As Chupplejeep had instructed, on his way to the office he visited the pharmacy between Dhesera and Suuj and enquired about the sale of insulin over the last month. A slender man, who matched him in height and build with glasses and thick black hair, told him that only two regular customers suffering with diabetes had purchased the drug.

Pankaj thanked the man for his time and turned to walk away, but at the entrance of the store something made him stop and turn around. 'Can I see the purchase ledger for the drug?' he asked.

His own words took him by surprise. But he was glad he asked the question because it was at this point

311

that the man, who claimed to be the proprietor, became flustered. He adjusted his glasses and his eyes darted here and there before he disappeared into the back room. Ten minutes later, he came out with a ledger showing that a quantity of the drug had been purchased – U-500, or 500 units of insulin per millilitre of fluid to be exact. Pankaj didn't know much about the drug but from a quick look online, he knew this was enough to send someone into a hypoglycaemic coma. The dosage was much higher than what Takshak had in his individual vials stored in the gallery. Pankaj studied the book and noticed that on the previous page, the same quantity of the drug had been ordered with a later date than the order on the last page. He queried this with the pharmacist.

'Oh, I missed a page by mistake,' the man responded with some confidence. 'It happens with these books. The pages get stuck together with the damp and the weather. I suppose I must get a better brand of book. I've only recently bought this place,' he said, looking around him. 'I'm still learning.'

'You're not from here?'

'I'm Goan, but I've been living in Bombay.'

'Family here?'

The pharmacist shrugged.

Pankaj accepted the answer about the purchase ledger, but it didn't sit well with him. In fact, he felt quite uncomfortable. He would need to discuss the matter with his boss and perhaps do a bit more digging around.

Pankaj parked his scooter and heard someone call out to him. 'Good, you're here. I want an update on my case.'

The police officer took a deep breath. Advani and his blackmail case. He had been so absorbed with Subrina Basi's murder, he had almost forgotten the artist's dilemma.

'Let me make some chai first,' he said, trying to bide some time while he thought about his response. He opened the office and Advani followed him in.

'What the hell? I don't want any tea. Don't try and blindside me with your sugary tea. I know you cops are all the same. You think tea will solve everything. That's why this state is going to pot. Remind me never to come to this state again. I have a serious fucking problem here and what have you done? Nothing. Christmas Eve is almost here or did you miss the memo? There were three children Christmas-carolling outside my window last night.'

Pankaj leaned forward. 'Memo?'

'Fucking hell. Not literally. Oh forget it. Tell me something about my case.'

'You know, sir, we're in the middle of solving a terrible crime that has taken place in Dhesera.' Pankaj took a seat behind his desk and gestured for Advani to sit opposite him.

Advani sat down, pursed his lips and pulled off a leaf from the money plant on Pankaj's desk. 'I hadn't forgotten that, no, but you see the threat against me is also serious. Okay, so my life is not at stake but one crime leads to another, does it not?'

'All crime is terrible.' Pankaj moved his plant away from Advani's reach. 'It's just unfortunate that this murder has happened at the same time.'

'How many police are based at this station?'

'Just Detective Chupplejeep and myself.'

'Oh, so you haven't even had time to look at my case?' Advani asked and his voice broke. Pankaj watched as he ripped the leaf in his trembling fingers into little pieces.

The police officer pulled out Advani's case notes from his drawer. He was certain now that Advani had lied to him about his secret. There was no way that Advani had passed off someone else's work off as his own. Pankaj was angry at Advani for wasting his time. He had to make it known to the artist, but he had never been any good with confrontation. To stall a little longer, in the hope that Chupplejeep would return, he enquired after the artist's assistant, the sneaky cobra.

'Oh, he's being such a drama queen,' Advani said, perking up a little. 'He wanted to stay back at the gallery. He's working on something. I've seen it. He's very good, you know. I'd never tell him. Imagine if he wanted to sell his works. Who would run after me then? Boys like Takshak are hard to come by. He is a good friend – forget friend. He is like my brother.'

'Really?'

'Don't look at me like that. I love Takshak. Of course I do, but I'm famous. My needs must come first.'

Despite Pankaj's mistrust of Takshak, he couldn't help but feel sorry for the man. 'You could give him some space on the walls of your gallery to hang his paintings. See what the public think. I think one would do that for a brother.'

'Don't tell me what to do. Do your own job first.'

Pankaj opened the file in front of him and looked through his notes. He knew without reading it what was written, word for word. As he formulated what he was going to say, the artist stood up. 'Enough of this,' he barked, leaning over and tapping the desk hard with his index finger. 'I want some fucking answers. And I'm not leaving here till I get them.'

Pankaj stood up, walked to the kitchenette and made two cups of tea. He placed one in front of Advani before sitting back down at his desk.

Advani pushed his cup away. 'Don't you have anything stronger?'

Pankaj took a sip of tea which strangely gave him a boost of confidence. 'This is a police station. What do you want?'

'Oh, never mind.' Advani pulled the cup of tea towards him and then raised the cup to his lips. He took a sip. 'Urgh! Bloody disgusting. Can't solve crime and certainly can't make tea.'

Pankaj took another sip of his drink and cleared his throat. 'Listen here Advani, we can only catch the person blackmailing you if you can tell me what your real secret is. You wasted my time by sending me on a wild goose chase.'

315

Advani raised his eyebrows then looked away. 'Well, if you were proper cops you would have known that from the beginning.' He started swinging his right leg which was crossed over his left.

Pankaj's eyes widened. He couldn't believe Advani had just said that. The man didn't deserve to be helped. He folded his arms across his chest, swallowed back his anger and took a deep breath. Advani was troubled. He needed support not someone shouting at him, that's what his mother would say. Pankaj uncrossed his arms and leaned forward. His tone softened. 'We're trying to help you. You came to us with a problem, which was a lie. You never used Vallabh's paintings, any fool could see that. I saw an image of his work – it was nothing like your work.'

Advani was silent.

'You wasted my time. And you certainly can't have expected me to solve a case based on untruths.'

'I had to say something,' Advani mumbled under his breath.

'Can't you see that if you tell me the real secret, we can look for the blackmailer's motivation in revealing it. It would narrow down the suspects considerably.'

'You have a long-list of suspects then?'

'Well,' Pankaj said, leaning back. So far he wasn't sure he had a single suspect.

'No, I didn't think you had. How do the government justify this outfit?' Advani asked. He looked around the station and Pankaj followed his eyes. The walls inside the station were as bad as the external walls, with peeling paint. The ceiling fan needed replacing too, the blades moved slowly no matter what setting you turned it to and did little to cool the place down. 'You could at least hang up some pictures. No wonder you don't feel like working. This place is utterly depressing.'

'We work very hard at this station to help people. But people who ask us for assistance and then lie certainly don't help themselves. I cannot continue with your case,' Pankaj said.

'Are you fucking serious? I'll call your boss and tell him.'

'The detective inspector in charge of this station has asked me to stop working on the case if you don't co-operate with the police.' Pankaj pulled at his shirt collar. It felt a couple of degrees warmer than when he first started talking to the artist. He hoped Advani wouldn't see the beads of sweat trickling down the back of his neck.

'What a joke.'

Pankaj was silent.

Advani scowled. 'Fine. You want to know? I'll tell you, but you better fucking catch this crook. And if I ever find out you've told anyone about this, I'll cut off your balls. You hear me?'

Pankaj swallowed hard. 'You have my word.'

Advani uncrossed his legs and crossed them again. He fiddled with his hair, pushing it behind his ears. Eventually he took his hat off. 'Hmm…where should I start?'

CHAPTER FORTY-THREE

Advani played with the end of his scarf. 'When I was born, I was not the same as other babies. I wasn't just male. I wasn't just female.'

'Huh?'

'I was intersex.'

Pankaj loosened his collar a little more. Images of Advani's art – the mutilated female genitalia – came into his mind. 'Sorry?' he said, feeling rather faint.

'I was born with both sexes. You know the term *hijra*?'

Pankaj nodded. Of course he knew of hijras, in fact he had experience of having one thrust her body at him. He had been waiting at the traffic lights in Mumbai when a hijra approached him. The eunuch tapped on his window and Pankaj had turned. He saw a face with all the facial features of a man, but painted with makeup – white powder and red lips. The face was almost farcical. The hijra was wearing a bright pink sari and as soon as Pankaj wound down his window, she had shoved her upper body through the open window and demanded money. He had given her ten rupees hoping she would go away, but instead she started singing a lewd song about genitals. She wouldn't stop. Since then, he never wound down his window for beggars again.

'So you know then that hijras are treated like the bottom of society. They are feared and hated. No one would ever buy art from a hijra – my reputation would be ruined,' Advani said.

Yes, Pankaj had a bad experience with hijras, but he knew it wasn't just him. Hijras had a bad name everywhere in India, known for their brash dressing, bawdy songs and ferocious begging. A shiver ran down his spine. Was Advani really a hijra? He didn't dress like one.

'I didn't know I was different from other children for a long time,' the artist continued. 'I mean you don't know what everyone else has down there when you are young, do you? When I was eight, I found a box with some girl's things inside. I thought I was getting a sister. I asked my father and he ignored me. I asked my mother and she said absolutely not. Then later that night I heard my father shouting at my mother. "We're never having another child," he said to her. "Not after what you gave me last time." I didn't know what the hell he meant. I was only small. What I did know was that I liked the pink clothing. The next morning I took a pink scarf from the box and wore it around my waist like a skirt. When my father saw me he hit the roof. "Get out," he told me. He screamed with such force I thought he was going to beat me. I ran to my room and my mother followed. She made me take off the scarf and then she took away the box of girl's clothing. I remember thinking I would rather a beating than them take away those pretty things.'

Advani paused then went on. 'Much later, I found out that when I was born my parents were going to bring me up as a girl, but there were some complications and the doctors at the hospital couldn't operate straight away to remove my penis, and as I grew my features started to become more and more male. So it was decided I was to be a boy. They bought me toy cars and guns, even though I asked for a dolly every birthday.'

'When did you find out that you were intersex?'

'Growing up, my father didn't want to know me. And for years I thought that ignoring your son was what every father did. Then when I was older I saw how my friends' fathers behaved with them. I saw them taking their sons to play football or out for ice cream. My father wouldn't even look at me. I knew then that something had to be wrong with me. My mother was different and I loved her. She made my favourite foods and showered me with affection. I think she was making up for my father's hatred towards me. But that day when I asked her why daddy didn't love me, she did a terrible thing. She explained how I was born.'

'That's not a bad thing. She told you the truth.'

'She said being that way, having male and female parts, made me even more special. And can you believe I fucking believed her! I told my friends what she had said and you know what they did?'

Pankaj winced. What a thing to tell other children. Children were the worst, with no sense of caring for how their words hurt others. He shook his head, remembering how he was bullied for having a lisp in school. A lisp he had thankfully grown out of. Poor Advani – he could only imagine the taunts from the other children when he told them he had both sexes.

'Those fucking children, they made my life hell. They pulled down my pants and pointed and laughed. They nicknamed me all sorts of things, the one I hated most was bitch. "Come and play, bitch," they used to taunt. Soon my teachers found out too. It hurt. It fucking hurt like hell.'

'That's terrible,' Pankaj said, feeling a little out of his depth. He didn't have the first idea of how to deal with what Advani was telling him. He willed Chupplejeep back. Just listen, he silently told himself. Just listen, and then you can decide how to help him.

'That was not the worst of it though. As I got older, people soon started to talk and they started giving my mother and father those looks of pity. My father couldn't stand it. First he was angry, used to come home from work and bang his fists on the table, but then he had episodes when he would just retreat into himself. That was something else. His anger I was used to, this quiet shell of a man I wasn't. Eventually, as my body started to change he stopped talking to me altogether. Then when I was fifteen, I came home from school and found my mother weeping at the kitchen table. "What's wrong?" I asked. "Has he been mean to you again?" Sometimes, for no apparent reason, my father would lash out at my mother for something small, like forgetting to buy the milk, and he would beat her. He used to beat me also, but I didn't mind. I thought I deserved it for what I was. She didn't, and by this time I was old enough to know that my father was an utter bastard.'

Pankaj wanted to reach out and touch Advani's hand. He had never heard such a story before and he could feel a burning sensation in the pit of his stomach that he recognised as anger. Anger for a man he had never met. 'Why was she crying?'

'My father had told her to pass on a message to me.'

'What was it?'

'That I was to leave the house.'

Pankaj leaned forward. 'What did you say?'

'For one hour I sat and cried with my mother. Where would I go? What would I do? All these questions came into my mind. I was only fifteen. I was failing at school. I was unemployable with no skills. I was too thin and weak to be a labourer or to work on a farm. I was scared, very scared. But at the same time I was relieved. I was fed up of living this life where people in my village were afraid to touch me. My body was doing all sorts of weird things, nobody understood me, and worst of all, my father didn't want me anywhere near him. I was an embarrassment to him, to the family. After my tears dried, I realised that this was my chance. My chance to get out of the family and to create a new identity for myself.'

'You found art?'

Advani frowned. 'That wasn't till later.'

'Oh.' Pankaj wondered how many other bad things happened to the artist after he left his father's house. Surely he had been through enough for one lifetime. 'There's more?'

'My father and those bullies at school were only the beginning. You know, I left home that very same day. My mother gave me her life savings, which wasn't much. We didn't have much.'

Pankaj nodded his understanding. If the family were wealthy, they could have paid for the necessary operations and hormone treatment for Advani. They could have put him in another school. They could have done so much more for him. But Pankaj also knew that even without money, his parents could have created a loving environment for him. Why did they kick him out? He knew the answer lay between Advani's father's inability to acknowledge his son and his mother's inability to stand up to her tyrant of a husband.

'I spent the first night in a small guesthouse two villages away from ours. I couldn't stay in our village because my father would not have accepted it. Plus, I wanted a fresh start, but I knew I couldn't afford to live in a guesthouse forever. I had to find somewhere economical and I had to find work.'

'So what did you do? Where did you go?' Pankaj touched his teacup. The tea had gone cold.

'I dropped out of school. I asked around for work in bars, at restaurants and in shops.'

'And?' Pankaj asked eagerly.

'Nothing. I found some work cleaning toilets one day and cleaning dishes another, but there wasn't much work in the village I had chosen. So I had no choice but to move on. I didn't want to waste my money on accommodation, so I slept rough. Luckily it was the summer so the nights were not too cool and the rains were still a few months away. On the third night a hijra approached me. She was so kind and gentle, not like the ones I had heard about. I was so dirty and tired, I was grateful when she took me back to the colony.'

'The colony?' Pankaj asked.

'The colony of hijras. I was so happy when I entered that place. Okay, so the men were dressed as women and they all stared at me when I arrived, but they were kind and I soon found out they were all like me. Some were eunuchs, some men that wanted to be women, some women born into a male body, some intersex like me. All sorts. For one week I didn't have to do anything. I bathed, I ate well and I slept like a baby. I thought, finally, this is my home.'

Pankaj smiled. He had heard terrible things of these colonies of hijras, that ostracized from society they had set up groups in slums around Mumbai and other parts of India. But perhaps that was untrue.

'But I was wrong,' Advani said, as if reading his mind. 'It was all a trick but I didn't see it at first. And I suppose I needed them at that time. Imagine if I had stayed living on the streets.'

Pankaj thought about this. It was a terrible consideration and he couldn't imagine it, for himself, at least.

'After the first week, one of the hijras, Ragini, came to my bed in the dormitory where at least five of us slept. She was beautiful, she didn't have any masculine features at all. She always had a yellow hibiscus flower in her hair and she wore bright orange lipstick. She sat on my bed and she said my name was to be Vanca. It means wish. I said to her that it was a woman's name. She laughed and gave me a peacock blue *gagra choli* to wear. At eight I may have wanted to wear a skirt, but by fifteen I knew I didn't want to be a girl. Okay, at that time I wasn't sure if I wanted to be a boy either, but to have this sex thrust upon me by someone else, well, it pissed me off.'

'No!' Pankaj said.

Advani nodded. 'She said that it was my time to work. I asked her what I had to do. Sweetly, she told me that I would have to go begging. Now, this really bothered me. I came from a poor family, but not so poor that we had to beg. I couldn't do it and so I told her just that.'

'What did she say?'

'She said I owed them for my keep over the last week. She said I had no choice. And at this point I knew she was right. I didn't have a single person in the world to turn to and I had no money. So that day I put my dress on and Ragini did my hair and makeup. My hair was short like a man's so from that day on I was told I had to grow it. I wish I had never listened to them.'

'Why?'

'Why? Because once it grew long, begging was not the only thing I had to do.'

Pankaj gasped.

'It was fucking degrading. Two years of my life I worked for the guru of the colony.' Advani took a sip of his tea.

Pankaj shook his head.

'I try not to think about my time spent there. It was awful.'

'What happened to the money you earned?'

'Most of it went to the guru. Ragini said the guru would pay for me to have my penis removed and so that I could have my SRS.'

'What's that?'

'Sex reassignment surgery.'

Pankaj began to feel quite ill. He stood up and walked to the window, turned the handle and pushed it open. He took a deep breath.

'Can you believe they wanted me to become a woman? My female genitalia had never fully developed.'

Pankaj shook his head.

'That's when I started getting worried. If dressing up like a woman every day taught me one thing, it was that I didn't want to be a woman.'

'Did you tell the guru that?'

Advani nodded. 'He didn't want to know. I was more valuable to him as a woman, not a man. I realised they would never let me leave so I concocted a plan.'

'A plan?'

'Yes, a plan indeed.'

'I had managed to save some money,' Advani said, 'from my working days. Not much but I had some savings. I also plucked up the courage to visit an old woman who lived near our slum.'

'She helped you?'

'I had met her the previous year when I was out begging. Only when other hijras were around I would chant and sing songs, but otherwise I begged in silence. Some of the eunuchs would go up to a man in a group of people and threaten to flash him if he didn't give them money. It was horrible. But it was on one of those days when I was alone that I met the old woman and started talking to her. She explained that her son was getting married and she wanted a hijra at the blessing.'

'I've read it's good luck you have a hijra at the ceremony. Some people believe that.'

'Yes, and she was one of those people. She was kind and I agreed to do the blessing. I didn't tell the guru back at the slum and I kept the money she gave me. After that, I used to occasionally bump into her when I was out. She always invited me for tea on her patio and she was kind. We used to spend an hour or so talking about art and literature. I often paid for this time out of my begging schedule by doing extra work at night. I hated it, but at least with the old woman I felt like a human being. Having my own time to speak with her made doing all those other things bearable. But in her company I felt so foolish dressed as a woman, because I knew I wanted to be a man. A gay man. One day, I was so depressed about what I had become I couldn't hold it in any longer. I ended up telling the old woman my story. We became even closer and I found we had much in common. She introduced me to the great artists and she showed me books full of paintings. I lapped it up.'

'Didn't the others find out?'

'After her son married she too was lonely, so after a while she started to pay me for my time. She knew how the colony worked. This suited us both. The money was coming in so no one questioned me. The other hijras never found out. If they did, they never said anything.'

'And she wanted to help?'

'Not at first. I think she thought I was trying to trick her, but after we became friends she made me an offer. She said that if I ever wanted to get out of the colony, she would help me. She kept to her word.'

'You went to her?'

'The day they started me on the hormone drugs, I knew it was only a matter of time before I went under the knife. I took what little savings I had and in the dead of night, I left the colony. I stayed at the old woman's house that night, but in the morning there was a knock on the door.'

'It was one of the other hijras?'

'It was the guru. I was upstairs cowering in the corner of the bedroom, scared the old woman would give me away, but she didn't. I heard the guru say I was dangerous and that I had mental problems. She said they were looking for me before I harmed someone. How could they say that?' Advani said. His words caught in this throat.

'If you want to stop, you can,' Pankaj said, taking a box of tissues out from his drawer and placing it on the desk. He looked at the old clock on the wall. Advani had been talking for at least an hour.

'No, I want to finish. The old woman said she hadn't seen me. After she closed the door on him she came into the room, saw my wet face and dried my tears with her *dupatta*. I told her that I should go back. I had seen other hijras try to leave the colony only to be brought back and beaten into subservience. But the old woman persuaded me not to. She made me hot tea and some *Achar Ke Aloo* to eat. When I had finished, I felt stronger. She told me to leave that evening in case the guru came back. Then she handed me a suitcase full of her late husband's clothing and an envelope full of cash and told me to go and do something I wanted to do, for myself, no one else. I cried all over again. But this time they were tears of joy. Finally, after two years I had a way out. That evening, before I left, she ran me a bath and cut my hair. I put her husband's old clothes on and I felt free. For the first time in two years, I felt free.'

'Lovely,' Pankaj said, his own eyes moist.

'I left that part of the city. I changed my name to Advani and I enrolled in an art college. There I swore never to reveal my past to anyone. I had been given a second chance and I was going to make the most of it. You know the rest.'

Pankaj took a deep breath and put his cup down. 'That's one hell of a story.'

Advani closed his eyes for a couple of seconds. When he opened them, he seemed like his normal self again. 'So, now you know my secret, cop, what are you going to do?'

CHAPTER FORTY-FOUR

'Thank you for telling me,' Pankaj said. It made sense that Advani didn't want anyone to know this secret and he could understand why he had lied before. The artist hadn't hurt anyone. It was his secret and his alone. So, the hijra community had lost one of theirs and he had left them under the cloak of darkness but that was his choice. They had saved him in the beginning but ultimately they had abused him and kept him against his will. Being a sex worker, singing bawdry songs on the streets and begging for money was not what Advani had wanted, let alone becoming a woman. And he had been so young – too young to find his way in life. He had every right to leave the way he did. The poor man had been through enough.

He had thought that in knowing Advani's secret, the case would have been simple to solve. But this was unlike any secret he had imagined. This wasn't a petty theft Advani had committed, or being an accessory to a crime, like Pankaj had hoped for. This was something far more personal. It wasn't anyone's business and yet someone wanted to expose the artist. An unfamiliar feeling of a tightening in his chest made him clench his fist and bring it down hard on his desk. How could someone hold this over Advani? 'You can't let someone threaten you with this,' he said.

'What choice do I have?'

'Your parents excluded you. They are the ones that should be suffering for this. Not you.'

Advani leaned back in his chair and smiled. 'You're different from other cops. Most cops would have kicked me out of their office by now. Cops are the worst. I saw the way they used to beat hijras for no rhyme or reason when I lived in the colony.'

Pankaj shook his head. 'The world is changing. Even India has recognised hijras as a third gender.'

Advani folded his arms over his chest. 'Not all the hijras in the colony were bad. Most of them were like me, just trying to live. But I'm happy living as I do now. I am Advani. This is all me. But I can't let this secret out. Why should I? It's mine. I'll make the payment if you cops can't find this blackmailer.'

'Call the press. Tell them your story, before anyone else gets the chance. If you make the payoff this time, there will always be another time. If you tell India your story, no one can hold this over you ever again. It will be a relief.'

'I don't think I can do that. You don't know what the hijra community will do to me. They were so angry when I left. I heard through various people that they wanted my blood.'

'With the money you get from your story, you could donate it to other people who find themselves in the same situation you were in. Or go back to the community and give the money to them. Things may have changed there. It was a long time ago. In the least you could help people in that community.'

Advani smiled and uncrossed his arms. 'I don't know.'

'Think about it.'

'I suppose it's an idea. I never once thought about telling my story. I guess it could work in my favour.'

'I have a contact in the press here,' Pankaj said, thinking of Bonaparte. 'I could give you his details.'

'But if I do this, if I contact the press today and tell them my story, how do I find out who was blackmailing me? I need to know that. Now that you know my secret, you must find out who did this.'

Pankaj sighed. Knowing did not help in the slightest. He felt guilty, like he had tricked him. 'Do you think someone recognised you from when you were younger? It could be one of the hijras from the colony that sent you the letter. You think nobody knows your story, but many of them do. They may have seen a picture of you in the press and put two and two together.'

'Not a chance.'

'How can you be so sure?'

'I've had work done to my face,' Advani said, pointing to his chin and his nose.

'Oh, I see,' Pankaj said, taking a closer look. He would never have guessed. 'Hmm, then I suppose we should perhaps look at previous lovers as suspects, because they would know.'

'There have been lovers, but not many. Most are high-flying politicians and I have more secrets on them than they have on me. They would not benefit at all if my secret came out. In fact, it would make things worse for them.'

'What about Dinesh? You said you had relations with his father.'

Advani shook his head. 'Yes, but if he threatens me, I threaten him. He is an MLA and he has a family. It will be worse for him.'

'Who else in Goa have you had relations with?'

'No one in this small state.'

'Takshak?'

'Takshak is beautiful and there was a time early on in our relationship when I wanted him. But he was with someone else then and it didn't seem right. After that time passed, I never thought about it again and he became like a brother. I know Takshak too well to ever be his lover.'

A brother that you treat like your slave, Pankaj thought. Someone who would have reason to want to harm you, had you not saved him all those years ago. But as Chupplejeep had said, you couldn't be grateful to someone indefinitely. Perhaps Takshak's gratitude had dried up. 'But you two spend a lot of time together. You have known him for years. Have you never felt like telling him?'

'Often. I have come this close to telling him.' Advani lifted up his hand and held his thumb and forefinger a centimetre apart. 'But I never did. I was too scared.'

'You get drunk with Takshak?'

'Too frequently. He doesn't drink too much though. He shouldn't drink at all because of his diabetes, but he does.'

'Maybe you told him when you where drinking? You said to us before that you rarely remember what you say when you've been drinking.'

Advani bit his lip. 'I…err…No, I couldn't have.'

'He's the only one that has been here in Goa with you the whole time. He could have slipped that note into the post box at any time.'

Pankaj opened Advani's file. He looked down at the fingerprint analysis in the file, hoping that there would be an answer there. Of course there were none. 'I sent off the letter for fingerprint analysis. But it hasn't helped,' he said, wanting Advani to know that he genuinely was trying to solve the case.

'Why?'

'Only your prints and Takshak's were found on the letter. And we know that you both touched the letter so it doesn't shed any further light on the matter.'

When Advani didn't respond with one of his quick jibes, Pankaj looked up. 'Are you okay?'

'Takshak's prints were on the letter?'

'Yes, but I know you and Takshak work very closely – '

'He never touched the letter.'

'But you came in here with Takshak when you first reported it?'

'He never fucking touched the letter. I made sure of it. Don't talk to me like I don't know what I'm saying. I know he never touched it.'

'Can you be certain?'

'I didn't give him the letter because after I read it, I was so afraid I hid it. And also…I know this sounds stupid now, but I was afraid that Takshak would read something in it that I couldn't see.'

'Like what?'

'Like my secret was written on that piece of paper in between the lines.'

Pankaj nodded. He understood. Chupplejeep often said that anxiety and fear caused people to imagine all sorts of things, to dream up situations that could never happen. 'He never read it. Why don't you believe me now? Minutes ago you were accusing him yourself. Perhaps I *did* tell him when I was drunk.'

Advani scratched his chin. Pankaj noticed his hands were shaking. 'I do remember one evening, about a year ago, I had a run-in with an old lover, a disgraced politician, who said my body made him feel sick. I drank myself silly that night. Don't even remember how I got home. I must have called Takshak to pick me up. The next morning I woke up with a helluva hangover and Takshak was there in my apartment. He was acting all strange. I remember because he kept saying "It's okay." I could tell he wanted to talk, but my head was pounding so I told him to leave me alone and I didn't tell him nicely either. Fuck. I must have told him that night.'

Pankaj looked at the fingerprint analysis again. The partial fingerprint on the back of the letter in ink was Takshak's. Even if Takshak had touched the letter, he wouldn't have had the same ink on his hands to create a print on the back of the note. How had he missed this obvious detail the first time he read the report? Chupplejeep would not be impressed. This was what he often referred to as shoddy police work. He braced himself for Advani's sharp tongue too as he told him, but nothing came.

'Why would he do this?' Advani asked.

It made sense, now, why Takshak would do this. Pankaj recalled his conversation with him when Chupplejeep was interviewing Advani. He had saved Takshak from his tyrannical father and they had been close in those early days before Advani found fame.

'He was my closest and dearest friend,' Takshak had said. But he had also said that he wished that Advani was a nobody again so that he would respect him a little bit more. He was tired of the way Advani treated him and complained that the artist was like a toddler. Pankaj had witnessed it himself – Advani screaming for Takshak to bring him water, wine, tablets, whatever the hell he wanted. Was this Takshak's plan? To expose Advani and ruin the image the artist had built up over the years, just so they could go back to eating chapattis and *daal*, with no one else for company?

But perhaps it wasn't just that. The handwriting analysis had been more accurate than he had given himself credit for. It indicated the author was creative, but unable to hit their goals. Takshak had ambitions, ambitions held back by Advani. Advani had as good as admitted this just over an hour ago. Perhaps Takshak wanted to expose Advani, weaken his confidence and then use him and his forty lakhs as a stepping stone to create his own success story. It must have been hard for Takshak to work under someone as selfish as Advani – someone who would never listen to reason or the needs of another person. Perhaps Takshak thought this was his only way out. Was that why he was acting strange when Pankaj went to question him? He must have thought his visit related to Advani's case and not Subrina's. That's why he was so calm when he was talking about the insulin. That's why he instantly calmed down when he realised, on that first visit Pankaj and Chupplejeep had made to the gallery, their visit was about Subrina's death and nothing to do with the blackmail case.

'Takshak's my friend. Why would he do this?' Advani asked again.

Pankaj took a deep breath. 'He wants the old Advani back and he too wants fame.' Takshak said that Advani had encouraged his work, sold a painting or two for him and said that one day he too could have his own gallery. But years had passed since those early days when they were starting out and Takshak was no closer to owning a gallery than when he first started painting.

338

Advani looked at Pankaj like he was talking in Urdu. Then Advani suddenly looked up. 'Subrina tried telling me, you know.'

'She did?' Pankaj asked.

'She said that Takshak had asked to meet with her. She did as he asked, but when she met him he warned her not to get my place back at Malabar Hill.' Advani shook his head. 'She said he had asked her to do him this one small favour. Why? He didn't say and she didn't ask. She found it all too funny. She left my gallery telling me to "Be careful of the Cobra."'

'And you didn't think to mention it?' Pankaj said. That was why Takshak had met Subrina – the meeting Indu, the maid, had referred to.

'I wasn't quite sure whether to believe it. Subrina could be quite the drama queen. Oh Takshak, what have you done?'

'He's tired of watching you succeed. He too is an artist.'

'But I am *the* artist.'

'I know little about art but I have seen some of his. It's good. But it's in the back room of your gallery, not on the walls. Maybe you could help him succeed?'

Advani crossed his right leg over his left. 'After what he did? He wanted money! My money!'

'And you must pay him well so there is no need for him to want money.'

Advani opened his mouth and closed it again, looking away. 'Of course, I pay him well.' He took a sip of his now ice-cold tea.

'I still think you should tell everyone your secret. I'm sure you can use it to your advantage. You shouldn't be ashamed. Think of how many other children in India that face exclusion because of this. You could give them strength.'

'It would be hard living without Takshak. I've known him for years.' Advani put his hat back on and pushed his chair back.

'Talk to him.'

The artist shrugged, then he stood up and left.

CHAPTER FORTY-FIVE

As labourers came and went, in the quiet corner of the taverna over a lunch of fish curry and rice, the farmer told Chupplejeep how he saw Rohit and Subrina the day that poor Nitin was killed.

'We were all being in the shop,' Mario said, 'means, the small shop between Dhesera and Suuj. At the time it was the only shop between the two villages. It was selling things like milk, eggs and flour as well as shampoo and other such items. The owner was very, how you say, enterprising. Getting anything his customers wanted. And what we wanted in those days? Nothing much. Now the shop has long gone. It's a pharmacy instead. I bet half those drugs in that store were not invented twenty years ago!'

Chupplejeep smiled and nodded as the farmer let nostalgia take over.

'I remember that day clearly because afterwards, on that terrible night, everything changed.'

'Tell me,' Chupplejeep encouraged, wiping his mouth with a paper napkin.

'I was in shop getting eggs for my mother. First, I saw Rohit – a small boy, must have been eleven or twelve. I was older than him. Subrina and I used to be laughing about this boy behind his back. Why? Because he had a crush on Suki. Also, I knew him from the village. There were fewer houses then, everybody knew everybody. We still do. But now the residents of Dhesera and Suuj don't mix. I don't know why. The only time we see each other is when we have to go to pharmacy. I helloed the boy. We made small talk. Means, I must have asked after his parents. He is telling me his mother had sent him to the shop to buy something. Then Subrina entered the shop. I helloed her, also. We talked. She was there to buy a new red lipstick. I remember because she had put it on right there in the store. There was big party happening that night. She was very excited. Some boy she liked was going and she had managed to convince her father to let her go. There was one condition though.'

'What was that?'

'That she took her sister.'

'Oh.'

'Her sister was quiet. She studied a lot. Subrina had plans for her.'

'She did?'

'Subrina's parents wanted her to become a doctor, but slowly, slowly she convinced her father that Suki was better suited for medicine because she liked her studies. Subrina planted the ideas in her father's head so that she could be free of this burden and become an actress. Suki became her project. After some time, her father started believing Suki was better suited to medicine. He also thought Suki's quiet nature would rub off on Subrina. He made them go out together, hoping one would rein in the other. And of course Subrina liked this, because she could force her sister to go out with her out of guilt. She would say, "Papa won't let me out unless you come," and then Suki would give in and go with her. It suited Subrina nicely because she also had company wherever she went and she liked this.'

'And then?' Chupplejeep said, trying to move the conversation along.

'Oh yes, the shop. We were in the shop. I remember sharing a joke with Subrina in the shop. We both laughed. When I looked down I saw Rohit there with his jaw hanging open. He was shocked, you see,' Mario said with glee.

'Shocked?'

'That a lowly son of farmer was talking to a girl from a rich family. Things like that don't happen here. Well, at least they never used to. I remember that moment well. I felt a warmth in my chest and I wanted to hug Subrina for her kindness in talking to me in front of everyone, for being my friend. Means, I liked the fact that Rohit was shocked. I felt proud to have a rich and beautiful friend.'

'When did you see Subrina again?' Chupplejeep asked.

Mario's face hardened. 'It wasn't until the next day. After the accident. I saw Subrina by the well crying,

343

sobbing. I asked, what's happening and she confessed to what she did. It was the first and last time I held her.' The farmer looked up at Chupplejeep. 'I had to,' he said defensively, as if he was being accused of doing something he shouldn't have. 'I told her no good would come of what she had done, but she wouldn't listen to me.'

'No good would come of it?'

'Let me explain,' Mario said to Chupplejeep, and he did.

It was three in the afternoon when the farmer left the taverna. Now it all made sense. Pieces of the puzzle were finally coming together. Chupplejeep paid the bill and stood up. He was almost certain as to who had murdered Subrina Basi and knowing this made him relax a little. He had to speak to Pankaj.

As he walked out to his car, his heart began to beat a little faster. He would shortly be making an arrest. But this wasn't an episode of Poirot, there was no hurry. This criminal wasn't going anywhere fast. He took his phone out of his pocket, punched in a number and held it to his ear.

Chapter Forty-six

'Sir,' Pankaj cried as Chupplejeep entered the office.

'What?'

'I solved it!'

'The murder of Subrina Basi?'

'No sir, the blackmail case. And I know Advani's secret. His real secret.'

'Good,' Chupplejeep said, helping himself to the open packet of cashew nuts on Pankaj's desk. He released a couple from their pink shells and popped them into his mouth. 'Where is the call list from Subrina Basi's phone? Did you check it like I asked?'

'One number came up the day before her body was found that we cannot attribute to anyone.' Pankaj handed the folder with the list to Chupplejeep.

'You called it.'

'The phone has been switched off.'

Chupplejeep opened the folder, ran his finger down the list and smiled.

'You look very pleased with yourself, sir.'

'That is because I've solved the murder.'

'You have?' Pankaj gasped. Chupplejeep was always one step ahead of him.

The detective nodded.

'Tell me,' Pankaj demanded. 'Did you find Ayesha Saxena's body? Is she dead? Did Dinesh do it?'

'Why don't you tell me how you solved Advani's problem first?'

'Okay, sir.'

Their conversation was interrupted by the shrill sound of the telephone ringing on Chupplejeep's desk. They both looked at the green lump of plastic. The detective walked over to his desk and lifted the receiver. 'Hallo.'

Pankaj watched Chupplejeep listen intently to the person on the other end of the line. Finally, Chupplejeep spoke. 'We're on our way now.'

'Where?' Pankaj asked as his boss disconnected the call. What could be more important than discussing who murdered Subrina Basi? And not just a theory, his boss said he had solved the case.

'Come on,' Chupplejeep said walking towards the door. 'We can talk on the way.'

~

'Sir, must you drive so fast?' Pankaj said, holding onto the dashboard to stop himself from sliding in the seat of the old Maruti. He had just told Chupplejeep Advani's story and that Takshak had been behind the blackmail.

'I'm proud you solved your first case.'

'But, like I explained, I solved it by accident. I never knew Takshak hadn't touched the note. That was very naive of me. I should've known exactly who had touched the letter before I sent it to the lab for analysis. And the print in ink on the back of the letter. I should have checked that as soon as I received the fingerprint analysis.'

'Sometimes we solve cases by accident. That's not the point. You still solved it before the deadline. Don't be so hard on yourself. I'll make sure the Inspector General knows about all the effort you put in.'

Pankaj couldn't help but smile.

'So now I need to know, what did you find out about Abhik?'

'Oh yes, I had almost forgotten. He's wanted in Nepal. He ran away.' Pankaj looked out of the window as they passed the hawkers selling *bhajis,* and stray dogs eating at an overflowing bin. In less than ten minutes they were nearing Mandovi Bridge. Pankaj could see a queue of traffic already forming.

'What did he do?'

'The sub-inspector said it was murder.'

Chupplejeep turned to face Pankaj.

'Sir, at this speed please keep your eyes on the road!'

Chupplejeep turned back to face the road and swerved to avoid a plump pink and black pig running for its life. 'Murder, you say? Who'd he kill?'

'Well, sir. It wasn't so much murder. But nevertheless, blood was shed.'

347

'What are you saying?' Chupplejeep said, looking ahead.

'He killed a cow.'

'A cow!' He turned to look at Pankaj, then back at the road.

'It's illegal to kill cows in Nepal. It's a felony. They have a beef ban there like Maharashtra made earlier this year. And sir, a cow is a big animal. You don't go around killing such big animals. They are mostly docile creatures. If you killed a cow, chances are you are capable of killing a human also.'

'In whose opinion?'

'In my opinion. And he used a knife. He slit the animal's throat.'

'Of course, he would use a knife. You hardly strangle a cow, do you?'

'Sir, you don't seem concerned.'

'Tell me, why did he kill the cow?'

'It was making a mess outside his house. The sub-inspector told me that every morning Abhik would find a large cowpat outside the door to his dwelling, or so he said in his statement. He tried everything to deter the cow. He even bought those prickly shrubs to plant outside. They are called duranta, I think. You know, sir, the ones cows don't like.'

Chupplejeep didn't know what shrubs Pankaj was on about but he nodded anyway. He looked below the bridge at the murky water, the tourist boats blaring out Hindi music as they sailed past.

'One evening Abhik returned from a long day at work to find that the cow had not only done its mess outside his house, but it was sleeping in front of the main door. He couldn't get access to his own house. He tried shifting the animal but you know, sir, how cows can be. They are seriously stubborn sometimes.'

'And then?'

'Then he took a knife to its throat. That was it for him. In Nepal he is wanted.'

'I see.'

'Just "I see," sir? You don't kill a cow like that unless you have serious anger issues. Perhaps he got into a rage after Subrina Basi had snubbed him. And he used a knife. A knife was used on Subrina's wrists and his prints were on the weapon.'

'I agree that killing a cow shows violent tendencies, for sure. But this murder was carefully planned and executed. It wasn't committed in the heat of the moment. Someone took their time to figure out how to murder Subrina, then they put her sunglasses on her and painted her lips red. Does that sound like something Abhik would do?'

Pankaj was silent for a moment.

'So do Nepal want Abhik back to press charges?'

Pankaj shook his head. 'No, sir. They said we were welcome to him. Their caseload is too high at the moment for them to bother. Are we going to press charges against him?'

'It's not really our jurisdiction and if Nepal are going to let it slide then there isn't much that we can do. Not that it's something I think we should pursue. Let's leave the man alone.'

'Sir?'

'Yes.'

'So, if it wasn't Abhik who murdered Subrina Basi, who did? And why?'

'That, Pankaj, is exactly what you are going to find out.'

Chapter Forty-seven

The old blue Maruti screeched to a halt. 'Come on,' Chupplejeep said to Pankaj as he got out of the vehicle.

'Sir, what's happening?'

'You'll find out soon enough. We don't have time to waste.' Pankaj got out of the four by four and, for the first time ever, he saw Chupplejeep run. He was running towards a maroon saloon car in the distance. Two people were standing next to it carrying large boxes. Pankaj looked up at the building in front of him and the towering green ashoka trees that stood in front of it. He shook his head and followed suit.

'Stop,' Chupplejeep said, gasping for breath. 'Stop right there.'

The two figures quickly put their boxes in the boot of the car and got inside.

'Stop that car, Pankaj.'

Pankaj could see his boss was struggling. He ran as fast as he could, past his boss towards the other car. Before the driver had a chance to start the car, he caught up with it. He put his hand through the car window and retrieved the keys. He clutched them in his hand, breathless. Sweat trickled down his brow.

'That was close,' Chupplejeep said to the driver, as he approached the vehicle. 'You almost got away then.'

'We're free to come and go as we please. Give me back my keys. We've done nothing wrong here.'

'Let's see about that, shall we?' Chupplejeep peered further into the car. 'Sister Valentine, or are you just Suki now? Not wearing your tunic and habit anymore? Decided to leave the convent? That was a bit sudden, no? It's a good job Sister Perpetua called me to let me know.'

Suki tucked her hair behind her ears. 'I made my decision a long time ago.'

'Hmm, I'm sure you did. You had this all planned out nicely. Do you mind stepping out of the car?'

Both the driver and the passenger ignored the request.

Chupplejeep leaned against the vehicle. 'Are you in a hurry, Pankaj?'

'No, sir.'

'Good. We can stay here then until these two decide to do as I have asked.'

Pankaj looked at the couple. He could see a slight resemblance Suki had to her sister. She was much smaller than the voluptuous Subrina Basi, but she had the same almond-shaped eyes. Then he looked at the driver. He gave a little gasp. He had seen him only a few hours ago and he seemed distracted then, as Pankaj asked him those questions about the purchase of insulin. A pharmacist was like a magician, giving people potions to make them better. A pharmacist was what Balbir was referring to. His visit earlier must have been the trigger that made them decide to run. Pankaj looked carefully at the man with thick-rimmed glasses. He hadn't seen it earlier, but now he recognised some of his own features in the face of the driver. It was all starting to make sense. No wonder Balbir had mistaken him for his own son, Rohit. If Rohit took his thick-rimmed glassed off, they could have been brothers.

The car doors opened and Suki and Rohit got out.

'What's this about?' Rohit asked.

'Surely, you must know.'

'Suki and I haven't done anything wrong.'

'We have information.'

'What?' Suki asked.

'Who killed your sister, of course. Surely, you want to know before you leave. Can I ask you where you are going? And whose car this is?'

'It's my car,' Rohit said, 'and as to where we are going, that, Detective, is none of your business.'

'Oh, but I think you'll find it is my business – '

'We're just going to Rohit's house,' Suki interrupted.

'You asked me to let you know as soon as I had any news.'

Suki played with the silver cross pendant that hung around her neck. 'Yes, of course.' She hesitated and looked at Rohit before turning back to the detective. 'You have news of my sister's death? I want to know. Who killed my sister?'

353

A crow landed on a wall close to where they stood.

Chupplejeep looked at the bird. 'Funny that.'

'What?' Suki asked.

'When I first met you, you said that your sister warned you when she was young that she would come back as a crow to watch over you if she died before you, no?'

Suki studied the black bird. She tapped her fingers to her lips three times and nodded.

'You want to know who murdered your sister. Let me tell you.' Chupplejeep twisted the end of his moustache. 'Over a week ago you, Suki, got a call from your estranged sister, did you not?'

'I can't remember.'

'Well I can. The maid remembered her pleading with you to meet. Subrina was desperate to meet you, was she not?'

'That much is true.'

'She begged you to meet with her, but you were apprehensive.'

'I hadn't seen her in so long. She virtually cut me out of her life when she moved to Delhi. They all did.'

'Only your mother kept in regular contact, keeping you up to date with Subrina's news. How she was getting small parts in movies and making a name for herself in the *filmi* scene. In Delhi she had created a new life for herself. The life she always dreamed of having.'

'Good for her,' Suki said.

'Do you think she remembered poor little Nitin?'

Suki shrugged.

'Nobody in Delhi knew about poor little Nitin, the boy who was killed when Subrina ran him over, so it was a perfect place to run away to.'

'Yes,' Suki said. 'She ran away from it, from what she had done. I stayed.'

'You could say that the death of that little boy did Subrina a favour, because your parents agreed to move to Delhi after that. And that's where her career started. There was a much better chance of a career for Subrina in Delhi than in a small Goan village, no. She must have been thrilled with what she had accomplished.'

Rohit flinched. Suki was silent.

'Yes, Nitin was your brother,' Chupplejeep said, looking at the tall man with glasses. 'It must have been a difficult time for you.'

'I don't need sympathy from a cop. I've had enough of you lot. Say what you have to say, and then we leave. We have every right to go where we wish. India is a free country.'

'Hear me out, no. When I heard that a child had been in an accident caused by dangerous driving, it made me think. You, Suki, were confined to a nunnery and Subrina had gotten away with murder, so to speak. I thought, how could this be?'

'Subrina chose her path. I chose mine,' Suki said.

'Pankaj,' Chupplejeep said, turning to the police officer, 'it would be a little unfair if your brother was living a full life after he had killed someone and you had imprisoned yourself in a place like this?' Chupplejeep looked at the imposing convent which towered over them, its whitewashed walls blackened by the recent monsoon.

'It would be completely unfair,' Pankaj said.

'What's your point?' Rohit snapped.

Chupplejeep ignored the question. His point would be made clear very soon. He looked back at Suki. Her face was plain, her eyes wide and watery. 'Reluctantly, you met your sister the day after she called you. The day before she died. She came to Verna and you spoke to her at length.'

'I told you all this already.'

'You told me that you spoke to your sister, yes. But you didn't disclose to me what you discussed. In fact you said that you spoke about "this and that."'

'She told me about her failed marriages, that she wanted to marry Dinesh.'

'Perhaps she did. But I think she wanted to meet you after all this time to discuss the death of baby Nitin.'

Suki put her hands on her hips and stepped away from Rohit. 'But she didn't.'

'She did, and you're lying.'

'I would not lie outside God's house.'

'I think you would. Do you know how I know that you are lying?'

'How?'

'The bruises on your sister's shoulders. At first, we thought her boyfriend made these bruises, but I spoke to the coroner and asked him to check the bruises again. He confirms the bruising is consistent with the hands of a woman. The bruises on her arms were made before those on her legs. They happened twenty-four hours before her death. I think when you met Subrina and she spoke the truth of Nitin's death, you got angry and you shook her by her shoulders to make her stop talking.'

She said nothing and Chupplejeep went on. 'You were satisfied with that and left her, but when you got back to the convent, you started thinking about what she had said and you were afraid. You knew she wouldn't let it go. Not after all this time. You see, you may think that Subrina forgot about Nitin's death, that she left Goa to escape while you remained and submitted yourself to God. But the death of little Nitin played on your sister's mind for years. Twenty years to be exact. But the older she got, the less she remembered of the accident. Her mind was confused. Do you know she had even contacted the police in Delhi saying that she had murdered someone?'

'Well, she had,' Rohit said. 'So what if in the final hour she was beginning to repent. You want us to say "poor thing"? She never paid the price for what she had done.'

'Until now?' Chupplejeep said.

'I know what you are trying to do, Detective, and it will not work. We have done nothing wrong. Perhaps God took matters into his own hands.'

'Would you agree with that, Suki? When I spoke to you before, you said your sister could have committed suicide.'

'She could have.'

Rohit shook his head and took a step closer to Suki.

'But it wasn't just the bruises that brought me to that conclusion. Your sister was a complex person. She wasn't the shallow person everyone believed her to be. At least, she was not always so affected by fame.' Chupplejeep looked at Suki, Rohit and Pankaj. Pankaj looked more intrigued by what he was saying than Suki and Rohit. But Suki looked uncomfortable. His plan was working. 'I spoke to a friend of your sister's. His name is Mario. You may not remember him. He's a farmer in Suuj. Where you and Subrina grew up. He told me something very interesting, confirmed some of my suspicions.'

'Subrina friends with a farmer! Ha! This is why you cops are so pathetic,' Rohit said, letting out a deep laugh. He opened the car door, but Chupplejeep walked up to him and closed it.

'You're not going anywhere just yet. You said you wanted to know how and why Subrina was murdered and I'm going to tell you just that.'

Chapter Forty-eight

'Rohit's right,' said Suki. 'My sister wasn't friendly with any farmers. She looked down her nose at labourers and those who worked in the paddy fields. Everyone knew what she was like. It must be a hoax.'

'Oh, this is not a hoax,' Chupplejeep replied. 'After I spoke with Mario I made a call to a journalist I know. He has contacts in the village so he checked the farmer's story for me. He tracked down two families who lived in Suuj. They recall your family – the two sisters. They confirmed what I needed to know. Subrina was a kind person before she moved to Delhi. Yes, she had her faults, don't we all, but she was kind. She only turned her nose up at people after the accident, after she moved to Delhi. Perhaps it was a defence mechanism. Didn't want people to get too close. You change when you are forced to live a lie for so long.'

Suki frowned.

'Surely, you must remember how kind your sister was? Acted like a mother to you? I heard that when you were young your sister loved life, she didn't mind who she spoke to. Whether they had one thousand rupees or fifty paise, she was happy to be friends with everyone. In fact, I think it was you who was the snob in the family, was it not?'

'What rubbish! I'm a nun. Everyone is equal in the eyes of the Lord.'

Chupplejeep's smile faded. 'Not a nun anymore, though. And please do not hide behind such clichés.' He looked away before turning back to the couple. 'Twenty years ago, your friend here, Rohit, witnessed Subrina laughing with this farmer the same day Nitin was killed.'

'What are you taking about?' Rohit said, adjusting his glasses.

'Think back, Rohit, it was some time ago.'

'I will never forget that day. I don't need to think back.'

'You were young.'

'Maybe so, but some things you never forget. Do you have a brother, Detective?' he asked.

Chupplejeep shook his head. He had no family at all.

'Well then, you don't know what it's like to lose someone so close. Nitin was only small but he was like an extension of me. Not another person, but part of me. Do you understand? I remember that day.'

'Then you remember going to the store to buy something for your mother.'

Rohit looked into the distance. 'The store?'

'You know the one. There was only one at the time – between Suuj and Dhesera. The shop that is now your pharmacy.'

Rohit began to nod his head. 'I remember, I remember. Yes. My mother sent me to buy some medicine for Nitin. He wasn't feeling well. That woman was there. I do remember her laughing with a man. Those bright red lips of hers, yes, I remember.'

'Subrina was pretty back then and you were a young boy with a crush on her little sister.'

Suki took a deep breath and Rohit reached for her hand. 'Get to the point, Detective.'

'Subrina Basi came to Goa not just for the International Film Festival of India but because she wanted to discuss the accident involving Nitin with Suki. Her so-called boyfriend, Dinesh, confirmed to me that your sister was carrying, in his words, "a lot of baggage".'

'And? So what?'

'Subrina wanted to clarify some points of that fateful day with her sister. Because at the time of the accident, she had been drinking. That much is true. Everyone knew that Subrina was a wild child. She wasn't interested in studies, only going out and meeting boys. The whole village knew that. You, Suki, were the clever one. Always achieved good grades. Your father wanted you to become a doctor, no?'

'That was a long time ago.'

'But Subrina liked to have company when she went out and your father wanted you to accompany her. Keep her out of trouble. Subrina used you so she could go out.'

Suki nodded.

361

'That night she told you to have a few drinks at the party and you did. She wanted you to loosen up a little. If you were to be her chaperone like your father wanted, she wanted you to be a little fun and she thought alcohol would help.'

'Yes. Yes, she did.'

'You also wanted to be a little like your sister. Wear her makeup, drink like her. The older one, the cooler one?'

'Maybe, a little.'

'You were not used to drinking like that.'

Suki shook her head.

'But the alcohol made you feel more confident. It gave you some courage. Perhaps you even spoke to some people you wouldn't have normally spoken to.'

'So?'

'So, Subrina was in no fit state to drive, but you felt like you could. You didn't realise just how drunk you were. Subrina conceded. She gave you the keys. Back then there was no drink-drive policy in Goa. Even today, if I am honest, it's rare if you get caught here for drink driving.'

'We're not here for a lecture,' Rohit said. 'Suki doesn't drink anymore. I rarely touch the stuff. Subrina was behind the wheel that day. She admitted to it and even if she hadn't it wouldn't have mattered, remember, I saw her. I saw her lose control of the car. I saw her behind the wheel when she killed my brother.'

'No you didn't.'

'What are you saying?'

362

'I'm saying that Suki was the one driving the car when your brother was killed. She was drunk and she should never have been behind the wheel. Neither of the girls should have. The accident sobered Subrina up. She quickly realised what had happened and she knew it was her fault that Suki was behind the wheel. So she quickly came up with a plan. Seconds after the car hit Nitin, she jumped out of the car and told Suki to move over to the passenger side. What did you do when you saw the car hit Nitin?'

'I screamed for mama and papa and then I ran to my brother,' Rohit said.

'You didn't watch the sisters?'

'Why would I?'

'In the commotion they traded places. Subrina knew that Suki was the golden child, the one set for great things. Not her. Is that not true, Suki?'

Suki began to shake her head. 'It's all lies. Why would Subrina do that? And even if she did, why would she not confess after my father paid off the family?'

'Because by then the lie was already too big. She lied partly to protect you and partly because she blamed herself. She thought she was doing the right thing. The trouble was, the accident changed Subrina. She started to drink heavily. She probably even did drugs. It affected her mind. Soon she started believing in her own lie.'

'This is nonsense.'

'First, she tried to block it out of her mind. Suki, you told me that you never discussed the death of Nitin after that night. In Delhi, she punished herself by believing her lie. She began to shut people out and started treating people badly. At the end of her time in Delhi she wanted to confess. She tried to when she called the Commissioner, but she didn't pursue it. Something held her back. Maybe in her heart of hearts she knew she wasn't to blame and in a moment of sobriety and clear thinking, she realised that there was more to that night than she remembered. So she decided to come back to Goa – to the village where it all started, to find the truth. When she was here in Goa, she started to remember what actually happened that night. But Subrina didn't trust her own mind fully. In fact she said those exact words to her maid at the Golden Orchid. So, whom did she trust?'

Silence.

'You, Suki, she called you. You were the one person who really knew what happened that night. And that is what she asked you when you met. I don't think you could lie to her, because Subrina already knew the truth and when she looked at you, you could see that she knew it. It was only a matter of time until the truth came out. The truth always surfaces. Sometimes it takes time, twenty years even, but it always comes out.'

Rohit took Suki's hand. 'You're not listening, Detective. I know what I saw. I saw Subrina behind the wheel.'

'Unconscious transference.'

'What?'

'That's what happened to you. You saw Subrina earlier that day buying lipstick, wearing the red lipstick.

You remembered seeing her in the store and in your mind you transposed the two sisters, misidentifying who was behind the wheel. Suki looks similar to Subrina, even more so at that age and she was wearing her lipstick that night. Dinesh even remembered Subrina telling him that little piece of information. It was Suki behind the wheel, your mind just thought it was the woman you saw earlier that day.'

Rohit turned and looked at her.

She looked away.

'No!' he screamed, pulling his hand away from her. 'Tell me it's not true.'

'You always loved Suki,' Chupplejeep continued, now looking at Rohit whose anger was barely concealed in his clenched fists. 'The farmer told me you had a crush on her when you were young. You were younger than her but you still liked her, you always held a torch for her even when you were away at college. Over the years, despite the distance between you, that crush developed into something more, didn't it? After college, when you came home you told your grandmother you wanted to meet with Suki. That was when it all started to go wrong for you. Chaaya was angry. First she lost her grandson, then her daughter-in-law and then her son began to lose her mind. She blamed everything on that accident, on that family. When she found out that you were in love with Suki she disowned you, didn't she? She made you choose and you chose Suki.'

Rohit relaxed his hands and pulled off his glasses. 'This can't be true. It's not true. Suki, tell them.'

'Your love for her must have been strong, given that you had only exchanged letters with her over the last twenty years.' Chupplejeep looked at Suki, her shocked expression. 'Yes, Sister Perpetua found them and told me just over an hour ago. She is more cunning than you think.'

Chupplejeep turned back to Rohit. 'Suki let you believe that it was her sister who killed your brother. I'm guessing after you finished your degree in Bombay, you came back to Goa and bought the pharmacy in Dhesera. Then you decided to find your first true love and marry her. That is what you set out to do. Did you go to the church to find her?'

Rohit nodded.

'And Suki, you fell for him at a time when you were growing dissatisfied with the church. Twenty years ago, you decided to punish yourself by giving yourself to God. It was all going well for you, wasn't it, up until you met Rohit? You never expected to see him after all those years. But you did and he pursued you – you fell in love. You were already growing tired of being a nun and he was offering you a way out. Perhaps you thought you had served your time.'

'I fell in love with Rohit, yes,' she said looking at him, her head tilted, her arms outstretched towards him.

'But then Subrina came back into your life and threatened to reveal what had really happened all those years ago. Rid her conscience of her demons. Her baggage, as Dinesh put it.'

'This is all lies,' Suki said, shaking her head and tapping it gently with the palm of her hand. She looked at Rohit. 'You have to believe me. It's lies. All of it.'

'When Subrina made contact with you after all this time, your anxieties returned, didn't they? The tapping – I noticed it when I first met you, and Sister Perpetua had noticed it too. She thought it was because you were doubting the church, but when you first arrived at the convent you exhibited the same behaviours. Now they resurfaced because your sister had got back in touch with you and you were concerned as to what she would say. When Subrina met you that day, she asked you about that night and for once you discussed what really happened. What did she say to you after all these years that made you want to murder her?'

'I never killed her. I have an alibi. You know that. I was at the convent all night.'

'Oh yes, we'll get to your alibi,' Chupplejeep said.

Rohit stared at Suki.

'Subrina pieced back the fragments of that night. She had told Dinesh how you wanted to wear her makeup that night. She told him how you were going to be a doctor. It must have been disappointing for her when you decided to become a nun. She admitted to a crime she didn't commit so you could make something of yourself and you chose a new religion. Is that why she cut you out of her life?'

'You don't know what you're saying. If, now after all this time, she had said that I was the one behind the wheel that night, what would it have mattered? The family had been paid off. It would not have meant that I would go to jail. And who would believe a drunk over a nun?'

'Rohit may have believed her. Because Subrina wasn't going to tell the police what she remembered. She didn't care about justice, she cared about lying to the family. She wanted to see Nitin's family. The family still live here in Dhesera. Subrina took the artist Advani to see the house. He painted the green bungalow from memory because it looked so typical of Goan architecture. I noticed it hanging in his gallery because it was such a standard picture amidst all the other abstract paintings he has there.'

Pankaj nodded. He knew the painting Chupplejeep was referring to, he had seen it himself.

'This was your problem,' Chupplejeep said. 'Subrina knew your secret and she was going to confess to Chaaya who would have told Rohit immediately. After you met, Subrina called you. We checked her phone records. She made a call to a mobile, not Dinesh's, but the phone Rohit had given you so he could call you. Another thing Sister Perpetua told me about. They found it in your room earlier and gave me the number which I cross-checked against her phone records. You had an argument.'

'No.'

'The maid heard an argument between Subrina and someone. We thought the person she was talking to was Dinesh. Subrina was heard saying, "The truth must be told." I thought she was referring to the fact that Dinesh was seeing a woman Subrina abhorred, Ayesha Saxena. The maid who overheard her thought that as well. But it wasn't him she was arguing with, it was you. She knew about you and Rohit too, the maid overheard her saying she blamed him – because of Rohit, she said, she would never be free. Why? Because he had categorically stated that it was Subrina behind the wheel when it wasn't. She wanted him to know it wasn't her driving that day. But you couldn't stand the thought of losing him. She was going to tell Chaaya, Rohit and Balbir the truth and you had to stop her.'

Rohit stepped away from Suki and leaned against the car. 'You called me after you met her. You were so angry. You said that she deserved to die.'

'Shut up!' Suki screeched. 'Shut up, you fool.'

'Yes, I've been a bloody fool. I had ordered the insulin on the twelfth, for a client I sometimes supply off the record. He's a psychiatrist and sometimes uses insulin to reduce the control on his patients' thoughts and memories.'

Chupplejeep shook his head.

'Suki asked me for a drug that would not be traceable after it was administered. She said it was time that Subrina paid for the death of my brother.'

'Shut up! We'll go to jail!'

Rohit slid against the vehicle to the ground. He squatted on the floor with his back against the car. 'I thought I was avenging my brother's death, but I am no better than a murderer. How could you do that to me? How could you let me believe that Subrina was the one who killed Nitin when it was you all along? I won't live a lie like you have. My grandmother was right. You and your family are evil.' Rohit started muttering to himself. 'She said that no good would come of blood money and she was right. Without that money I wouldn't have gone to college. I wouldn't even have known what insulin is.'

'You went with Suki to Subrina's room at the Golden Orchid?' Chupplejeep asked.

'We waited at the rear of the hotel until we saw Dinesh's car leaving. We were not expecting him to leave, but we knew, from what Subrina had told Suki when they met, that they were sleeping in separate rooms.'

'So you lied when you said Subrina told you they wanted to marry,' Chupplejeep said. Suki ignored him.

'We saw the light in her room. We used the rear staircase, near the kitchen, to avoid the front desk and Suki knocked on her door. I stayed back. But I could hear water running so I knew Subrina was running a bath. It was perfect.'

'She was happy to see her sister. Family had become important to her,' Chupplejeep said.

'They sat and drank together. It must have been an hour later when Suki peered out of room and called me inside. When I stepped inside the room Subrina had passed out on her bed, in her dressing gown. I lifted her up and Suki injected her with the insulin in the beauty spot on her bottom, which Suki already knew about.'

'I'm not listening to your lies,' Suki said. She started to walk towards the convent, but Pankaj stopped her.

She wriggled in his grip, but he was firm. He pulled out his handcuffs and cuffed her hands behind her back, then walked her to where Chupplejeep and Rohit were.

'You carried her to the bath and lay her down in the water?' Chupplejeep asked.

Rohit nodded. 'She was slowly dying but I thought she deserved it. I put the sunglasses to cover her eyes in case she opened them. I didn't want to see her dying.'

'The lipstick?'

'The day my brother died...it was all I could remember about her. That red lipstick, that laugh. I thought she was laughing behind the wheel.'

'She was laughing in the store earlier that day,' Chupplejeep said, remembering what the farmer had told him. 'She was happy, that was all.' A warm breeze ruffled the leaves of the ashoka trees and they swayed gently in the wind.

Rohit looked away. 'I didn't know that. I never realised that. I saw the lipstick near the sink. I just applied it to her lips. I wasn't thinking.'

'Why then did you slit her wrists?'

'I didn't.'

'You didn't?'

'It was Suki. She said that if the insulin broke down sufficiently and was not traceable, the slit wrists would indicate suicide. We could get away with it.'

'And you, Suki, knew to slit the wrists vertically because you looked into it when you considered taking your own life after Nitin died. You told me you had thought about killing yourself after the accident, remember?'

Suki spat at the detective's feet. 'I'm not saying anything. You cops can't take an admissible confession from me here. I'll say you beat it out of Rohit. You'll be fired right there and then.'

'The insulin didn't break down though,' Rohit said, as if just realising this fact for the first time.

'Not all of it, no. We'll have to arrest you both for the murder of Subrina Basi.'

'I'll deny it. I'll deny all of it. It's not true. I was at the convent all night,' Suki said.

'Not all night,' Chupplejeep said. 'Yes, let's get to the story of your alibi. That was the final piece of the puzzle. You couldn't have committed the crime if you were at the church all night with another sister. I tried to speak with this sister but it turns out the sister you were with was Sister Carmina, who has taken a vow of silence. Very convenient.'

'But she provided a note. Sister Perpetua confirmed this to you.'

'When Sister Perpetua told me you were making a hasty exit from the convent, she also told me how she had asked Sister Carmina again about your presence at the vigil. Sister Carmina clearly wrote that you had left at midnight and she hadn't seen you again till the next morning. In fact Sister Carmina was confused that we did not already know that as her previous note to us had stated just this. It was then that I realised what you had done.

'You followed Sister Carmina and watched her place the letter on Sister Perpetua's desk. Her room is never locked, because after all it is a convent, she trusts all of you. When Sister Perpetua was praying in the chapel, you swapped Sister Carmina's letter for one you had already prepared. You did this before I called Sister Perpetua to confirm your story. You were quick and what you did with Sister Carmina's letter I will never know. But I'm guessing you destroyed it in a fire, maybe? Your forgery was good, it fooled Sister Perpetua, but not when she compared Sister Carmina's real note with yours. You will do anything to protect yourself, no?'

Suki looked at Rohit with a pained expression in her eyes. 'I never killed your brother. It was Subrina. I love you. You have to believe me. I love you.'

'You planned this murder very well, but you forgot one thing.'

Rohit looked up.

'What?' Suki asked.

'Can I ask where you found the knife you used to slit your sister's wrists?'

Suki laughed.

'The kitchen,' Rohit said. 'Suki went back down the stairs, back outside and then entered the kitchen from the rear entrance. She took it from the drawer closest to the oven. She told me it was the logical place to put a knife in a kitchen like that.'

'But for some reason you took your gloves off...maybe they got wet in the bath water. You handled the knife and you missed wiping the fingerprints. You

373

were so busy making sure Subrina's fingerprints were on the knife you failed to wipe yours and Suki's, and when the knife fell to the bottom of the bath you forgot about this last-minute addition to your plan. It was a small mistake because you wiped your fingerprints off everything else, even the lipstick. We took four sets of prints from the knife. Subrina's were instantly ruled out. We know she could not have made such cuts herself. Two sets have been matched and eliminated, the gardener and the chef. The fourth, I'm guessing, will match yours.'

The black crow, which was still on the wall next to where they stood, took flight.

'I think Subrina has her answers, don't you?' Chupplejeep said, looking towards the flying bird and then at Suki and Rohit. 'Let's get you both to the station.'

CHAPTER FORTY-NINE

Christabel opened her delivery of wedding invitations in peach and pink at the same time that Pankaj asked Chupplejeep how many fried foods he had eaten over Christmas.

Chupplejeep rubbed his round belly. 'I'm just not feeling right today. But I don't think it is the samosas.'

Pankaj frowned. 'You're worried about Dinesh's arrest and what his father will do?'

Chupplejeep nodded. He had good reason to be afraid. Soon after they had arrested Suki and Rohit, Gosht had called to tell him that Dinesh's father wanted to see 'heads roll' over his son's false arrest. He wanted Chupplejeep to lose his job, but in the days that passed nothing further had been said. It had gone eerily quiet.

'But nothing has been mentioned.'

'This is what worries me, Pankaj. This is the calm before the storm.' Chupplejeep didn't tell Pankaj that his impending wedding was also playing on his mind. With the case and Christmas out of the way, Christabel was talking about wedding decorations and dresses at every opportunity, giving him bouts of indigestion and sleepless nights.

'Perhaps he's forgotten,' Pankaj said. 'Gosht was pretty happy we solved the case so fast. He may even put our station forward for the funding.' Pankaj looked around the office. 'New paint, new computers, maybe even someone to help with the paperwork.'

'He said fast? The last time we spoke to him he said we were too slow.'

'Well, it's always one or the other,' Pankaj said with a grin. He lifted up the newspaper on his desk. 'Look what made the headlines.'

'Nishok was fired from the Golden Orchid for freeing the ducks?'

'Of course not. Though I do feel sorry for him.'

'Don't worry about Nishok. I happen to know that the wildlife sanctuary in Utorda has just hired a silent man who is very good with animals. No more killing and plucking chickens for Nishok, or being bullied by Abhik for that matter.'

'Really, sir?'

Chupplejeep nodded.

'That is good news, sir. But you haven't guessed what's in the papers?'

'Ayesha Saxena has been found, alive?'

'No, sir. That's not it. To tell you the truth I had forgotten about her. Has she really been found?'

'Alive and well in an ashram near Amboli somewhere. Apparently being disconnected from her smartphone when she was with Dinesh gave her a new perspective on life. She decided to check into one of those ashrams where they don't even speak.'

'Let me guess, now she wants to put the high life behind her and work with the poor.'

'Nothing doing. She met a Scandinavian artist there. She is getting married next month. She's planning a big wedding,' Chupplejeep said.

'A big wedding! I bet they put it in *Icon Bites*. There are sure to be some celebrities there.'

'Well, at least it's one less body we need to concern ourselves with. Now what was in the papers?' Chupplejeep took the copy of the *Larara Express* that Pankaj was holding. 'So Bonaparte got his story: *Murder, Masala and Mayhem*. Typical of Bonaparte, coming up with such a tasteless headline. What's the masala he's referring to?'

'The sisters swapping places in the car when baby Nitin was killed.'

'I hope my epitaph is never referred to as a masala.'

'I don't think it will be, sir. But it's not just Subrina Basi's murder that got into the paper. Look at the lower half of the front page.'

'At this rate, Bonaparte will be getting his job back in the city,' Chupplejeep said, looking at the paper. 'Advani took your advice. Good for you, you should be proud. Well done.'

'I hope revealing his secret finally gives him and others courage, sir.'

Chupplejeep smiled at his officer. 'I never thought you would say nice things about Advani.'

'I'm warming to him. Now that I have just about erased that terrible canvas of his from my mind.'

'Ah, speak of the devil. What brings you here?' Chupplejeep asked, as Advani poked his head around the front door.

'*Hai*, my two favourite policemen,' Advani said. He pushed his way through the front door carrying a large brown parcel. He placed the package against the wall and adjusted his bright orange shawl over his black *kurta* pyjamas. 'I'm leaving Goa today.'

'Back to Mumbai?'

'The interview I did with that handsome boy, Bonaparte, appeared in the *Times* two days ago before it was issued in the *Larara Express*. One of the directors at Malabar Hill saw it. They want to offer me a three-year contract. Apparently, with this story so hot in the press, I can put my price up. My paintings, it seems, have doubled in value overnight. And to think I was scared of sharing my past. People want to know everything these days, warts and all.'

'Good for you,' Chupplejeep said. 'And Takshak? What did you do with Takshak?'

'What could I do? He tried to swindle me. He knew my story and he wanted money from me to keep quiet. I couldn't be around someone like that. It's too much negative energy and I don't need that in my life anymore.'

'You let him go. You don't want us to arrest him?'

Advani shook his head. 'I had a long talk with him. It turns out I'm not the amazing person I thought I was. I see now that I treated people badly. I treated *him* badly and that was wrong. I see the error of my ways.'

'Wow,' Pankaj said.

'Don't get me wrong, some idiots deserve to be spoken to like that.' Advani smiled.

Pankaj laughed. 'Of course.'

'I gave Takshak the forty lakhs he wanted. You were right, Pankaj, he too is an artist and his work must be seen, not hidden in a backroom. The money will be enough for him to set up his own gallery. I think he is going to stay here in Goa. It's cheaper here. The money will take him much further.'

Chupplejeep let out a low whistle. 'That's a lot of money.'

'Don't make me want to change my mind. It's done and I suppose he put up with my shit for years. But anyway, enough of Takshak, before I leave this quiet little village I thought I'd drop in to say bye and I also wanted to say thank you to this man for finally setting me free. I will not forget you.' Advani tilted his head to one side and looked at Pankaj like a proud parent.

Pankaj blushed. He stood up and offered Advani his hand.

'*Hai,* don't be so formal,' Advani said, before walking over to Pankaj and embracing him. He turned to look at Chupplejeep. 'Firstly, I want you assure you that you have nothing to worry about in regards to that man Dinesh and his family.'

'How did you know?'

'It's Goa, darling, word gets around.'

'Oh,' Chupplejeep said.

'Well, don't you worry about them.'

'How can you be sure of that?'

'Let's just say I did a little blackmailing of my own. It's not just the types like Dinesh that know people. I know people too. And I know what his father likes in bed. Let's just say I took care of it. I don't think he'll be coming after your job anytime soon.'

'I don't know what to say,' Chupplejeep said.

'Good. Don't say anything. Secondly, I'm here because I've brought you a little something,' Advani said, looking back at Pankaj. 'While I'll never forget what you did for me, you may forget me. And just the thought of that makes me feel all nauseous. So to prevent that, I want you to have this.' Advani pointed to the large parcel.

Pankaj swallowed. 'Th-thank you.'

'Well, don't just stand there. *Hai,* open it. I want to see your face, Pankaj.'

'So do I,' Chupplejeep said, suppressing a laugh. 'Open it.'

Pankaj loosened his collar, walked around his desk and pulled at the string holding the brown paper together. As the wrapping fell to the floor, Pankaj took a step back. The violent black and red brushstrokes he had desperately erased from his mind were now in front of him, burning an impression on his brain.

'Velutia,' Advani said. 'Her name is Velutia.'

'It has a name?' Pankaj asked.

'She. It's a she and yes, her name is Velutia. Do you like it?'

Pankaj nodded.

'He's too emotional to speak,' Chupplejeep said, walking towards the painting. He put his arm around Pankaj's shoulders. 'It's a very generous gift. Are you sure you want us to have it?'

Advani looked around the tired office. 'It'll liven up this place, don't you think? Although you should possibly paint the walls before you put Velutia up.'

'I think we'll do that.'

Advani smiled. 'If you're ever in Bombay, give me a call. I don't usually hang around with cops, but I think I can make an exception with you two.' And with a wave of his hand, he left the station.

'So what do you think, Pankaj?'

'Sir, it absolutely cannot stay.'

'Really? I was thinking we could put it behind my desk, then you can look at it all day.'

'It, sir? Her name is Velutia!' Pankaj put his face in his hands while Detective Chupplejeep laughed.

Acknowledgements

Thank you to my friends and family, particularly my dad for sharing with me his heritage and beautiful ancestral home. Thanks also go to Urmi Kenia for her expansive knowledge on India and her attention to detail. Any mistakes are my own. My editor David Wailing and JD&J for their fantastic cover design. And of course a big thank you goes to Abingdon Writers' Fiction Adult Group for their continual support and critique.

About the Author

Marissa de Luna is a passionate author who started writing in her late twenties. After spending her early years growing up in Goa, Marissa returned to England where she now lives. The Body in the Bath is her fifth novel.

Other novels by Marissa de Luna

Goa Traffic

The Bittersweet Vine

Poison in the Water

Under the Coconut Tree – A Chupplejeep Mystery

Coming soon

Jackpot Jetty – A Chupplejeep Mystery

www.marissadeluna.com

36295665R00227

Printed in Great Britain
by Amazon